THE DREAMING

Amanda Sheridan

The sequel to Rapid Eye Movement

Amanda Sheridan

First published in e-book format by self-publishing via Amazon (Kindle Direct Publishing) in 2020.

During lucid dreaming, the dreamer may be able to have some control over the dream characters, narrative, and environment.

Wikipedia

Prologue – Sayeed Qahtani's compound. Unknown location, Syria.

Only in the darkness did he permit thoughts of her to infiltrate his mind. He had forced himself to forget about his home, his family and the people he loved while he was pretending to be someone else. But for tonight, for this one brief moment, he permitted his mind and his soul to escape the horror that surrounded him and he embraced the thoughts of home and the woman he loved almost beyond reason.

Brief though it was, he needed the escape, even if only in his mind. He needed to imagine her cradled in his arms. He needed to imagine they had been making love. She had been tender, yet passionate, and he could almost feel his arms around her as he held her tightly to him and they basked in the aftermath of their passion. Her face rested lightly on his chest and he needed to imagine he could smell the faint traces of shampoo in her hair and the unique scent of her skin. He needed to imagine that her warmth eased the icy coldness of his soul and for a little while, in the darkness, it was almost as if she was right there with him.

This welcome invasion into his thoughts was a small, precious island of love and happiness that he clung to while surrounded by the sea of terror he found himself drowning in. He could almost see her. He imagined that he could almost reach out and touch her.

His hand unclenched and relaxed as he felt her fingers interlocking with his, tightening and holding his hand in hers, refusing to let him go. He stared into her blue eyes, gentle yet sometimes mysterious. Often playful and mischievous, but always loving. Always loving *him*.

Her smile was his smile and her laughter mingled with his laughter. Her strength was his strength and it was her love that he lived for. In the darkness, she gave him hope when he should have no hope.

But that hope was false and he knew he would never see her again.

Chapter 1 – Tel Aviv, Israel.

It should have been a black SUV. Wasn't that how they did it in the movies or on television? A big, masculine-looking SUV. Black in colour. Always black. And polished until it shone. Now and then it would be a Toyota Land Cruiser, but most times it was one of those big Fords. An Explorer or an Expedition maybe. And there would be two similar vehicles following it. They would screech to a halt on the road outside the house and men in black suits would spill out of it. They were the security detail – distinctive because of their black suits and the black sunglasses they wore, even on a dull day, and the way they whispered into their sleeves. They would scan the area from behind the sunglasses with cold, experienced eyes, taking in everything around them. From old Mr. Stein pottering about in his beloved garden, to the jogger running past them, and the two eight-year-old boys from a couple of houses down the street racing their bikes along the pavement. The men would watch carefully as the boys raced towards the makeshift ramp they had fashioned from old bricks and a plank of wood. The kids would seem out of place, and therefore suspicious, because kids nowadays preferred their iPads or smartphones to bicycles or skateboards.

They would quickly assess the jogger as harmless. She was. She jogged past the house every day as part of the surveillance. They would look at Mr. Stein and the kids on their bikes and deem their threat level to be extremely minimal. It would have been zero but for the garden rake and the bucket of dead leaves he was carrying and the potential injury a kid on a bike could do to their principal.

But it was not a big, black SUV. It was a little Honda Civic and it did not screech to a halt either. The driver crawled along the street then manoeuvred carefully into a parking space like a little old lady on her twentieth attempt at her driving test, grittily determined to pass it this time. It was silver in colour with a dent in the rear wing and a bumper sticker that wasn't as funny as the bumper sticker writer hoped it would be.

A nondescript little vehicle – dirty, battered and unkempt. It had all the appearances of a teenage boy's first, inexpensive car. A car on its last legs, with too many miles on the clock, ready to shudder to a halt any day now. And it was covered in dust. Jennifer was surprised no one had scrawled 'wash me' on the side of it yet. The kids probably would as soon as they got a chance.

The engine should have sounded ill. It should have coughed and spluttered as though ready to die. But – and this was the part that gave it away – the engine in this decrepit little banger *purred sweetly*. It had been fine-tuned and well-maintained. Jennifer knew what a well-maintained, fine-tuned engine sounded like. Hadn't her father been a car mechanic for most of his working life?

Jennifer also knew who owned the car. It belonged to an organisation rather than an individual. She couldn't help feeling a little disappointed that they would come for her in a beat-up looking Honda instead of a big, black SUV.

It parked across the street from her house and two men climbed out of it. The younger of the two, the driver, was wearing faded black jeans and a red T-shirt. He was obviously a fan of Liverpool football club as the T-shirt sported their well-known Liverbird logo across the left breast. He was dark-skinned, with a mop of curly black hair and he wore the obligatory dark sunglasses. Jennifer didn't know him.

The second man seemed familiar to her but she couldn't place from where, or how, she recognised him. He was better dressed, in smart, casual attire – light brown canvas trousers

and a neatly ironed white shirt, the sleeves of which were rolled up and folded neatly at the elbows. His hair, what little he had, was grey and cut short against his scalp and he wore a pair of rimless glasses. Not sunglasses. He was around her age and he had an air of seniority about him.

Jennifer knew why they were outside her house. And

why she could see them from her living room window. She knew it would be bad news and she placed her palm against the wall to stop herself from falling.

Hope flared in her heart when they disappeared from her sight. Maybe they were going to another house. Maybe they were door-to-door salesmen. Maybe she had imagined them.

Then the doorbell rang.

Maybe they were strangers to this part of town and they were lost. It would be ironic if that was the case, and the first person they asked for directions was the foreign woman.

She took a deep breath, let it out slowly and wiped her palms on the legs of her jeans as she walked slowly from the living room to the hall. She was aware of a slight tremor in her arm as she reached for the door handle and opened her front door.

'Mrs. Ben-Levi?'

It was the younger man who spoke. She was surprised at that. She had anticipated the older man would have been the one to initiate the conversation.

'Yes. Can I help you?'

'Would you mind coming with us?'

Jennifer frowned. 'Why?'

'We will explain everything in due course but we need you to come with us. It is a matter of urgency.'

'Where to?' Jennifer asked.

The two men exchanged a look between them that Jennifer couldn't quite interpret. Exasperation, with a large pinch of sympathy thrown in for good measure. That, in itself, was enough to cause her to worry.

'Oh, it's somewhere nearby,' the younger man replied. The casual tone of his voice was so obviously false. She picked up on it immediately and a cold dread settled in her bones. There was something else going on here.

'Israel is a small country,' she said conversationally and attempted to make light of her fear. 'Everywhere is nearby.'

'You are quite correct, Mrs. Ben-Levi.' The older man

spoke for the first time and she turned her attention to him. 'Now, if you don't mind, we would like you to accompany us right away. There is... a matter of some urgency that we need to discuss with you.'

Her impulse was to flee. Slam the door in their faces and run out the back door as fast and as far as she could. But it was a small country. They had all agreed on that point. She could only run so far.

'Let me just get my coat and my bag and lock up,' Jennifer said with an attempt at a bright and cheerful smile. She refused to let them hear the fear in her voice.

Jennifer welcomed the silence from her two travelling companions and took the opportunity to admire the scenery from the back seat of the little Honda. The interior of the car wasn't much to look at and it smelled faintly of wet dog. Definitely not something one would expect from a government vehicle.

The journey from her home on the outskirts of Tel Aviv to the large military base at HaKirya took the best part of an hour. It shouldn't have taken that long but major roadworks and two traffic collisions ensured that, when it wasn't at a standstill, the traffic could only crawl along. But, to Jennifer, that hour felt like a lifetime as she watched the buildings and the city pass her by. Her gaze was drawn up to what little she could see of the sky. Blue and cloudless today with a winter sun that was shining brightly. She studied the contrails of a jet as it flew to its destination somewhere in the world. She wished she was on it.

As they crawled along, it seemed as though, with each metre she travelled, her life was passing by along with the landscape and she was moving farther and farther away from the person she was. Jennifer found herself wondering who she would become when she reached her destination.

She regretted not sending a WhatsApp message to Nurit, her stepdaughter, to tell her where she was going –

some record if something should happen...

Jennifer pushed the insane notion out of her head. She knew she was being ridiculous. Nothing was going to happen to her. All they were going to do was formally notify her of the bad news or perhaps ask her, as next of kin, to identify the body. She would telephone Nurit once she had done that. As soon as she managed to compose herself – get over the shock, so to speak.

But it might take a few hours. There was bound to be paperwork involved.

Maybe I should have messaged her to nip round this afternoon and feed the cats.

The building they were driving towards was a military base, although its outward appearance resembled a hospital. Jennifer knew it was a military base, but her hands still grew clammy and a wave of nausea threatened to force its way to the surface at the sight of it. Normally, a military base wouldn't disturb her but she knew they often had hospital wings. And just like regular hospitals they had morgues which were usually hidden away in the basement or around the back of the building. Safely tucked out of sight of the living in case a glimpse of what could be their final destination might encourage them to get there sooner.

So, it *was* a body they needed her to identify.

Yet the thought didn't fill Jennifer with as much horror and dread as she expected. After eight months without him, all she felt was sadness and cold acceptance. There was nothing else for her to feel. Maybe when she saw his body, or what was left of it, it would dawn on her that she had lost the love of her life. Then, perhaps, she would react. But how? Would she howl and scream? Or would she weep silently as she gazed at his cold, decayed remains? Would she even recognise him after all this time? Would his body *be* recognisable? Would her heart break? More than it had been broken when, eight months ago, he sat down in front of her and gently told her he was going away for a long, long time?

As they slowly approached the security barrier a guard

stepped out of the small, reinforced glass and metal hut. He raised his hand for them to halt and quickly walked towards the driver's side window. The guard was dressed in army uniform and he carried an automatic rifle.

From the rear passenger seat, Jennifer strained to listen to what they were saying. The guard seemed to know the driver but he still asked for identification from both him and his older front seat passenger. He inspected both ID's carefully and gave her a questioning glance. She began to fumble in her bag for her driving licence and her own te'udat zehut – the identity card that all Israelis were required by law to carry with them. It hadn't occurred to her to bring her passport with her, either her Israeli one or her old British one, although it had expired a little over a year ago.

Jennifer reached forward and gave her driving licence and identity card to the guard who glanced from them to her a couple of times before handing both documents back to her.

'She's with us,' the older of her two travelling companions said by way of an explanation. He did not elaborate any further.

The guard nodded, hit a button to raise the barrier and waved them through. They made their way to the main carpark at the front of the building and found an empty parking space about three rows back.

Chapter 2.

Jennifer took a deep breath, opened the door and climbed out of the car. She squared her shoulders, and did her best to ignore the thumping of her heart, as she allowed her two travelling companions to escort her into the building. They entered through glass doors that opened automatically into a small foyer. A body scanner and an x-ray machine, similar to those found in airports, met her just inside the front door. She placed her bag on the conveyor belt and, when asked to, stepped forward into the body scanner.

It didn't ping or beep and no klaxon alarms sounded. No armed guards came rushing to surround her and no steel shutters crashed down, sealing the building and all inside it. This meant, obviously, that she wasn't carrying a weapon and her bones weren't made from metal. As a result, Jennifer was waved forward. Her handbag had also made it through the x-ray machine without causing concern. She retrieved it, slung it over her shoulder and glanced around her.

Personnel in both civilian clothes and military uniform were everywhere to be seen, reinforcing the fact that this was definitely not a hospital. Which meant there was no morgue tucked away in a basement or around the back of the building. And that was a good sign.

Wasn't it?

Jennifer and her two silent companions took a short downward journey in the elevator and then a long walk along a corridor to a door. The small metal plaque on the door read 'Room 308' in Hebrew with the English translation underneath the Hebrew characters.

The door was unlocked and they ushered Jennifer inside. It was obviously an interview room. That much Jennifer knew from a diet of TV cop shows over the years. It was empty apart from a desk, bolted to the floor, and two chairs on either side of the desk, also bolted to the floor. She noticed a camera mounted high on one corner, and a large mirror that most likely had an observation window on the other side. Her travelling companions invited her to take a seat.

'We will be right back,' they told her.

'Hey! A cup of coffee would be nice!' Jennifer yelled as they left, closing the door behind them. 'How about a vodka and diet coke? No? Okay, I'll settle for a glass of water. Please.'

At least they haven't handcuffed me to the desk. Well, not yet.

They came back five minutes later with a fingerprint scanner and a digital camera.

Jennifer sat up straight in the chair, confused and more than a little fearful. This was no longer about identifying her husband's body.

'Look guys, if this is about me leaving the car in that no-parking zone last week, I swear, I was literally only five minutes. Seriously, I was taking delivery of dog and cat food for my shelter. Eight big bags. And they were too heavy to carry all the way to the carpark, so I'm happy to pay any fine. With interest, if necessary,' she joked as she tried to make light of a situation that was becoming more and more strange, and more frightening, by the minute. 'Come on guys, it was for abandoned animals. It doesn't make me a career criminal.'

'It's not what you think, Jennifer,' the younger guy told her. His voice was gentle and friendly as he quickly scanned her fingers – her prints were now stored forever in their database – and motioned her to stand against the wall so he could take her photograph. 'We need your fingerprints for our records and your photograph for your ID pass.'

'So, I guess I'm hired then?'

He laughed, and his laugh seemed to be genuine but she wasn't a hundred per cent convinced. 'Yeah, I guess you could say that.'

They didn't bring the vodka and diet coke Jennifer had requested but they did give her coffee and a pre-packed sandwich. They also handed her a bottle of water.

Both the coffee and the sandwich turned out to be delicious, despite them obviously coming from a vending machine.

As soon as Jennifer was finished eating, they ushered her out of the room and the trio followed the long corridor back to the elevator. This time they went up. The first room she had been in had been one floor below ground, now the elevator stopped four floors above ground.

They placed her in another room, identical to the last one, leaving a fresh bottle of water on the table and telling her that someone would be along to speak to her shortly.

The minutes ticked slowly by and, once more, the fear began to settle around her like a shroud. Paranoia was in there too. *Have I really done something wrong?*

The parking comment had been a joke, obviously, but now Jennifer searched her mind for something she might have done or said out of place. But nothing sprung to mind. She never mentioned Ilan, or what he did, in public. She kept herself to herself and, other than her work at the animal shelter and her weekly trips to the shopping centre, she rarely spoke to anyone. It had been like that since he had left.

Nurit – Ilan's daughter and her step-daughter – was the only other person in Israel that Jennifer was close to and considered a friend. She quickly grabbed her phone out of her bag, surprised they had allowed her to keep it, and dialled Nurit's number.

A voice, in Hebrew, told her that they were sorry but her call could not be connected at this time and that she should try again later. She ended that call and tried calling Nurit on both WhatsApp and Messenger but there was no Wi-Fi signal. She tried to send a text message and watched the spinning circle until it told her that her message could not be sent. She looked at the screen in surprise. There was no signal at all. For anything. Her phone was useless.

Of course, there isn't going to be a signal. A big high-

security building like this would have the technology to block private cell phones.

The longer Jennifer sat there the more worried she became, but she couldn't put a solid reason to her concern. That, in itself, made her all the more worried. And she needed to pee. Not desperately. Not yet. But she would be more comfortable if she could use the bathroom.

She was about to start yelling and waving her arms to get the attention of whoever was watching her on camera when she heard a click and the door behind her opened. She stood up and turned around to see a tall, distinguished looking man in his late fifties or early sixties enter the room. He was carrying a leather briefcase.

He looks like a lawyer. A defence lawyer. What the hell do they think I've done?

He took a seat opposite her and, without a word, pulled a thick paper file from his briefcase and set it in front of him on the table. Jennifer glanced at the cover and saw her name and address in English and in Hebrew written on the front of it. A small, passport-sized copy of the photo that had been taken earlier, when she had been fingerprinted, was attached to the front of the file.

'You are Jennifer Ben-Levi, nee Scott, is that correct?' he said in heavily accented English.

Jennifer swallowed hard and nodded. Now, she was very concerned.

He leafed through a couple of pages in the file but didn't read them. She suspected he had already read every word.

Then he took off his glasses and smiled at her.

'My name is Saul Mueller,' he said. 'I am very pleased to finally meet you, Jennifer. I have heard so much about you and to meet you in person is a delight.'

'Why have I been brought here? Is it something to do with Ilan?' Jennifer asked.

'I know Ilan well. I have known him for many years.'

'Is he dead?'

'Unfortunately, that is a question I cannot answer because, quite simply, we do not know.'

'Is he, what do you call it? MIA? Missing in action?'

'Again, I am afraid we do not know. We have had no contact or sightings of him in a little over five days.'

Five days? Not even a week? Well, that's not very long. I haven't seen or heard from him in almost eight months. It's not that much, is it?

'Why are you concerned after only five days?' Jennifer naively voiced her opinion. 'It could be there's a problem with his phone? Or something.'

'It doesn't work that way, Jennifer. He doesn't use a cell phone. He makes non-verbal contact with us by... other means every two days and has done so without fail up until now. That is why we are so concerned.'

Oh God. He is dead.

The finality of it hit Jennifer like a punch in the guts. Tears welled in her eyes. Grief and loss tore through her and she wanted to scream, to swear and to lash out at this man in front of her who had just broken her heart. She wanted to slap him. Punch him. Kick him. Scream at him. Anything to make him stop breaking her heart.

But she merely sat there, arms folded in front of her and she fought back the tears, and would not permit herself to give in to them.

'Does this mean he's dead?' Jennifer needed to hear it aloud from this man in front of her.

'Not necessarily. We believe the people he is working with have moved to another area but, unfortunately, we are unable to locate them… and him. And it appears he can no longer make contact with his… ahh… with the person he was supposed to contact.'

You're talking about his handler. I've curled up on the sofa watching too many spy movies to not know what you mean.

'Why am I here then?' Jennifer asked, a hitch in her voice that she struggled, and failed, to disguise.

'Because, as I said, we have not heard from either Ilan or his contact for almost a week. We have informants working in the area who have been looking for them – questioning locals and the like – and, so far, they have come up with no leads whatsoever. Believe me Jennifer, we *are* looking for him.'

'Okay, I get that, and I'm relieved you haven't given up on him. But what has this got to do with me? Apart from notifying me. Obviously.'

'We need your help with something.'

Jennifer's mouth dropped open.

'My help?' Her words came out with a squeak and it was so unlike her own voice that she almost turned around to see who had spoken.

This was nothing to do with Ilan, Jennifer realised. And she had no idea what they wanted from her or how on earth she could help them. They were spies so maybe they wanted her to spy on someone? The notion was absurd. She had no idea how to be a spy. She was an ex-interior designer who now worked in an animal rescue centre. She might have been – no, she still was – married to a spy, albeit a missing spy, but she was no spy herself.

'I'm not sure how I can help you. Unless you want to adopt a dog or a cat, or you want your living room re-designed and redecorated. But other than that, well…'

Saul burst out laughing. A genuine laugh that in other circumstances would have been infectious.

'We think you can help us. In fact, we are very confident that you will be able to help us. And, naturally, we will assist you to do so.'

'Naturally.' Jennifer threw it back at him with a frown.

'We should begin,' he told her. His voice became serious as he opened the file. His voice told Jennifer that she had no say in the matter.

'I still don't know what you want from me. But go ahead.'

This time Saul did read the first page.

'You suffered a serious head injury when you and Ilan were involved in a traffic accident in Cyprus, is that correct?'

Jennifer's blood ran cold as the memories she had managed to keep buried for so long threatened to reassert themselves in her mind. She clasped her hands tightly together under the table and tried to ignore the thoughts that, all of a sudden, filled her head. They had no place in her life now and she did not want to remember a single moment of that time.

But this man in front of her was forcing her to remember it all over again.

'It was more than a traffic accident,' she told him. 'We were being chased, but yes, I was injured when we crashed. You already know all of this. Why do you need to ask me again?'

'And because of that accident, and shortly after you and Ilan were flown to Israel,' Saul continued, ignoring her question. 'You collapsed and were taken to hospital suffering from a… brain injury which required surgery after which you were placed in a medically-induced coma for nine days. And during that period, you claim that you experienced a dream state in which you connected with a woman in England?'

'Er... yes.'

'Her name was…' He glanced at the file again. 'Lucy Wilson. She was a photographer and married with two children. She also was involved in an accident, a fall, a few hours after you were involved in the traffic accident. Is that correct?'

'Yes,' Jennifer nodded. 'Well, I think it was maybe about twelve hours later. Around the time I collapsed.'

'She required surgery for a head injury, similar to yours, and she was also placed in a medically induced coma. And she died the day you awakened. Is that also correct?'

'Yes.'

'Where did you know her from?'

'I didn't know her from anywhere.'

'You are both English, and of similar age. I find it hard to believe, given the connection you had with her, that you did not know her.'

'I'm telling you; I didn't know her. I got to know her when I dreamed about her, but I didn't know her before.'

'Before what?'

'Before I started dreaming about her,' she glared at him.

'Why did you move to Cyprus from the United Kingdom?' Saul changed tack.

'The weather.'

Her sarcasm met with disapproval. It wasn't much, but Jennifer took it as a small victory.

'That's not what I meant.'

'Well, it's true. Ask any Brit who moves abroad and one of the main reasons they give you is the weather.'

'So, apart from the weather, what other reason did you have for moving to Cyprus?'

'My brother set me up in a job with a friend of his. As an interior designer. Surely you know all that.'

'Yes, we do. But I still need to know why you decided to move there. It appears to be a sudden decision.'

'What if I don't want to tell you?'

'I think you should, Jennifer. Trust me, it will not leave this room.'

'So that's a real mirror and the camera up on the wall in the corner is a dud?'

'I think you know what I mean.'

'I think you already know why I moved to Cyprus.'

'Did Ilan know?'

'No.'

'Why not.'

'I thought, I mean... I didn't want him to know. He didn't need to know.'

'That you were involved in an affair with a married man?'

'I didn't know he was married until after we got together.'

'But you continued the affair until his wife found out?'

'Not really. I had more or less decided to end it, but he didn't want to. Then she found out about us and that was when I moved to Cyprus. I had been planning to move anyway.'

'How did you know Lucy Wilson?' Saul changed direction once again.

'I've already told you. I didn't know her. I swear, I didn't know who she was until I met her in my coma.'

Scepticism was written on his face and in his raised eyebrows.

'I wish you would believe me. Ilan did.'

'How exactly then, did you connect with her in your dreams?'

'I don't know. It just happened. I lived her life through the dreams I had when I was unconscious and she lived my life with Ilan. She knew all about him through the dreams she had. She knew he worked for the Mossad. She knew everything about us just as I knew everything about her and her family. I can tell you everything that happened. I just can't tell you *how* it happened.'

He seemed disappointed by her answer. But it was the truth and the only answer she could give him. Jennifer watched as he made some notes. She still had no idea why she was here and it was time to try and find out.

'What has this got to do with Ilan's disappearance? I mean, this was… like three years ago. I'm sorry, but I'm not seeing the connection.'

He ignored her question and continued scribbling on the file.

'Tell me how you feel about Israel?' he asked.

Jennifer blinked in response to the sudden change of direction once again. It was unnerving and probably a deliberate interrogation tactic.

'Israel in general, or living here?'

'Both.'

She took a moment to formulate her answer. 'In

general, I never really thought about it. I'm sorry if that sounds shallow but that's me. It's a country with a long history of conflict. I support some, well most, of its actions because I know survival is precarious, but there are a few I'm not comfortable with. But then no country or it's government can ever be perfect. As for living here? I love it. It wasn't our choice to move here but since we did, I learned to love it. I found the language difficult at first, because I've never had much of an ear for languages. But the people are great. Ilan has shown me so much of the country and taught me a lot about the history and culture and I've been happy here with him. I'll be honest with you; I probably never would have made it my choice to live here. But I am happy and I do like it.'

'How much of the language have you learned?'

'I took an ulpan. One of those intensive adult learning classes. Do you know what I mean?'

Saul smiled and nodded.

'I'm sorry. That was a stupid question. But it's a really fantastic method of teaching a language. And I did okay. In fact, I did better than okay. Languages have never been my strong point, but this helped me so much and now I can understand Hebrew very well now. The spoken word anyway. The written word was, still is, more difficult because I found the alphabet very tricky at first. Like I said, languages aren't my strong point, but after three years I can more or less speak Hebrew like a native. Although my accent would probably give me away. But writing maybe not so much. I've mastered it enough to get by, though.'

'Do you have an Israeli driver's licence?'

'Yes. And a passport.' Suddenly a thought occurred to her. 'Am I being deported?'

'Why would you think that?' Saul asked.

'Because I have no idea why I am here and why you are questioning me like this. I assumed it was something to do with Ilan – that he was dead or captured or something – but I don't know and I'm worried. And more than a little frightened.'

'We have no wish to deport you. That is not our intention.'

'Then what is going on?'

'We will tell you everything in due course, but for now I ask that you please be patient with me. I have some more questions and then some forms for you to fill in. If you find anything in them difficult, we can assist you. Once they have been completed then we will be in a position to make things clear to you. Please believe me, you have nothing to fear from me.'

Jennifer stared at him. She didn't believe the 'you have nothing to fear' part at all, and she knew she should tell him to go to hell, but her curiosity got the better of her. 'Okay, let's get it over with.'

Saul took a few moments to go over his notes again before he continued with his questioning. 'Are you completely recovered from the brain injury you suffered three years ago?'

'Yes.'

'There have been no side effects or long-term disabilities?'

'No. Well, I get more headaches than I used to and every now and then I forget... um, I forget... words,' she joked. 'And I'm less grown up and sensible than I should be at my age.'

He smiled and raised his eyebrow at her. 'Somehow I suspect that has nothing to do with your accident.'

'That is entirely possible.'

'How do these side effects affect your day-to-day life?' Saul continued.

'They don't. Well, not much. The headaches are annoying but not overly severe and the words – well everyone forgets words now and then.'

'Do you still dream?'

'No. Okay, maybe I do. I probably do. I think everyone dreams but, if I do, I don't remember them.'

'Do you have trouble sleeping?'

'Not now, although since Ilan left I don't sleep so well. But after the accident I couldn't sleep properly for a long time. I think I was afraid to go to sleep. I was afraid that I wouldn't wake up or I would…' she stopped, unsure what to say. How much she should tell him.

'Go on.'

'Sorry. I was afraid that I would end up in Lucy's life again.' Jennifer decided that she might as well be completely honest with the man sitting in front of her. 'I was afraid that she would want revenge for living while she died. I was terrified I would see her again.'

'How did you overcome that?'

'I would love to tell you that it was all down to yoga, long walks on the beach at sunset and healthy living, but I'd be lying. It was plenty of whiskey and sleeping tablets. Although I did do the therapy. For a while. And the long walks. I still take long walks.'

'And how is your general health now?'

'I'm reasonably fit. I eat a healthy diet… most of the time and I try not to drink too much alcohol. I don't always succeed at that, but I do try. I've never smoked and I take plenty of exercise. More now than I ever did.'

'Have you ever been able to control your dreams?'

'What? I… I don't understand what you mean.'

'Have you ever, before you went to sleep, thought about what you wanted to dream about – going to the beach for example. And when you woke up, you found you had dreamed about a day at the beach or some other scenario that you thought about deliberately before falling asleep?'

'Um... no. Unless you want to count the one about Kevin Costner? I mean, who doesn't think about *him* before going to sleep.'

Saul ignored her flippant comment and continued with his questioning. 'Before your accident and subsequent coma did you dream often?'

'I don't know. How do you define often?'

'Two or three times, or more, in a week?'

'I don't know. Yeah. Probably.'

'Were you able to remember these dreams in any detail?'

'Sometimes I'd remember them. But not very often. Most of the time they were only fragments and usually they disappeared seconds after I opened my eyes.'

'Did you ever have recurring dreams?'

'I did when I was young,' Jennifer admitted. 'It happened when I was around eight or nine. My brother and a couple of his friends rented some horror movies and I watched one along with them. It was that very well-known vampire movie, from the Stephen King book, and it frightened the shit out of – sorry – I mean it really frightened me. For a few weeks afterwards, I kept dreaming about the little boy who had been turned into a vampire. I would wake up believing he was scratching at my bedroom window for me to let him in. It terrified me and I would start screaming and I'd waken everyone in the house. This was happening every night and, believe me, it didn't go down too well with my mum and dad. In the end, dad hung a string of fake garlic on the window. Although I didn't know it was fake. He told me that vampires were afraid of garlic so it – the little boy vampire – couldn't get in. I already knew that from the movie, so the garlic reassured me and the dreams stopped. That was the only time I remember having recurring dreams. Until Lucy, that is.'

'Do you miss her?'

'What? No. Of course I don't. I think about her from time to time and I'm sorry she died. I do feel maybe a little bit guilty, but I'm also thankful I was the one who got the chance to wake up and recover.'

Jennifer didn't mention the nightmares she suffered in the first few months after her discharge from hospital. Nightmares from which she would awaken, terrified and screaming. Caught up in their grip and trapped there until Ilan took her in his arms. He held her tightly to him, rocked and soothed her until she finally calmed down. Nightmares in which Lucy was the driver of the car that had been chasing them. Then they crashed and Lucy had gotten out of the car and walked towards Jennifer. She pulled the door open and dragged her out and she was carrying a gun which she pointed at Jennifer and she told her she was going to finish the job. Then, as she pulled the trigger, Jennifer woke up screaming.

She had experienced this dream in which Lucy tried to kill her again and again. Only Ilan knew about this particular nightmare and it was through his help and comfort that she was eventually able to stop it recurring.

'Do you miss your home in Cyprus?' Saul asked.

'Yeah. I do. But I've accepted that we cannot go back and we have a lovely home here so I'm okay with it.'

'Do you miss the United Kingdom?'

'No. It was my decision to move to Cyprus so, no I don't miss it.'

'You were an interior designer, quite a successful one I am told. Do you miss that?'

'A little. But I can live without it. I enjoy working at the rescue centre. The work's hard and it can be distressing at times. But for every sad story there are many ones that have happy endings. It's rewarding and I love being there.'

'Do you consider yourself happy?'

'Uh, yeah. I suppose so. Obviously, I was happier when Ilan was here. I miss him every single day and I wish he was home, but other than that I'm more or less happy.'

Saul made some notes, impossible to read from her side of the table, and Jennifer wondered if he was writing everything down word for word. She suspected the whole interview was being recorded to be analysed by experts and his notes were merely his own observations. It would be helpful to see what he was writing. She fidgeted as she waited. Her need for the bathroom was more urgent now.

Then Saul closed his notebook, put his pen into his jacket pocket and abruptly stood up. 'Will you excuse me for a moment?'

He was out of the room, her file and the notebook she wanted to get a look at tucked under his arm, before Jennifer had a chance to ask him for a bathroom break.

Fifteen minutes crawled by and Jennifer felt the anger bubbling to the surface. It broke when Saul walked through the door, the file and his notebook still tucked under his arm. He sat down in front of her again.

She was up on her feet immediately and slung her bag onto her shoulder as she did so.

'I'm sorry,' she said, trying to keep her voice as level as possible. But the anger was there and she was ready to verbally lash out at him. She forced it down as best as she could. 'I've answered all your questions, even though some of them were a little more personal than I was comfortable with, and I've been patient and I've behaved myself, which actually surprised me, but I think it's time you tell me what the fuck is going on? Or I'm walking out of here.'

'I only have a few more questions,' he said.

'Tough shit,' Jennifer replied. 'I want some answers and I need to use the bathroom. Like right now.'

'I apologise sincerely, Jennifer. I will have someone escort you to the ladies' facilities where you can freshen up before we continue.'

Saul glanced briefly at the mirror on the far wall and gave the slightest of nods. Seconds later the door opened and the two men who had brought her to this place were standing there.

They guided her down the long corridor and stopped outside the female bathroom. It was obvious they were going to wait outside for her. She ignored them as she forcefully pushed open the door. Thankfully the bathroom was empty and she made her way to the first stall. She locked the door and sat down on the lid of the toilet. Her anger gave way to fear and she shivered. She hid her face in her hands and closed her eyes.

An image of Ilan appeared in her mind and Jennifer began to cry. Softly and quietly. She missed him so much. His smile and his laughter. The smell of his aftershave and his arms around her. She missed making love and how he would hold her tightly to him afterwards. She wanted him home. With her. She didn't want to spend any more of her days and her nights missing him.

'Please come home, Ilan,' she whispered through her tears. 'Please. Please. Please.'

When her tears finally subsided, Jennifer blew her nose and wiped her eyes with some toilet tissue and then remembered she really did have to pee.

As she washed her hands and her face and caught a glimpse of herself in the mirror, Jennifer remembered the evening she had woken up in the hospital. She had asked Ilan to take her into the bathroom where she had stared at herself in the mirror. At first, she hadn't recognised the woman staring back at her. She wasn't sure if she was Jennifer or Lucy. But the image of him standing beside her had grounded her in the reality of who she was and where she was. She had called him her anchor to this world and those words were as true now as they had been back then. She was adrift without him. Lost at sea, with no hope of returning to shore. She could never return until he did. She knew that now. But she did not know if he would ever come back to save her from drowning.

Chapter 3.

Agitated, her interrogator leafed through some papers on the desk and tapped his tablet impatiently when Jennifer came back into the room and sat down opposite him.

'Thank you. I have only a few more questions for you,' he said.

'I have one or two of my own,' Jennifer told him.

'Carry on,' Saul said and she could detect the exasperation in his voice.

'Firstly, why was I brought here? What do you want from me? And where is Ilan?'

'I understand your concern Jennifer, and your questions will be answered in due course. All your concerns will be addressed, but we need to get through this stage first. I promise you that everything will be explained to you shortly.'

'I want to go home.'

'That will be arranged as soon as we are finished.'

'So, I can't go now.'

'At this moment, no.'

'Then I'm under arrest?'

'No. You will be free to go shortly. As soon as we complete these final questions. They are extremely important.'

It was obvious Saul was as stubborn as she was but Jennifer knew he had the upper hand, so she nodded for him to continue. This time he didn't look at the file. Instead, his eyes bored into hers.

'In one of your therapy sessions, you –'

'My therapy sessions? Those are confidential. How did you get a copy of my doctor's reports? And why?' Jennifer glared.

'We subpoenaed them. It's a matter of national security.'

'The fuck it is! Those are private!'

'I am sorry Jennifer. We had no choice and you will

understand fully in due course. May I continue?'

He held her gaze, his eyes determined and relentless, until, with a shrug of her shoulders, Jennifer backed down.

'Now,' he continued. 'You said that you were able to meet Lucy in a setting that you described as a street café in a large city. Why a café in a large city? Which city? And what is the significance of why you decided to meet her there?

'There is no significance and I have no idea what city. It seemed... well, it seemed generic. Maybe it's because I like city centre cafes. It's something I love to do – sit at a sidewalk café, drinking coffee, or maybe wine, and watch the world go by. That's all there is to it.'

'But you said that Lucy told you she saw a picnic table in a forest.'

Jennifer looked down at her hands, examining her fingernails as the memories of that conversation came back to her. Lucy had been adamant that they were in a forest while she had been convinced that they were in a city. It had been then that both of them realised they were somewhere else – in their respective dreams, or minds maybe, and that, in real life, something had happened to them to cause this. That, and the creepy, telepathic waiter who anticipated their wine orders almost before they even thought about another glass.

'Yeah, she did,' Jennifer told him.

'Why do you think that happened? And how do *you* account for the particular settings both of you found yourselves in?'

'I don't know. It's possible we saw what we wanted to see because our minds took us to a place where we would feel happy and relaxed. Even safe.'

'How did you manage to do that?'

'I didn't. I mean I did meet her there but I wasn't able to make it happen. I didn't contrive it.'

'But you said that you and she had planned to meet?'

'Yeah, we did. But it wasn't like that.'

'How did you communicate with her?'

'It's hard to explain, and you have to remember that in real life none of this happened. Okay?'

Saul nodded and Jennifer continued. 'There seemed to be a time lag of a day – I would dream what she had been doing yesterday and she would do the same. I was in the house alone one day. But you have to please remember that all this occurred in Lucy's dream. In her dream, I was in the house alone. I think Ilan had nipped out to get a newspaper or something. And I decided that I didn't want to experience her life in my dreams any longer. I already knew by this stage that she was experiencing my life the way I was experiencing hers. So, while Ilan was outside I stood in my living room and spoke aloud to her, knowing she would get my message that night when she went to sleep. Or at least Lucy dreamed that I did this.'

She could tell he was sceptical. *Who wouldn't be?*

'I know it sounds insane but this is what I went through.'

'Go on.'

'Well, I dreamed that she did the same the next evening. She was a little bit drunk and she ranted and raved a bit but she agreed that we should meet and discuss it. But neither of us knew how do to it. It's not like it's something you can Google for a 'how to' demonstration on YouTube. There was a bit of back and forth, er... discussion between us, that seemed to last for ages, then shortly afterwards we sort of... arranged to fall asleep at the same time, or at least we dreamed that we would arrange to fall asleep at the same time. That was when we met outside the street café, or at the forest picnic table as Lucy called it.'

'So, you did contrive to meet her?'

'It wasn't contrived. Not in the sense you mean. Neither of us knew how to meet. I mean, we didn't know the mechanics of it. We spoke about it in our dreams and then it happened.'

'As if you willed it to happen?'

'I dunno if we actually willed it to happen or not. More

like we dreamed it and it happened. But saying that we willed it is a bit of a stretch.'

'Have you ever willed something to happen and then it did?'

'I don't know what you mean?'

'How did you first meet Ilan?'

Another change of direction threw Jennifer and, exasperated, she puffed out her cheeks and sighed as she tried to keep up with her interrogator.

'Uh, we met in a bar in Cyprus.'

'Did you contrive to meet him?'

'No. Of course not. I went into the bar that evening for a drink because I was bored sitting in my apartment every evening. Yes, of course I noticed him. It was hard not to. I was on my own and he was good looking and he appeared to be on his own. So, when I was ordering my drink, I said hello and chatted him up a bit. Then he bought me a drink and we found a seat, continued chatting and carried on from there. I planned that part from the moment I spotted him at the bar but I didn't 'contrive' to meet him in the way you're suggesting.'

There was a light tap on the door and Saul stood up to open it. One of the men standing outside handed him a large manila envelope. He set the envelope down on the table and looked at her again. His expression seemed softer to her now, his eyes a little more compassionate. Jennifer found this worrying. Maybe the envelopes contained photographs of a body they needed her to identify as Ilan?

But, if that is the case, why all the questions and answers? What is going on here? What does he want from me?

Saul continued to question Jennifer further about Ilan and their relationship. She was as forthright as she could be with her answers, but she got the impression he believed she wasn't telling him everything. Of course, she wasn't telling him everything. She didn't see a reason why she should tell him the details of their marriage. What business was it of his what happened within their marriage?

Eventually he stopped. Either he was satisfied with her answers or he had run out of questions. He opened the envelope and took out a document – three pages stapled together. Jennifer could see that it was written in Hebrew. There was also a photographic ID pass attached to a plain blue lanyard. Her photo, the one that had been taken earlier, was on the pass. He produced his pen from the inside pocket of his jacket.

'I would like you to sign this Jennifer, and then we can proceed.'

'Um, what is it? I'm not comfortable signing something I haven't read.'

'It is a non-disclosure agreement. Basically, it is our equivalent of what in the United Kingdom you would call the Official Secrets Act. I can give you time to read it or I can get you a translation but that would take a while and I am sure you would like to get back home.'

'Can't I take a translation home read it and then sign it? What is this all about anyway?'

'Unfortunately, I cannot tell you until you sign the document but basically, we would like to recruit you because we believe you can be very helpful to us regarding a certain matter.'

'Recruit me? Seriously?

'Yes, Jennifer. I am very serious.'

'This is insane. I don't know if I want to be recruited. By you or by anyone.'

'You are, of course, at liberty to walk out the door and that will be the end of the matter. But I do wish you would join us, because I believe it would be in your interests to do so. I will not force you but I will tell you that it is connected to Ilan and his well-being.'

Despite the insanity of Saul's suggestion, a part of Jennifer was intrigued. She could not deny it. And of course, they were dangling Ilan in front of her. If it helped him, how could she not? It was for this reason alone that she took the pen from him and signed where he indicated she should.

Saul presented her with the ID pass, dangling from its blue lanyard.

Jennifer turned it over in her hand and studied it. The ID pass gave her employment as a typist and secretary. She had joined the civil service.

Chapter 4.

It was early evening when Jennifer returned to her home. The same two men who had collected her that morning drove her back to the house, in the same little Honda. Still covered in dust and dents. And still smelling of wet dog. Both men were more relaxed and much more conversational on the return journey – much shorter this time because the roadworks had been lifted, and the rush hour traffic had all but dispersed. They asked her question after question about her life in Cyprus and in the UK. They also asked her the standard question – was it true that it rained every day in England? They had both been to Cyprus but neither of them had ever visited Britain so their curiosity was piqued, and they made the most of the opportunity to talk to this striking Englishwoman who spoke almost flawless Hebrew. But with a funny accent.

By the time they parked outside the house, Jennifer and her two travelling companions were on first name terms. She even promised Ari, the younger of the two, that she would help him select a rescue dog for his girlfriend if he dropped by the shelter some weekend soon.

'But it must be a dog that has lots of energy,' Ari told her jokingly. 'My girlfriend likes to hike everywhere. An energetic dog means she can take the dog hiking with her and leave me in front of the television!'

Despite their friendliness, Jennifer was glad to watch them drive away and she was relieved to be back home. But as soon as she opened the front door and walked inside the loneliness and the isolation hit her all over again.

She leaned the back of her head and shoulders against the door and closed her eyes as she took a moment and a deep breath, thankful to be back home again where she could sit down and relax. But the cats had other ideas. They ran to her and entwined themselves around her ankles as they meowed and begged for food.

She pushed herself forward and went into the kitchen

where she filled their food bowls. They quietened down and ignored her as they ate. As far as they were concerned, she was home and had fulfilled her duty by feeding them. They would give her attention later when they decided they wanted to do so.

With the cats fed, Jennifer opened the fridge door and considered her own supper. Nothing appealed to her, other than a bottle of white wine. She poured a glass and added two ice cubes from the freezer. She had adopted Lucy's old habit of adding ice to her wine but only when the weather was hot. This evening though, even in the chill of mid-December, she wanted it with ice. She pulled on a sweater, carried the wine outside onto the patio, took a seat and tried not to think about the extraordinary turn of events her day had taken in the company of Saul Mueller.

The sun had long set and it was completely dark now. The only light came from the traffic and the glow of the nearby houses and the street lights but that was enough tonight. The air was chilly and Jennifer wrapped her arms around herself. A hot toddy instead of the wine probably would have been the more sensible option for this winter's evening.

It'll be Christmas soon. Two weeks to go and I haven't done a thing. Not that we ever do much other than exchange gifts and cook a nice meal. Something a little bit more formal, with the table set. Crystal wine glasses and napkins instead of paper kitchen towels. But I haven't even sent cards to everyone back at home. Oh, it's probably too late now anyway.

It was true, they didn't celebrate Christmas. It was not part of Israeli culture. In Cyprus they put up a tree every year – a big brute of a thing, decorated with birds and lights and tinsel – to celebrate the winter solstice. They did the same in Israel but on a much smaller scale and used a potted palm tree instead of a fir. But it was mostly because Jennifer loved any excuse to have a plant inside the house rather than any Christmas symbolism. And of course, she loved candles, so she always had some lit at Hanukkah.

And we always exchange gifts on Christmas Eve. I hadn't even thought about what to get him this year. Now I won't have to.

In the darkness, the temperature had fallen and Jennifer was glad she had put on a sweater before coming outside. But she continued to sit there, sipping her wine and allowing her mind to stray in whatever direction it chose to go. Naturally, it insisted on leading her to Ilan and, by extension, to what had occurred this afternoon.

As soon as she had signed the document – the Israeli version of the Official Secrets Act – Saul had explained what they wanted from her.

At the time, it had seemed a perfectly reasonable request but, sitting at home in the darkness, she was filled with a lot of doubt and more than a little fear. Now, on the surface, it sounded insane – beyond the realms of possibility. It was only the thought, or the hope, that it might bring Ilan home that made her determined to try and go through with it.

Jennifer sat there for the longest time, wishing he was beside her, thinking of tomorrow and what it would bring. The thought of what she was about to do suddenly became terrifying, and already the old memories were beginning to haunt her. She suppressed a shudder because she knew she had no choice. To do nothing was a betrayal of Ilan and their love for each other and, in promising Saul she would try and do this, she was also promising Ilan that she would do all that she could to bring him home safely. She hoped it would be enough.

Her phone pinged an incoming WhatsApp message. It was from Nurit.

They've seconded me in to work with SM and briefed me on what u r going to do. I know we're not supposed to discuss it but I want to tell u that ur a hero! Is there anything I can do to help? xx

For a moment or two Jennifer stared at the message and had to think who SM was. *Saul Mueller. Of course!*

She smiled and sent a reply. **Can u ask Reuben to look after the cats plz.**

Nurit texted back immediately. **You have to ask?! When do u start this?**

Wednesday.

Ok. B in touch.

With that, Jennifer came back into the warmth of the house and closed the patio doors against the coldness of the evening. She switched on the lights and plugged her phone into the charging socket, then poured another glass of wine and sat down on the sofa. With her glass of wine and her thoughts, she spent the time in an attempt to mentally prepare herself for what the day after tomorrow would bring. But she couldn't. There was no point of reference. How could there be? What she was about to undertake was a step into the unknown.

She tilted the glass and drained the last mouthful and decided to go to bed. An early night and a good sleep would help her to prepare herself. Or at least stop her thinking about what lay in store for her in the coming days. She was rinsing the wine glass in the sink when the doorbell rang.

Nurit stood on the doorstep. She was carrying two bottles of wine and a Chinese takeaway.

With a smile, Jennifer stepped back to let her enter. Despite her plans of only a few minutes ago, Ilan's daughter was a welcome sight.

Nurit placed the wine and the food on the kitchen worktop and turned to her stepmother. 'I thought you might need company. And food, because I know you well enough to know you won't bother making anything for yourself. I brought food and, more importantly, wine.'

'I was about to go to bed, but now that you're here, yes I definitely need the company. Todah! Thank you!' Jennifer put her arms around the younger woman and hugged her tightly. 'Thank you so much.'

Nurit was tall. She was beautiful and had Ilan's dark hair and pouting smile. She looked so much like her father that Jennifer couldn't help but feel a deep affection for her.

When they first met, both women had been formal and stiff towards one another. Jennifer made a point of not casting herself in the role of stepmother and, although Nurit seemed to appreciate this, the younger woman maintained her distance – friendly, but polite and not inclined to give too much of herself to this woman who was now a vital part of her father's life. When both women discovered they had a similar sense of humour and a love of light and colour, they gradually let down their respective barriers. From then on, their relationship began to slowly develop towards friendship.

One afternoon, Jennifer overheard Nurit in conversation with Ilan about decorating their newly-built home and that neither she nor Reuben had the expertise to do it alone. Jennifer cautiously jumped in with a few subtle suggestions on what might work for them. Before she knew it, Jennifer found herself nervously planning the interior design of the whole house. When Nurit invited her over one day to see the results of her designs, she hugged Jennifer tightly and told her it was exactly what she had imagined. That day their friendship had been sealed.

'Ahh, I'm here to check what food you want me or Reuben to give Holly and Possum.'

'Liar. You both know exactly what they eat.'

'Okay,' she shrugged. 'I'm here because Reuben is watching a football match and the kids are fast asleep and I can't relax because of… well, you know. I need to be drinking wine and eating junk food along with some good conversation. And you need to not be alone tonight.'

'I'm afraid I can't guarantee good conversation,' Jennifer told her.

'If there's wine, I think I can survive,' Nurit replied.

'Okay. I'll get the glasses and pour the wine while you dish out the food.'

They made small talk while they ate. It seemed Nurit was reluctant to discuss anything too important until the distraction of dining was out of the way and Jennifer hadn't realised just how hungry she was until the food was set in front of her. The last bite she had eaten had been the vending-machine sandwich at lunchtime. She tucked in, relishing the taste as well as the carbs.

When they were both finished, Nurit sat back in the chair and looked at her stepmother intently.

Jennifer recognised that look. It was one of Ilan's best and it always meant a serious conversation.

'What?'

'Are you sure about this?' Nurit asked.

'As sure as I can be,' Jennifer replied. 'Why?'

Nurit picked at a few stray grains of rice on her plate as she thought about what she wanted to say. 'If it can help bring my father home then, naturally, I'm all in favour of what you are trying to do. But I don't understand much of it other than what they told me during the briefing, and that was just the very basic details. They want me to be a part of your support system and they're bringing me in because, with my background in military intelligence, I have the necessary security clearance. When Saul Mueller himself asked me, I jumped at the chance because – sorry, but it does sound fascinating. But I also want to be there with you. So, I agreed without hesitation. I couldn't not agree, but I'm –'

'Thank you. I really appreciate this so much.'

'You're welcome. But I'm not sure what it involves. My father told me some of what happened to you in Cyprus but not all and I don't understand how this can be connected.'

'Okay, I'll tell you all about it,' Jennifer said. 'But It's a long story, Nurit. We need more wine first.'

Jennifer quickly rinsed the plates in the kitchen sink then took another chilled bottle out of the fridge. They made their way into the living room where they got comfortable on the sofa.

The two women drank wine like it was going out of fashion. Jennifer had placed a bowl of potato chips on the table and Nurit sipped her wine and, despite the meal she had just eaten, munched her way through half of the potato chips as she listened intently while Jennifer told her the full story of all the dreams she had experienced while in a medically induced coma.

Nurit interrupted her now and then to ask Jennifer to clarify something she didn't understand as Jennifer told her how she relived ten years of the life of a woman in England called Lucy Wilson. She told Nurit how this all came about because Lucy had suffered a brain injury roughly around the same time she had collapsed the day after she and Ilan had crashed their car that night in Cyprus. As a result, Lucy had experienced the same dream state wherein she relived Jennifer's life.

Jennifer paused as she found herself growing uncomfortable under the intense scrutiny of the younger woman's gaze. Relating it to Nurit once again brought the painful memories back to the surface. Memories she had buried for so long that she had almost begun to believe the whole thing had never happened. Now, the memories were fresh and clear and it seemed she was caught up in the whole nightmare all over again.

Nurit set the first bottle on the coffee table, drained of its contents, in a not-so-subtle hint that they needed another one.

Glad of the momentary reprieve, Jennifer unfolded her legs, got up and went to grab another bottle of Pinot Grigio from the fridge. She returned with the wine and more potato chips which she placed within easy reach on the coffee table. She filled their glasses up again and sat down again on the comfortable armchair opposite the sofa on which Nurit was half-sitting, half-lying, with a cosy throw draped across her legs.

This is what it will be like. Jennifer felt a shiver run through her as the memories surfaced once more.

'Are you okay?' Nurit asked.

'Yes. It's just a bit... painful to remember it.'

'It's hard to believe.'

'But do you believe me?'

Nurit thought about it for a moment as she sipped her wine. Then she nodded her head slowly. 'Anyone else telling me this I would be sceptical. Fuck! I'd be more than sceptical. I wouldn't believe them and I'd call them crazy. But I know you and I know my father and he told me a little of it – not all the details, merely the fact that you had some bad hallucinogenic experiences during your coma after you were injured. I believed him when he told me and yes, I believe you now.'

'Thank you,' Jennifer said, struggling to keep the tremor of relief out of her voice. 'But calling what I went through a bad experience is probably too strong a word. And I'm not sure hallucinogenic would be the correct word. That implies I imagined it all and I didn't imagine or dream it. It was real at the time and it was real when I checked out Lucy's life and then visited her grave. She existed. But the experience wasn't all bad. There were times when I found it interesting, and even enjoyable…' she paused when she saw the surprised look on Nurit's face. 'Don't look so horrified. It happened and I lived through it. And naturally some of it was good and some of it was bad. I don't see the point in dwelling on the negative. I learned that from your father – always search for the positive.'

'Yeah, that sounds like him...' Nurit paused and smiled at her stepmother and friend. But her smile was wistful. 'I miss him terribly, Jennifer.'

'I miss him, too.' Jennifer took a long mouthful of her wine as she also tried to keep her emotions in check.

'So, how does this help them find him?' Nurit asked.

'They're going to try and recreate what I experienced.'

'I know that part. They told me all about that. What I mean is how are you, and they, going to do it.'

'I have no idea. They didn't go into the details. I

suppose they're going to put me in a medically induced coma again, similar to what I experienced after the crash in Cyprus, but this time they're going to help me try to control my dreams.'

Nurit frowned. 'Isn't that risky? I mean the coma part.'

'Probably. But what else is there?'

'There's gotta be some other method. Something safer. Hypnosis maybe,' Nurit shrugged. 'Something...'

'Maybe there is. I'm not saying this is what they're gonna do. It might not be a coma and it may well be they'll use hypnosis or something like that. Honestly, I have no idea what they're planning. They haven't explained the ins and outs of it to me. But whatever method they use, and I'm open to trying anything, it all depends on whether or not I can do it.'

'So, you can you connect with Dad and find out where he is?'

'I think that's the aim.'

Nurit blew out a long breath. 'It's a long shot.'

'I know,' Jennifer shrugged. 'But what else is there?'

Chapter 5.

Jennifer opened her eyes and peered at the clock beside the bed. She groaned, threw back the bedsheets and staggered into the bathroom. Still half asleep, she pulled off the T-shirt she was wearing – an old one of Ilan's – and stepped into the shower. The cascade of hot water slowly awakened and refreshed her.

It had been much later than she realised when they had called it a night and gone to bed. Nurit was more than a little bit drunk and her mood varied between concern about her father, and interest in what Jennifer was going to be doing, to her latest repertoire of dirty jokes.

'So, there was this guy who… um… was married to a woman from Turkey, and she… No wait. He was from Turkey and she was Australian. I think. Anyway, he had the biggest dick. Ever. And… and… shit. I can't remember,' she said as Jennifer helped her into bed.

'Don't worry. You can tell me in the morning. Now, go to sleep,' Jennifer whispered as she pulled the bedcovers over the already asleep younger woman.

In her own bed, Jennifer, snuggled under the covers and lay awake for a while, painfully aware of the empty space beside her, until she eventually fell into a deep and dreamless sleep.

It was the only wayward strand of long dark hair that indicated someone was underneath the duvet as Jennifer carried a mug of strong black coffee into the spare bedroom. She nudged Nurit's shoulder gently until she heard a muffled groan and a curse. Holly was asleep at the foot of the bed and she opened one eye to see who it was that dared to disturb her slumber.

'It's morning, Nurit. Time to get up. I brought you some coffee.' She set the mug down on the nightstand.

'Todah,' Nurit replied with a sleepy yawn and a groan.

'Thank you.'

'There's plenty of hot water if you want a shower.'

'Yeah, okay. Give me five minutes.'

It took a bit longer than five minutes but eventually Nurit appeared, showered and dressed and looking decidedly hungover. She made immediately for the coffee machine, poured herself another mug of coffee and added two sachets of sugar. Jennifer watched her as she stirred it with a spoon.

'Bad hangover?'

'Ken,' she replied in Hebrew then glared at the empty bottles beside the re-cycling bin as if they were to blame for her suffering. 'I'm not used to this much wine in only a couple of hours.'

'Do you want something to eat? It will help you.'

'No. I couldn't face anything. This will do,' she said and held up her mug. 'How do you drink all that wine and still look fresh and sober first thing in the morning?'

'Years and years of practice,' Jennifer grinned. 'And, if you can remember, it was you not me, who got stuck into the second bottle.'

'Me bad. Me never, ever drinking again.' She thought about it. 'Well, until the next time.'

'That's my girl,' Jennifer laughed. 'Now, if you don't mind, as soon as you've finished your coffee, I need you to get out of here so I can get ready for... work.'

'When do you have to be there?'

'Tomorrow morning at eleven.'

Nurit nodded. 'I can stay tonight again, if you need some company.'

'No, I'm fine. I think I need to spend some time by myself and I have stuff to do. Get my affairs into order, so to speak.'

'Don't say that! That's frightening!'

'I didn't mean it that way,' Jennifer replied. 'I need to pack a few things and phone the rescue centre to let them know that I won't be available for a while. Talia is going to be annoyed. She's short-staffed as it is with Naomi out on sick leave.'

'Do you want me to come with you tomorrow? Drive you there?'

'No sweetheart, I'll be fine. They're sending a car to pick me up. But thank you for offering. I do appreciate it.'

'Okay. But are you sure you want to be alone? I can come back this evening if you want. Just for an hour or so, and no booze. Definitely no booze.' Nurit shuddered as she topped up her coffee mug.

'I know and I appreciate the offer but I... well, I think I need to spend some time by myself. Gathering my thoughts and trying to get my head around this. I might go for a long walk later. Maybe on the beach, or something. And then a quiet night by myself.'

'Are you sure about this, Jennifer?' Nurit asked with a frown on her face.

'Yes. I'm sure. I just need some time to... prepare. And I do need to pack a few things. I have no idea how long this will take. If I can, I'll call you when I get there. But if there's no cell reception…'

'I'll be there, working with you. I mean, are you sure about the whole putting-yourself-into-a-coma thing?'

'Yes. I'm sure,' Jennifer replied, keeping her voice strong and steady.

'Okay. I just hope it works and Dad is found and you are not harmed. I'll see you at um… work. And don't worry about the cats. Between Reuben and myself, they will be well looked after.'

Nurit finished her coffee and rinsed the mug under the tap, then put her arms around her stepmother's shoulders and embraced her tightly. 'Please bring him home, and if for some reason that isn't possible but if you do get the opportunity to talk to him in a dream, will you tell him... tell him he's the best father in the whole world and I love him with all my heart. And I'm so very proud of him. Will you tell him that for me? Please.'

'I will do my very best,' Jennifer said. She fought back the tears as she returned the hug.

Jennifer watched from the doorway as Nurit, with a casual wave goodbye, set off on her way home. She walked at a brisk pace that soon turned into a gentle jog as she made her way up the slight incline and then she turned left and disappeared from view. Jennifer knew she would run the kilometre to her home to dispel any traces of the hangover that the coffee had missed.

Jennifer went back inside, took a can of cat food from the kitchen cupboard and prised open the can. This brought the two cats running into the kitchen. They meowed and weaved themselves around her legs as she scooped the meat into their respective bowls. She opened another can into a larger bowl, took it outside and placed it near the front door. The feral tabby cats would wait cautiously in the nearby shrubs until they knew it was safe to come out and eat.

She spotted them sitting there, waiting patiently, as she closed the door behind her.

Now, she didn't know what to do. Well, she did. She had to pack and maybe give the house a bit of cleaning before she left. And she had to telephone Talia at the rescue centre and let her know she wouldn't be available for a few days. When she stopped and thought about it, she actually had a lot to do.

Instead, Jennifer made herself another large mug of coffee. Then she sat down at the table with her hands curled around the coffee mug. She stared out of the window and she wondered how and why her life had come to this.

Chapter 6 – Syria.

The cold he felt came not from the icy wind that blew around him. Nor did it come from any illness. This coldness came from the isolation of being a stranger adrift in a harsh, uncompromising land, and in the company of some very dangerous people. And he couldn't escape the feeling of foreboding that had crept up on him in the last two days. A feeling that something was about to happen that he would be powerless to prevent. He still didn't know what this 'something' was, despite his high standing within the group.

'Jamal?'

He turned to face the voice behind him that spoke his name quietly but with authority.

'Yes, my brother?'

'Sayeed wishes to speak with you. He expected you to meet with him after morning prayers. I searched for you but I could not find you until now.'

There was nothing he could say in reply. He merely nodded his response. His face a mask of calmness and serenity that hid his true emotions and the rage that boiled in his heart. That, and the fear.

'Are you troubled, my brother?' Asif asked him with a frown.

'No. Why do you ask?'

Asif looked at him. 'He expected you earlier.'

'I did not know this, but please inform Sayeed that I will be with him shortly.'

The smaller man hesitated. He had been sent to bring Jamal to the meeting and he did not wish to disobey, but this tall, dark-haired man also commanded respect and he was as equally afraid of him as he was of Sayeed.

In the end it was the darkness in this man's eyes that won and he courteously nodded and said that he would convey the message back to their leader.

Jamal turned away and looked out towards the horizon again, stealing a few more moments before his meeting with the man who was in charge of the camp. The sun had climbed higher in the cloudless sky, but it brought only a hint of warmth to the lands beneath its fiery eye. Nothing stirred as his gaze searched the distant horizon.

Would he ever see his home again? Would he ever see her again? Was she standing at the back door staring in his direction and wondering where he was? Did she worry about him? Or had he been away too long?

He shivered once more then he turned and walked calmly back to the camp.

Chapter 7.

After Nurit left, Jennifer went into the spare bedroom and dug out her large holdall from the back of the wardrobe. She carried it into their bedroom, placed it on the bed and opened it. For a few moments she could only stand there and stare at it as her memory flew back to that night in Cyprus, when a similar type of holdall had been dragged from the back of a wardrobe and hurriedly packed. That was the night their lives had changed forever. Now, in a way, history was repeating itself. How would this change manifest itself? Jennifer had no idea.

She shook her head to clear her thoughts and concentrated on what she would need. Changes of underwear, comfortable causal clothes, sleepwear, toiletries, a paperback or two and some other odds and ends. She packed, added a light sweater and a couple more tops, then carried the holdall into the living room and looked around to see what else she wanted to bring with her. She picked up her favourite framed photograph – one of Ilan standing behind her, his chin resting on her shoulder and his arms surrounding her. She placed it carefully in among some T-shirts.

From the kitchen she got two bottles of wine and placed them in the holdall inside the legs of her jeans, more to protect them than hide them. And that was it. She was packed and ready to go.

Cleaning wasn't Jennifer's favourite method of passing the time but she needed to do something to prevent herself from sitting on the sofa brooding and the house had been neglected far too long. She never had been obsessively house-proud but she wasn't a complete slob and usually spent at least one day a week giving it a complete going over. But her interest in housework, among other things, had waned over the months since Ilan left and Jennifer had found she couldn't be bothered. It was so much easier to spend her evenings on the sofa in front of the television, watching mind-numbing rubbish and drinking wine.

Jennifer tackled the housework with a vengeance. She went from room to room, gathering up old magazines that were lying around. Throwing out the many empty bottles of wine that had gathered in the utility room cupboard. She dusted and polished until the furniture gleamed. Scrubbed and wiped and swept. She cleaned the bathroom until it was pristine and wondered how on earth a blob of toothpaste could land so high up on the mirror that she had to stretch to clean it away.

As she polished the mirror, Jennifer realised just how much she had let things go since Ilan left. As she continued cleaning and tidying, she made a promise to herself that she would change her ways.

By the time she had cleaned every room, the house was gleaming and Jennifer finished her housework by sweeping up the fallen leaves on the patio. She stopped and looked at her watch, dismayed to realise that it was only a quarter past twelve. Her whirlwind of nervous energy had only managed to pass a couple of hours.

This is going to be a long day, and probably a longer night.

She dropped a teabag into a mug as the kettle came to the boil. As she stirred the dark liquid, Jennifer wondered why they hadn't asked her to come this evening. It would have been preferable to start the ball rolling sooner rather than later, because no matter how hard she concentrated on cleaning the house she couldn't stop thinking about what was in store for her. The more thought that went into it and the more she wondered what exactly they were going to do to make this work – *if* it even could work – the more frightened she became.

What if they put me into a coma and something goes wrong and I don't wake up? Would they pull the plug and let me die? Would that be murder? Probably not. They'll make sure my death certificate is a carefully worded document, citing accidental or natural causes as the reason for my 'oh, so tragic' demise. Or would they stage a car accident or a suicide?

Her paranoia was a galloping horse as she imagined all the possible scenarios in which her death could be covered up.

But what if I don't die? What if I don't waken up and I remain in a coma forever?

She had heard stories of that happening. People remaining in a permanent vegetative state for years, sometime fully aware of their surroundings and situation but unable to communicate. Unable to scream for help or beg release from the prison of their mind. One case in particular she had read about where a patient, for year after year, could only weep when he recognised the faces of his family.

That wasn't living. It was only existing on the most basic level. Jennifer prayed she would never end up like that.

I should have got something in writing. Some sort of living will with a guarantee that they switch me off if I don't wake up. Something legal. But it's too late to do that now.

Despite the pleasant warmth of the winter sun, Jennifer shivered and folded her arms defensively in front of her. She had already agreed to do what they asked, but that didn't stop all these terrifying thoughts from running through her mind. She needed something else to focus on so, as soon as the laundry was finished, she grabbed her car keys and sunglasses and headed out the front door.

Less than fifteen minutes later, she found a parking space close to the rescue centre where she worked. With a deep breath, she opened the front door and made her way inside.

The reception counter was unmanned and she could hear the sounds of loud barking coming from the rear of the premises. *Sounds like lunch is being served.*

Jennifer opened the office door and poked her head

through.

'Hi there,' she said.

Talia looked up from her accounts and smiled. She set her pen down and stretched her arms and shoulders to work the stiffness out and relished the chance to ignore the paperwork, even if only for a few minutes.

'Isn't this your day off?' she asked.

'It is but I need a long walk to clear my head and I might as well exercise one of the dogs while I'm at it.'

'Thinking of Ilan?' Talia's look was fully of sympathy. She knew Ilan was working abroad but, like all Israelis, she knew in a general sort of way what he was probably doing, even if she didn't know the specifics.

Everyone knew the old 'joke' in Israel, that when someone – maybe a young reservist soldier living at home with his parents – is called up for a special anti-terrorist mission, the conversation between him and his parents would consist of them asking him where he was going and him telling them he was going nowhere. Then they would ask him what was he going to do. His reply would always be the same – nothing. The parents knew where he was going and they had an idea of what he was going to be doing. Then they would watch him leave and sit at home and worry until he returned.

This so-called 'joke' also applied to spouses. Jennifer had heard it many times and hated it. It wasn't funny the first time she heard it and it still wasn't funny.

'Yeah. I think about Ilan all the time but maybe a bit more these days. And I'm missing him terribly. More than ever.' Jennifer nodded. She wanted to say more. Tell Talia that Ilan was 'missing in action' and that they didn't know why and they were concerned about him. It would have been nice to share these concerns with someone she considered a friend but she knew that it was impossible.

Official Secrets Act, or whatever it's called here.

Jennifer glanced around the small, untidy office. The paperwork was piling up, but that was a good thing and no one was complaining. The rescue centre was busier than it had been in a long time, but only because recently there had been more adoptions than intakes. Every member of staff, both regulars and volunteers, kept their fingers crossed that this trend would continue. It probably wouldn't, but they made the most of it when it did.

'Most of the time I manage okay. I have my own routine and I'm content enough and then out of the blue it hits me and I start missing him. And sometimes I miss him so much it physically hurts me. That's when I need to get out of the house for a while. Like now.'

Talia nodded but didn't speak. Her husband had died of a heart attack two years ago and she knew exactly how lonely a house became when the person you shared it with was no longer there. For whatever reason.

'I'm being stupid, I know. It's not like this is the first time he's been away for a long time. You'd think I'd be used to it by now.'

'Do you want a coffee?' Talia asked.

Jennifer screwed up her face in a negative gesture. 'I need a good walk first. Maybe when I get back?'

'Sure. No problem. Could you take Benji? He needs some exercise and it's obvious that he prefers to go with you. What do you bribe him with? Ice cream?'

Jennifer laughed. Benji was one of their long-term residents. He was deaf and had been adopted twice but had been unable to settle into either of his new homes. Despite the experience and love of both his new families, he became depressed after only a few days. He refused to eat and came close to shutting down completely, much to the disappointment of the people who wanted to give him a loving home. They had no choice but to return him to the shelter where, on both occasions, he improved immediately and was back to his normal, happy self by the next morning.

It appeared Benji was institutionalised and considered the rescue centre his home. As a result, he got extra attention from staff and visitors alike. But, while he enjoyed the attention, it seemed his real reason for being there was to befriend and comfort the new arrivals, especially the puppies.

He was one of Jennifer's favourites and they shared a special bond with one another. Maybe he was aware she needed someone to comfort her every now and then, she didn't know, but she accepted his friendship and returned it wholeheartedly.

'Yeah, no problem. I'm always happy to spend some time with Benji,' Jennifer replied as Talia reached behind her for his harness – or his bra, as Jennifer jokingly called it. It was a type that he stepped into that fitted across his shoulders and around his chest. Benji's name, his microchip number and the telephone number for the centre was printed on a little disc attached to the harness. The leash clipped onto the rings at the top on the harness across his shoulders. Benji had a habit of slipping out of a neck collar so this 'bra' solved that problem.

Jennifer took the harness and got a leash from a row on nearby hooks on the wall. From a big plastic bucket in the corner, she scooped up some dog treats and poured them into a bag which she placed in her pocket. She glanced at her friend and boss. Talia returned the look with a quizzical frown.

'What?'

'I need to talk to you about some time off,' Jennifer told her. 'I wouldn't ask but it's important. It's to do with Ilan. Well, indirectly.'

Talia nodded thoughtfully. 'Enjoy your walk. Both you and Benji. I'll have coffee ready when you get back and we can have a chat.'

Benji was already standing up on the back seat of the car and whining frantically to get out as Jennifer pulled into the beach parking lot. She attached his leash to his harness and he leapt out of the car and stood by her side, waiting obediently but stepping from one paw to the other with impatience while she locked up.

Although it was sunny, it was still chilly enough to make Jennifer grateful she had brought a padded jacket and a woolly hat. She put on the hat and zipped the jacket up to her neck and glanced round her. At this time of the day the beach was, thankfully, almost deserted apart from one or two people far in the distance and a walk along the water's edge with only Benji and her thoughts for company would do her the world of good.

Benji's age was somewhere around nine or ten years old and he was completely deaf. He was a purebred golden retriever and had all the funny, loving and loyal traits of the breed. Apart from retrieving. Retrieving was something Benji did not do. His attitude when someone threw a ball or a frisbee and asked him to fetch it was: 'Excuse me. Since you were stupid enough to throw it, you can go and retrieve it yourself.'

Instead, he preferred to walk close to his human, relishing the sights and the smells, but with no inclination to chase anything. Except cats and, worst of all, motor vehicles.

Cars, trucks and motorcycles tended to be Benji's nemeses and he would be inclined to slip out of a neck collar and race off after them. In his mind, all vehicles were the enemy and their tyres should be ripped to shreds and they should be chased out of the country. His hatred of them had caused problems in the past, and had almost gotten him killed, so he was banned from walking anywhere near traffic. It was the same when he spotted a cat.

Because she walked him regularly, Jennifer was aware of this and always took him to the beach – one of the dog-friendly beaches. And sometimes she got the impression that he was relieved when she took him there because he knew this was the one place there would be no cats or cars.

Since she started interacting with him, Jennifer had developed a basic sign language which he learned remarkably quickly. It was nothing elaborate, merely some simple hand gestures and movements that indicated what she wanted him to do. She had reinforced his training with treats until he had learned what she was telling him and what she wanted from him. Now he was at the stage where he could anticipate her request before she made it. He was that intelligent.

His deafness was not a handicap and Jennifer often wondered if he preferred the quietness even if it meant he never heard a human voice telling him what a good boy he was and how much he was loved. Maybe he knew he was loved already and didn't need to hear the words. He was that intelligent.

She stuffed the car keys into the small zip pocket of her backpack, along with a bottle of water, a small plastic bowel and the bag containing small bite dog treats, a handful of which she placed in her jacket pocket. Her phone was in the other pocket – she wouldn't hear it ringing in the backpack – and they were good to go.

She raised her hand up in front of Benji, palm towards him. He wagged his tail and his ears pricked up in eager anticipation as she pointed towards the sand and the water beyond. This signal told him they were ready to set off on their walk.

Benji barked softly. Jennifer tapped the side of her leg and stepped forward. This was his cue and they set off down the short path to the beach. He woofed a happy hello to a passing jogger, but he didn't strain to run after him and Jennifer rewarded him with a 'thumbs up' gesture and a treat. He thanked her with a wag of his tail and a lick of her hand and they walked along the beach together at the water's edge. He lunged towards the small waves and he lapped at the water, snorting in disgust at the salty taste of it.

Benji found a shell half buried in the sand and grabbed it up in his mouth then dropped it at Jennifer's foot. He nudged it with his nose and looked up at her. It was a gift to her for loving him and, to his delight, she accepted it gratefully. She didn't have to tell him she would treasure it. He knew she would.

He remained by her side as they walked along, but

Jennifer wasn't fooled in the slightest by his compliant behaviour. If they were near a busy road, he would be pulling her arm out of its socket in his attempt to hunt down and kill some cars.

It was the same with cats. In Benji's mind cats were put on this planet for him to chase. Several faint scars on his nose bore witness to previous run-ins with his feline adversaries. It should have encouraged him to give up his fight once and for all but, if anything, it seemed to make him more determined than ever to get involved in… well, catfights. He may have lost a few battles in his day but Benji had no intention of ever losing the war.

This was the sole reason Jennifer and Ilan had, very reluctantly, decided not to adopt him. She was convinced he would have settled with them despite two failed adoptions already. He was content and very happy in her presence at the shelter and when out for a walk, and he went nuts with delight each time he met Ilan. It would have been perfect except for the cats. Holly and Possum were well settled and the two feral cats were comfortable enough to hang around outside. Bringing a dog into the mix, especially one who hated cats, was never going to work no matter how much Jennifer wished it would.

The woman and the dog kept up a steady but comfortable pace as they walked, but eventually Benji started to slow down. He was beginning to tire and he needed a rest. There was no one around so Jennifer decided it was time to take a break.

Still close to the edge of the gently breaking waves, they sat down on the sand. She poured water into the bowl and Benji lapped at it until his thirst was quenched. Jennifer watched him drink as she took a couple of mouthfuls from the bottle herself. Then Benji nudged her arm to remind her that she still had dog treats for him. She gave him four and kept the rest for later.

There was a slight breeze coming off the sea and, although it was chilly despite the winter sunshine, Jennifer was content to sit a while. She listened to the waves that lapped the sand and watched the gulls as they swooped and dived for small fish.

As they had a habit of doing, her thoughts turned to Ilan. *Where are you, darling? Are you safe? Are you well? Do you miss me like I miss you?*

Missing him was a dull ache in her chest. One she had learned to live with, even forget at times, but it was always under the surface. It was an ache that, especially when she was alone, brought tears to her eyes. This was one of those times.

Benji pressed his shoulder against Jennifer's arm, looked into her eyes and offered his paw to her. She took it as her tears fell in silent rivulets down her cheeks. They splashed on to her arm and onto the sand where they would, at the next high tide, disappear forever among the salty waters of the Mediterranean. Every now and then Benji turned towards her and licked away a tear. But mostly he allowed her to cry in peace and waited patiently for her tears to subside. When she buried her face in his fur, he knew then she would be okay. It was a ritual they often performed. He didn't not know the cause of her sadness. He only knew she was sad and it was his place to comfort her as best as he could.

'You want to know something, Benji?'

In his deafness he ignored her.

'Sometimes I think I hate him.'

He continued to ignore her, preferring to watch the seagulls.

With a heavy sigh, Jennifer fished a tissue out of her pocket. It smelled of dog treats but she blew her nose with it anyway and got to her feet. Benji jumped up, ready and eager to begin the walk back home.

Chapter 8.

There was nothing left to do. The house was clean and tidy and the laundry was up to date. Over coffee and pastries, Talia had agreed to give her indefinite time off work.

She had dismissed Jennifer's attempts to explain with a wave of her hand. 'You wouldn't be asking me if it wasn't important,' Talia had said and had given her a sympathetic smile that conveyed what words could not.

Pouches of wet cat food and a box of kibble for snacks sat on display on the kitchen counter, along with detailed instructions on which cat preferred which packet of food. She remembered to bring in some extra bags of cat litter from the garage and left them by the back door.

Jennifer was all packed and ready. She only had to get the evening and the night over and they would be there to pick her up at nine-thirty or thereabouts tomorrow morning. Driving there herself would have been the preferable option because it would be a way to retain some small degree of control in a situation that she felt she had little or no control over. Merely knowing her car was in the carpark and she could get into it and drive away any time would have made all of this easier.

Well, maybe slightly easier. It didn't change the fact that her husband was missing and she was the only one who stood a slim chance of locating him.

How crazy is that? The only way to find Ilan is for me to go to sleep and dream about him. Seriously? If that's all they have then he's in big trouble.

Hunger gnawed at her stomach but the thought of food almost made her feel nauseous. But not eating anything wasn't a good idea and the last bite of food had been the two pastries and a coffee with Talia after she returned a happy, though exhausted, Benji to the shelter.

She stood in front of the open fridge, but staring at the meagre contents didn't help. There was nothing that appealed to her other than the bottle of wine left over from last evening. It was three-quarters full and it seemed to be calling to her.

'No point in letting good wine go to waste,' Jennifer said aloud as she grabbed the bottle, got a wineglass from the cupboard and poured herself a healthy measure.

It was crisp and cold and delicious. She lifted another bottle from the wine rack and placed it in the fridge knowing that one wouldn't be enough. She remembered the two bottles she had hidden in her bag.

I wonder if I'll be allowed wine? Or any alcohol for that matter?

Even with the wine Jennifer couldn't relax. It never had been in her nature to spend her time hanging around waiting for something to happen, and this evening was exactly what she was doing. She was tempted to send a WhatsApp message to Nurit and have her call round, if only for an hour or two, but she didn't want to impose. Nurit had a demanding job, two small children and a husband to look after. Holding her stepmother's hand was too much to ask. Besides, hadn't she done that last night?

Ilan's e-cigarette kit with its charger and a bottle of vape juice was on the kitchen counter where he had left it all those months ago. The rest of the accessories belonging to it, spare coils and other bottles of juice in various strengths and flavours, he kept in a nearby drawer. The kit had been her birthday present to him last November and, despite her doubts that he would use it, he had taken to it like a duck to water. He tried it, decided he liked it, and quit smoking immediately, content to happily puff away on this instead of a real cigarette.

When he left, Jennifer never put it away. She would lift it every time she wiped down the counter, then put it back again. Keeping it there was her way of pretending he had only nipped out for a couple of hours and would be using it again as soon as he came back home.

Now it mocked her. A simple e-cigarette, with the battery probably flat by now, and a bottle of his favourite strawberry e-juice alongside it, told her he was no longer here to use it. It told her he hadn't cared enough to stick around.

The words she had whispered to Benji, her canine confessor, came back to her. Did she really hate him? No. Of course not. She would not be taking part in this crazy experiment tomorrow if she hated him.

I don't really hate you, Ilan. But I am seriously pissed off at you and I hate what you've done. You got bored with your desk job and the quiet life and you were away the first chance you got. And now you're missing. And it's your fault. And that's why I'm pissed at you.

It was the fact that he had left her that Jennifer hated. His promise to stay at home and be content with a desk job vanished like early morning mist the moment someone told him he would be ideal for this operation. She had seen the gleam in his eyes. The excitement and the anticipation. He was never meant to be parked behind a desk and deep down she knew that.

But she hated that he couldn't wait to kiss her goodbye with promises that he would be careful. That he would think of her every day. And that he would be back in a month or two. Three at the most he promised.

'Bastard,' she said as she poured another glass of wine and immediately apologised to Ilan in his absence.

I'm sorry darling. I know you're one of the good guys. I just wish you were here and we could chat over a couple of bottles of wine about how to put the world to rights. Instead, you're off somewhere actually putting it to rights. I shouldn't call you names and curse you. You're a hero and I love you, and I'm very proud of you. But that doesn't stop me worrying about you and missing you. And cursing you for risking your life.

She added a couple of ice cubes to chill it some more. It was going to be a long, lonely evening.

Seven-thirty. It was only seven-thirty in the evening yet it felt so much later. Jennifer poured another glass of wine, she was into the second bottle now, and tried to think of something to do that would take her mind off tomorrow. She'd tried watching TV but there was nothing that held her interest. Reading was the same. The latest novel by her favourite crime writer couldn't even hold her attention. Her concentration flew out of the window after only a paragraph or two – the words made no sense at all. She even tried a few games of Solitaire on her laptop but lost on the second game and her interest quickly waned. Losing at internet Solitaire and drinking a bottle of wine, two bottles if one was going to be picky about it, was for the sad and lonely.

It suits me well.

Even the cats had picked up on her mood and neither of them were eager to comfort her by joining her on the couch. She tried calling them and patting the cushion. Holly gave her a baleful stare as she concentrated on her intense bout of personal grooming. Possum opened one eye, stood up as if to approach her then changed his mind and settled down again on his favourite spot on the windowsill.

With a sigh, Jennifer topped up her wineglass again. She added more ice cubes and told herself that it was to keep the wine chilled and not because Lucy still had a degree of influence over her. She picked up a throw and her wineglass, then as an afterthought, grabbed the bottle out of the fridge, *no sense in running in and out for a refill*, and made her way out onto the patio.

The gentle breeze wafted the scents of the flowers around her as she sat down on one of the patio chairs and placed her glass and the bottle on the small table, the comforting throw draped across her shoulders. The moon, almost full now, shone in the cloudless sky and its cold light bathed the tips of the shadows around her in eerie iciness. It was beautiful so see and, as she sat with a glass of wine in her hand, Jennifer realised that this was the most sensible way to spend the evening for it was still far too early to go to bed.

I probably won't sleep anyway.

Then another thought struck her. Despite the pleasantness of the breeze, it left her shivering in its wake. *What if Lucy is still around? Well, obviously not Lucy in person, but her ghost or spirit or whatever.* She would be lying if she said there wasn't a part of her that missed Lucy. Despite all her protests to the contrary she had been intrigued by the time she had spent living this other woman's life through her comatose dreams. Well, mostly intrigued.

But what, after all that transpired three years ago, what if she is still there? Still somewhere? In a place where she could reconnect with me? At that sidewalk table outside that street cafe? Or what if I go to sleep tomorrow night to look for Ilan and I find her instead and we're back in that forest park of hers? And what if she is pissed off at me because I lived and she didn't? What if she tries to kill me again? What if she succeeds this time?

Jennifer's hand shook when she lifted the wineglass to her lips and the ice cubes clinked against the glass. She took a sip and suddenly hated the coldness in her mouth and the sensation of the ice against her lips. This was Lucy's habit, she reminded herself, not hers.

I need to stop thinking about her. Especially now. I need to be thinking of Ilan. Concentrating on him and building a connection to him in my mind. And he needs to be thinking of me. Please be thinking of me, Ilan. Please. I won't be able to find you if you don't think of me.

I also need to be thinking of going to bed soon or I'll end up drunk and sobbing like I usually do.

Jennifer finished her wine and went indoors. She shut the beautiful moon outside, determined to get a good night's sleep before the morning came with whatever it would bring into her life.

The cats were fed and settled. All the doors and windows were locked. A note for Nurit was left on the kitchen counter beside the kettle, telling her to make herself at home and take anything she wanted from the fridge rather than let it spoil. Although it would most likely be Reuben who would be calling twice a day to take care of the cats since Nurit was going to be working with her.

She dumped the empty wine bottles into the recycling bin in the garage and cleaned out the litter tray. Then a quick shower and two large glasses of water to counteract the effects of the wine and she was ready for bed.

As she climbed under the duvet, Jennifer didn't expect to sleep. She would most likely toss and turn all night. But her eyes closed and she drifted off moments after her head hit the pillow. Her sleep was deep and dreamless. If there had been any dreams, she did not remember them.

Chapter 9 – Syria.

She was standing before him and the sunlight lit up her face as it bathed her with its rays. He could see that she was smiling and, when their eyes met, she raised her hand and beckoned to him. She seduced him with her eyes. She enticed him to come to her. It was obvious she wanted him and all he had to do was step forward and gather her up in his arms, throw her down on his bed, and kiss her while he removed her clothing. He became aroused at the thought of her naked below him.

He stepped towards her willingly. Her hand reached out to him and she pulled him into her embrace. Her lips met his and she pressed her body against him.

He trembled with anticipation and his fingers fumbled with the buttons on her blouse. With a gentle laugh, she slapped his hand away and deftly undid each button herself, then shrugged the brightly patterned blouse off her shoulders where it dropped to the ground. She leaned her hand on his shoulder to steady herself as she stepped out of her long, flowing skirt and it joined her blouse on the floor. She wore no underwear and now she was naked before him.

His eyes travelled up and down her body. It was as familiar to him as his own. But had she lost weight? It was hard to tell. She seemed slightly thinner, yet she was still curvy in all the right places. He had never known her to put on more than a few pounds and she would strive to lose it as quickly as she had put it on. But now it seemed, to him, that she was a little more gaunt than usual.

His thoughts came back to the present as she impatiently tugged at his clothes, wanting him as naked as she was. Her hips swayed in a seductive dance and her fingers worked with a purpose – she did not fumble with buttons – until he was naked too. The warmth of her flesh met the warmth of his skin and she took his hand and led him to the bed.

She lay down before him. Her legs parted and in the

dim light of the nearby lamp, he could see her glistening wetness inviting him as she arched towards him. She offered her breasts to him, the nipples hard with desire.

'I want you inside me,' she whispered. She rose up and reached for him again.

He pulsated with heat and yearning as he gave in to her demands.

Without preamble he was inside her. He moved with a fluidity that was gentle at first but grew more forceful as his need for her increased. Then he stopped. He raised himself up on his arms and, although he was reluctant to leave her warm inner core, he abruptly pulled out of her.

She frowned and moaned beneath him as she tried to draw him towards her again. Back into her.

'Too soon,' he breathed the words as he kissed her, devouring her mouth. 'I need so much more of you first.'

His lips traced a path from her mouth down to her breast. He found the erect nipple and took it into his mouth. He sucked gently but firmly and, as she climbed higher and higher, her breath came in short, sharp gasps. His thumb and forefinger found her other nipple. They pinched and squeezed, and replicated the movements of his lips and tongue. Driving her, and himself, wild with anticipation.

His mouth left her breast to go lower, planting kisses on her ribs and around her navel, before continuing his onward journey.

He paused and looked up at her face. Her eyes were closed and she was biting her lip, needing more of his touch.

Not yet. Not yet.

'Not yet,' he told her. 'Not yet.'

Her fingers clutched his hair, making fists as she pushed him towards her. He resisted, still circling. He breathed deeply, inhaling the musky scent of her.

Then he began.

She gasped as he worked her slowly until she begged for release. He knew her so well that he could anticipate her reactions. She was close now. Almost there. He took her closer and closer.

Then he stopped. She was mere seconds away. Her eyes flew open in shock but before she could speak, he raised himself up above her and plunged deep inside her.

His body took the place of his tongue as he ground into her and against her. She writhed below him, arching her back to meet his thrusts.

He held it as long as he could, waiting for her to join him. When he sensed she was ready he hooked the back of her legs over his arms, raising her up higher so he could go more deeply into her.

He felt her contract around him as wave after wave engulfed her. He could see the tendons in her neck as her whole body arched rigid and she cried out. On her way back down again, she seemed to sink beneath him, becoming soft and inviting once more as she urged him to climax with her movements and gentle whispers.

He held on and his speed increased now that it was all about him. He fucked her as deeply and as hard as he could. She would be sore tomorrow. She would love that. She always loved it. For a day or two afterwards, every time she sat down, she loved that little aching reminder of what they had done the night before.

He felt it building inside him until he could fight it no more and he came. Harder than he had in a long, long time. He fell on top of her, his breathing shallow and rapid. Underneath him she shuddered as her arms held him close to her, reluctant to let him go. Her voice was a whimper.

'I love you,' she told him. 'I needed you so badly. I needed this so badly.'

Then she pushed him off her and she stood up. Her voice, and her eyes, hardened. 'Why did you leave me? Why did you leave what we had?'

He could not answer her and he watched helplessly as she drifted away from him. Her face was full of sadness and reproach as she left him.

He was alone once more and the cold loneliness settled over him again as he slowly awakened from the dream.

Chapter 10.

'Mrs. Ben-Levi. Hello. My name is Bina and I am here to assist you during your stay here. I understand the strain you might be feeling and if you have any questions, or if there is anything you might need, just ask and I will do my best to help you.'

'Thank you.' Jennifer shook the offered hand. The woman standing before her looked to be in her mid to late thirties. She was petite and slender yet she gave the impression she could fight her way out of a tight corner if she had to. Probably military, Jennifer surmised. It didn't take a great leap to come to this conclusion as the building they were in was, to all intents and purposes, a military establishment.

'I will show you to your room. Did you bring a swimsuit with you?'

'I… no. It never crossed my mind that there'd be a swimming pool and that I'd need a swimsuit.'

'Don't worry. We can get one for you. We have a pool and an excellent sauna. Also, a gym, a cafeteria and a bar. You are entitled to use any of the facilities here whenever you wish.'

'Cool,' Jennifer replied. It seemed she hadn't needed to smuggle the two bottles of wine inside her holdall after all.

Bina led the way along a wide, brightly lit corridor. There was a plain carpet under her feet and the whole place put Jennifer in mind of a modern hotel. All the doors were numbered which added to the hotel-like impression.

Bina stopped at one of the doors about mid-way along the corridor. She turned the handle and opened the unlocked door then stepped back to invite Jennifer in, closing it behind her as she followed Jennifer inside.

It definitely wasn't a five-star hotel room, Jennifer decided as she appraised the décor and the furniture in her new home away from home. It was adequate. Actually, more than adequate. It was comfortable and almost cosy. It wasn't a bedroom with an attached en-suite but a small self-contained unit with an open-plan living room and kitchenette area that held a table and four chairs, a sink and drainer, a cooker, a refrigerator and cupboards. There was a coffee machine, several mugs and a kettle on the counter near the sink. The living area had a sofa and chair, a small coffee table and a large flat screen television mounted on the wall.

Nearby, there were two wall shelves stacked with paperback books, all of them seemed to be second hand. Another small cabinet held a good selection of DVD's – mostly movies and box sets. Like the books, the DVD titles were in a mixture of Hebrew and English. A carpet in neutral beige covered the floor in the living room and the kitchen area was laid with wood-effect linoleum. A few scatter cushions and throws on the sofa finished the furnishings.

The décor was soft and gentle and finished in warm, soothing colours. Nothing too bright or too loud. It was designed for relaxation rather than dramatic effect. Jennifer liked it. The interior designer she had been in a previous life nodded approvingly.

But it was hardly a room where she would fall asleep and dream of her missing husband in an attempt to locate him.

She raised a questioning eyebrow at Bina. 'Where's the bed? Where all the action is supposed to happen?' *God, that sounds dirty.*

'That will take place elsewhere. Your bedroom is through there.' Bina pointed towards the open door to the left of the kitchenette. Jennifer set her handbag and overnight bag down on the coffee table and peered in through the door. The décor was similar to that of the living area and a double bed took up most of the space. It had a nightstand on either side and a bedside lamp on each one. There was a dressing table with a large mirror and a wardrobe. Another door led into a compact yet fully functional en-suite which held a bath/shower combo, a toilet and a wash hand basin. She noticed shampoo, conditioner, shower gel and body lotion on a tray beside the wash hand basin. A box of tissues in the corner and some extra toilet rolls were stashed in a small basket in the corner near the wash hand basin. Bina opened the door of a small, free-standing unit to show Jennifer that it contained freshly laundered towels.

'It has everything you will need,' Bina said.

The en-suite and the room itself looked, to all intents and purposes, like a typical small self-catering apartment or maybe a well kitted-out hotel suite. Jennifer glanced around quickly. There was no mini-bar.

'Take your time and get settled in,' Bina told her. 'You can unpack and then freshen up in the bathroom. Relax for a while and I will come for you in about…' she glanced at her watch. 'An hour and a half, if that is okay with you?'

'Yeah. That's fine,' Jennifer nodded as Bina left, quietly closing the door behind her.

As soon as she was alone, the doubt began to creep in. Jennifer looked around the small apartment that was going to be her home for the next while. *What am I doing here? I'm wasting my time. This'll never work. But it has to work. I have to try to make it work. But I don't know how.*

She retrieved her holdall from the living room, set it on top of the bed and unzipped it. The first thing she lifted out was the framed photograph. The best, obvious, place to set it was on the nightstand beside the bed. Although old, it was her favourite photograph of the two of them. They looked so carefree and happy back then.

Will we ever be like that again?

The two bottles of wine, carefully wrapped inside her spare pair of jeans, caught Jennifer's eye next. She took one out and looked around for a glass or a cup, anything she could use. There was nothing. With a shrug of her shoulders, she unscrewed the cap and lifted the bottle to her lips. It was warm now but that didn't matter. She sat down on the side of the bed, took another swig of wine, then picked up the photograph again.

A smile spread across Jennifer's face as the memories

of happier times came flooding back. She remembered the day that photo had been taken. It was in Cyprus, at their favourite beach, and the guy who ran the jet ski hire had taken it for them. In the photo, Ilan's chin was resting on her shoulder and his arms were around her as they both smiled for the camera. She was leaning back against him. Their body language showed a couple who were very much in love. She wondered if they had made love when they returned home after that photo had been taken. They probably had. They made love all the time back then.

A fragment of a dream surfaced in her mind. Jennifer hadn't been aware of any dreams last night. There was certainly no memory of one when she had awakened this morning. But now it all came back to her with a clarity that made her gasp.

They were having sex. Screwing. Fucking. Enjoying one another. The images weren't so clear but the sensations were. Jennifer remembered Ilan inside her. Then abruptly pulling out and going down on her. Doing that thing he did with his tongue that drove her crazy and she remembered coming twice in rapid succession when he entered her. He had fucked her hard. Almost hurting her.

Almost? I don't think so. He was hurting me. Like he wanted to hurt me and I wanted him to.

Jennifer hadn't cared about the discomfort. She had loved it and couldn't get enough of him. She wanted him to hold back as long as possible. She didn't want him to stop.

Just stay inside me forever, please.

Then it was over and she remembered in the dream feeling angry because he had gone away from her. It was his fault he was no longer in her life or in her bed. She remembered telling him so as she turned and walked away from him in the dream.

Jennifer took another long swig of wine. Was that a dream? Or a memory? It felt more like a memory but she couldn't be sure and that was a problem. After her accident it had been difficult to sift through the images and memories in her head and determine which were her own genuine memories and which belonged to Lucy. Ilan had helped of course, but it wasn't easy telling him about something she remembered and then asking him, embarrassed, if it had been real.

Stuff like – 'Did we really almost get caught having sex on the beach one night, or did I dream about Lucy and her husband having sex on the beach and almost getting caught?'

Oh yeah. Asking your husband those kinds of questions did wonders for your relationship!

Ilan was sympathetic to her confusion and did all he could to remind Jennifer which memories were real – 'your favourite place is the shower, or right here on the couch,' he said as he patted the couch and smiled. He would take her hand in his and tell her – 'no, we never had sex on the beach, because you hate getting sand in your underwear and you refuse to do it.' And which were memories that belonged entirely to another woman – 'no, you don't like beetroot. Or cabbage. You love guacamole and pizza, especially Hawaiian. You prefer Mexican and Italian food to Chinese. You like to read spy dramas, cop thrillers and occasionally romance novels. You love old black and white movies, but you also enjoy a good modern thriller. And you always cry when the dog or the horse dies. You have never owned a blue and yellow bicycle or a pair of old denim dungarees. And no, I can assure you we never made love under a tree during a hailstorm. Thankfully.'

Every day for months he helped Jennifer sift through the images and thoughts in her head until she got a clear picture of the woman she had been, and still was. It had taken a while but eventually she was able to lock the part of her that had become Lucy away. Out of sight and out of mind. Some of Lucy's memories popped up to the surface every now and then, but they were infrequent enough that they no longer disturbed her.

But if this had been a dream, and Jennifer was fairly certain that it was, then maybe, just maybe, Saul Mueller's crazy idea could work. Of course, a lot of details needed to be ironed out. She would have to figure out how to dream what she wanted, not some random scenario, and as far as she knew, Ilan would have to be asleep too. The more Jennifer thought about it, the more unlikely and far-fetched it seemed. But it could work and she would try her best to make it work. For him. For both of them.

She took another swig of wine, grimacing at the taste of it. Warm white wine was awful. *I should have brought red.*

A gentle knock sounded at the door and she heard Bina's voice asking if she could come in. Jennifer glanced at her watch, surprised that the time had flown by so quickly. She swallowed the mouthful of wine, almost choking on it, screwed the cap back on the bottle and stuffed it back into her holdall underneath her clothes.

'Just a second,' she said as she grabbed her toothbrush and toothpaste and hurried into the bathroom where she quickly brushed her teeth to kill the smell of wine on her breath. At least she hoped it would kill it.

She took a deep breath and opened the door.

'Are you ready?' Bina asked. She breathed deeply and gave Jennifer a look that bordered on suspicious.

Fuck! She knows I've been drinking. Or is my paranoia kicking in already?

'Uh, yes. Let's go,' she said and forced a smile.

'This is for you,' Bina handed her a key card. 'Naturally, you are entitled to your privacy when you are here.'

Yay! Sad party for one in my room this evening!

Jennifer slipped the card into the back pocket of her jeans, closed the door behind her and followed Bina back along the corridor.

It was a large building, or rather a large complex of buildings joined together by various connecting corridors. Jennifer wondered just how many people worked, and lived, here. She was tempted to ask Bina, more for conversation rather than a need for her to know, but there was always a chance that her questions could be misinterpreted as information-gathering. They might think she was spying or something.

One corridor they walked past had double doors with a sign that bore the legend 'AUTHORISED PERSONNEL ONLY' in Hebrew and in English. There were cameras mounted near the ceiling that covered the doors from both directions. There was a swipe card entry system, a palm scanner and a keypad and it was obvious that the only people getting through those doors were the people who were meant to go through them. Jennifer thought a sequence of knocks and a coded phrase – 'the bray of the donkey falls silent at midnight' – or a similar inane phrase would be proper spy stuff. And a hell of a lot more fun.

The two women walked on past these doors and along the shorter corridor. Then through another set of double swinging doors and they were in the cafeteria. Through the glass panelling near the seating area, Jennifer could see a near Olympic-sized swimming pool. Bina was busy prattling on about the excellent facilities that she could avail of during her stay.

Am I gonna be working for the government or joining a gym?

Bina glanced at her watch as they walked towards the counter and asked Jennifer if she wanted coffee and something to eat.

'Just coffee, please. I don't think I could eat anything,' Jennifer said as she looked around her at all the people going about their day. Most were in civilian clothes but she noticed quite a few in military gear. Nurit didn't seem to be among them. This was disappointing because a friendly face would have been very welcome right now.

'Relax Jennifer. There is no need to be nervous,' Bina told her as she carried a tray holding two coffees to an empty table.

'I know. I just have no idea where I am. Not exactly. I don't know what I'm doing here or what will happen. It's all a bit, well... overwhelming. Frightening too.'

Bina leaned back in her seat and gave her an appraising look. Jennifer tried not to squirm in front of her.

'I don't know exactly why you are here, Jennifer,' she said. 'Whatever it is, it's well above my paygrade to know and I'm only here to chaperone you until Nurit comes on shift. She is your stepdaughter, yes?'

Jennifer nodded.

'From what I can see, you are a strong, confident woman and I get the impression you will take everything in your stride.'

'I hope you're right,' Jennifer let out a long sigh, wishing she felt as confident as this woman believed her to be. She took a sip of coffee.

'Are you sure you don't want anything to eat?' Bina asked, eyeing the food on the nearby display with obvious longing.

'If you want something go ahead,' Jennifer told her. 'Don't worry about me.'

'Maybe later,' Bina replied, glancing at her watch again. Then she stood up, almost to attention.

Jennifer glanced around. Standing behind her was the man who had interviewed her and then recruited her. Saul Mueller.

'You can go now, Bina. Thank you,' he said. 'Mrs. Ben-Levi. It is good to see you again. May I call you Jennifer?'

Jennifer nodded.

'Would you come with me, please?'

Bina had already disappeared and Jennifer stood up, grabbed her bag and slung it over her shoulder. Saul gently took her arm and led her towards the double doors. The ones with the cameras and the keypad and the secret knocks. She bit her lip in an attempt to suppress the laughter that threatened to escape as she imagined him uttering the phrase about the donkey not braying at midnight.

His palmprint registered. He keyed in the correct five-digit code and his card was swiped. The doors opened electronically and Jennifer knew she was taking a massive step into the unknown. Or possibly Narnia.

Chapter 11.

'Take a seat Jennifer.' Saul motioned her towards the comfortable chair. 'I want to go through the procedure with you, if that is okay?'

Jennifer nodded as she sat down.

'Okay. We are going to wait until around ten o'clock tonight until we begin. Between now and then please don't relax too much or have a nap. We need you to be able to sleep as we want to make this process as natural as possible. So, if you are tired, but not too tired, it should work.'

'It should work?' Jennifer echoed. 'How do you know? Have you done this before?'

'In all honesty, no. Have you ever heard, or perhaps read, about the remote viewing programs carried out years ago by different agencies?'

'Only what I've read on the internet and seen as plots in some movies. Hallucinogenic drugs played a big part, I believe,' Jennifer told him.

'Well, I can assure you it won't be anything like that.'

'Damn. I was looking forward to the drugs.'

Saul threw back his head and laughed. 'Sorry to disappoint you. We're going to try more modern and less intrusive methods such as relaxation techniques and hypnotherapy.'

'So, no medically induced coma then?'

'Of course not. We have no wish to harm you in any way.'

'That's good to know. I mean it. Really.'

'What we will attempt to do is plant suggestions in your mind before you go to sleep, to ensure you are focusing on Ilan and... well, the best way to describe it is that in your dreams you are going to talk to him. Have a conversation with him as you would if he were sitting here beside you. Then you have to draw that conversation around to where he is and what is happening. It's a form of what is known as lucid dreaming but we want to take it a step further and have you speaking to Ilan and obtaining as much information as you can.'

'I've heard of lucid dreaming. I don't know much about it but I have heard of it. But doesn't it take ages to learn how to do it?'

'Normally, yes there is a learning process which requires time and dedication,' Saul nodded. 'But we believe that hypnosis can advance the technique.'

'Okay. So, how does this work from Ilan's side? I mean, how does he know to react in his dreams and know that it isn't just a dream but it's really me trying to contact him?'

'You will have to convince him of that. Did you and he ever have a safe word or phrase?'

It was on the tip of Jennifer's tongue to tell him they weren't *that* kinky, but then she realised what he meant.

'Yeah, sort of,' she said. It was something Ilan insisted on a short time after he told her he worked for the Mossad. 'Just in case,' he had said. She had laughed when he told her what to say to him if she was ever in trouble of any kind but she had agreed to use it if the occasion ever arose. It never had. It seemed that they might be using it now.

'Do you need to know it?' Jennifer asked. 'Because Ilan made me swear never to reveal it. Not to anyone. Under any circumstances.'

'No. Of course not. But it is something you could use when you are conversing with Ilan in a dream. Then he will know that it is really you.'

'And if that doesn't work? Being able to talk to Ilan, I mean.'

'Then you have to watch and observe. You have to pinpoint his location and find out what he is doing and why. Try and remember as much as you can. Even the little details, the surroundings and the people. We can learn from him through you.'

'It sounds impossible.'

'It does. I agree with you on that point Jennifer, but do

you not agree it is worth pursuing, yes?'

'I don't see why you can't just send a team in, shoot everyone, grab him and bring him back?'

'If it were that easy, we would have done so. To begin with, we do not know where he is. It is up to you to find his location.'

Jennifer sighed. It seemed impossible. It was the stuff of bad science fiction movies. And, while amazing and seemingly impossible things worked all the time in science fiction movies, they rarely, if ever, worked in real life. But then she remembered all the dreams of Lucy's life she had experienced. The times she felt as if it were her making love to Charlie. The pain of giving birth, twice, and the joy of holding Lucy's daughters in her arms. She even remembered how it felt breastfeeding. All those things had seemed as real to her as if she had experienced them herself. Was all of that a bad sci-fi movie?

Then there was the meal and the wine at the weird street café or the forest park that Lucy claimed she could see. If she and Lucy, two complete strangers, could meet when both of them were lying unconscious in hospitals, then she could find and communicate with Ilan. Couldn't she?

'Okay,' Jennifer nodded. 'Okay. I'll do it. Now that I know you aren't going to knock me out with a brick to the head.'

'Good girl,' Saul smiled and Jennifer could see that his smile was genuine. 'Now, I will have someone take you back to your room where you can get settled and then we'll meet back in the cafeteria at around nine-thirty this evening. All I ask is that you don't sleep beforehand so you will be able to fall asleep when we begin.'

He was on his feet, all business once more as he ushered her out of the room and back through the double doors where Nurit, in uniform, was waiting for her. It wasn't midnight, not yet, but the donkey still wasn't braying. Or if it was, she couldn't hear it.

'Wow! Should I salute you or something?' Jennifer

asked as she studied the uniform. It consisted of khaki combat trousers and matching shirt – open at the neck and the sleeves rolled up and neatly folded above her elbows. A pair of highly polished boots and a beret tucked underneath her shoulder epaulettes also caught Jennifer's eye. The captain's insignia patches on Nurit's sleeve and her service ribbons attached to the shirt above her left breast finished the ensemble. Her hair was tied up in a tight bun, but a strand or two hung loose and curled around her ears. Jennifer wondered if they had escaped of their own accord or had Nurit deliberately pulled them loose in an attempt to go for the 'slightly-less-severe-but-still-on-duty' look.

Nurit burst out laughing as they walked along the corridor towards Jennifer's room. 'Of course! You've never seen me in uniform before!'

'No. Only a photo of you in uniform. The one Ilan keeps on his desk in the study.'

'What do you think?' Nurit did a twirl. 'First impressions?'

'Very fetching.'

'Do you think so?'

Laughing, Jennifer shook her head. Then her face grew serious. 'Will you be here with me?'

'I'm not sure if they'll let me stay in the room with you while you're actually doing the sleep thing, but I promise I'll be nearby because I'm on duty until seven tomorrow morning. Don't panic, Reuben already said he would check on the cats for you while I'm here. He'll feed them and he has promised that he would sit with them for a while so they won't be too lonely.'

Jennifer made a mental note to thank Reuben with a case of his favourite beer.

'Guess what?' Jennifer said. 'They've decided that they're not going to put me in a coma. Or pump me full of drugs.'

'Oh, that's a relief. I was worried about that. What are they going to do instead?'

'Make me all relaxed, then hypnotise me and tell me to go and find Ilan. I feel like a tracker dog. Maybe they'll make me sniff an old shirt of his and say – 'Good girl. Now, go fetch!'

Nurit couldn't help giggling and wrinkling her nose. 'As long as it's not his socks.'

Jennifer swiped her card and entered what would be her home for however long this would take. Nurit followed her in, glancing around the room and nodding in approval when she saw how comfortable, almost luxurious, it was compared to some of the barrack accommodation she had stayed in.

'The bastards!' Jennifer exclaimed as she rummaged through her belongings.

'What?'

'They've taken the two bottles of wine I brought with me.'

'You can get a drink in the bar, although I wouldn't advise getting drunk considering what you'll be doing later. Maybe just a glass or two. And if you present your ID card, they won't charge you for it. Same applies to food and coffee and water. Anything you want.'

'It's the principle,' Jennifer muttered. 'I'm not crazy about them searching through my stuff and I'll want both those bottles back when I go home.'

'Do you want to be alone for a while? I can come back for you when it's time.'

'I'm feeling a bit nervous. I'd prefer if you stayed. Would you?'

'No problem.' Nurit parked herself on the chair beside the bathroom door as Jennifer unpacked her clothes and hung them in the wardrobe. She left the old T-shirt and pyjama trousers on the bed, ready to take with her and she tried not to think about what the evening had in store.

Nurit found the remote and switched on the television. An episode of a series they both followed was about to start and they watched it in silence. Then they watched the news when it came on. When it finished, they channel surfed for a while but couldn't find anything interesting. Nurit switched off the television and threw the remote onto the table. They sat together in silence for a while. It was nearly time and Jennifer felt nervous now with nothing to distract her. She would have killed for a glass of wine. She even found herself thinking of Ilan's e-cigarette lying on the kitchen counter at home. Did nicotine calm you? She wasn't sure. Maybe she should have charged it up and brought it with her even though she wasn't sure if she would know how to use it. Or even like it. Although, they probably would have confiscated it along with the wine.

Jennifer got up and paced around the small area. Then she yawned. That was a good sign, wasn't it? Nurit saw her yawning and gave her an encouraging thumbs up.

They channel surfed some more but could find nothing that appealed to either woman. Jennifer was about to suggest they check out some of the DVD's but Nurit looked at her watch. 'It's time to go, Jennifer.'

'I need to pee first,' she replied, making a dash for the bathroom.

She really did need to pee. Nerves did that to her. After ages, and what seemed like several litres, she finished and flushed and washed her hands.

She stared at herself in the mirror. *I can do this. I can do it for you, Ilan. It's easy. All I have to do is close my eyes, fall asleep and dream about you. How hard can that be? How many times have I closed my eyes and dreamed about you?*

'Let's go,' Jennifer said as she walked out of the bathroom, her head held high and her shoulders squared. With a determined frown on her face, she grabbed her T-shirt and pyjamas, rolled them into a ball, tucked them under her arm and made for the door.

Her dramatic exit failed when she had to turn back and lift her ID card and lanyard off the bedside table but, other than that, she thought she looked totally in control.

What they were calling the 'sleep room' wasn't quite what Jennifer expected. Not that she had known what to expect – aromatherapy candles and faint, gentle whale song playing on a CD maybe.

It was similar in layout to the room Jennifer was staying in but this one was all new and shiny and there was no sofa and coffee table and, obviously no TV or DVD player. The overhead lights were glaringly bright and gave off a cold light rather than a warm hue. Hardly ideal for sleeping, but the dimmer switch on the wall would fix that. The elephant in the room was, of course, the bed – a hospital-style single bed with several cables draped over the pillow. Against the far wall sat a workstation on which three laptops were all powered up and ready to go. Beyond the bed there was another door which, Jennifer assumed, lead into a bathroom. To the left of the bed, a window was hidden behind floor-length heavy blackout blinds that, when closed, would forbid even a sliver of light to enter the room. It did not look comfortable. It did not look like a room that would ensure a good night's sleep. Falling asleep was the point of this whole exercise, and if she couldn't manage to do that, then her mission could be doomed to fail before it could even begin.

Nurit was behind her, carrying the bag of toiletries she had forgotten all about. Jennifer took comfort from the presence of Ilan's daughter, who had made it abundantly clear that she was going to be a part of this process.

Jennifer glanced around. Apart from herself and Nurit, Saul and three other people were in the room. One man, a nerdy type, sat at the workstation. A woman in a white lab coat was standing by the bed and another man, dressed in jeans and a checked shirt, stood beside her. Saul had been leafing through a file he was holding and he set it down and stepped forward to greet her. He took her hand and gave it a reassuring squeeze. Nurit didn't exactly stand to attention and salute him, but she didn't slouch either and only allowed herself to relax when he nodded to her. Saul let go of Jennifer's hand and introduced her to the other three.

'This is Ben and he will monitor everything. As you can see, we will keep an eye on your heart rate and your brain activity so we can ensure you are remaining in REM sleep as long as it is safe to do so. This is Meira. She is a doctor and she is here in the event there are any complications of any kind.'

'Complications?' Jennifer frowned.

'Yes. You may become distressed and we may have to waken you immediately. It is only a precaution. We are not expecting anything to go wrong.'

'Maybe you shouldn't have said that. Tempting fate and all?'

'And this is Nathan Cohen,' Saul smiled and continued. 'He is a psychotherapist who specialises in sleep disorders and hypnotherapy. He is going to be your teacher and your guide throughout this procedure.'

'Hi.' The big guy who looked more like a farmer or a lumberjack than a psychotherapist gave Jennifer a small self-depreciating smile.

She was thankful for Nurit who took her hand and squeezed it tightly.

'Okay,' she took a deep breath and turned to face her audience. 'When do we start?'

'No time like the present,' Saul told her.

Chapter 12.

It turned out to be a relatively simple and completely painless procedure. And a lot less nerve-wracking than Jennifer had expected. Her routine was the same as though at home and preparing for bed – she slipped into the bathroom and quickly changed into her favourite, comfortable pyjamas, then brushed her teeth and washed her face. She took a deep, calming breath, nodded to her reflection in the mirror, then opened the bathroom door and walked back into the room feeling a little bit like a performer stepping out onto a stage. The audience she faced, though small, was vital to her role in this little play. Jennifer smiled at each one, pulled back the sheets and climbed onto the bed. She lay back against the pillows and pulled the light duvet over her legs and stomach. With her shoulders relaxed and her arms resting lightly by her sides she waited for them to begin.

Within moments they had surrounded Jennifer. All except Nurit, who stepped back out of their way to allow them to work. Jennifer locked eyes with the younger woman and focused on her rather than the people around her while they hooked her up. Small flat discs with the cables attached were placed on each side of her temples. Another one was positioned on her chest over her heart, and a blood pressure monitor was placed around her left arm. Everything she was hooked up to was attached to the computer monitors and terminals sitting on the workstation.

The big guy who Saul had introduced as Nathan Cohen, pulled the seat over and sat down beside her. He was around her age, maybe a few years younger, with wavy dark brown hair and a full beard. He was a big, muscular man who looked as though he should be outdoors working the land instead of sitting in this small room. He wore rimless glasses that emphasised the intelligence and highlighted the compassion in the dark brown eyes behind them.

Despite his man-of-the-outdoors appearance, it was easy to see him for what he was because he exuded such an air of calm authority that he put Jennifer at ease immediately.

In a quiet, almost hushed, voice Nathan explained briefly what they would be doing. He told her that she had no cause to worry and that he would be right beside her the whole time.

'If anything, you will feel great – relaxed and content,' he said.

'Okay,' Jennifer replied. 'Let's do it.'

Nathan began with deep breathing exercises to relax her. Despite a few lapses of concentration – like her stray thoughts on the calming benefits of scented candles and how it might have been a mistake to forget the whale song – Jennifer eventually found herself feeling drowsy. She began to yawn.

Someone dimmed the lights and Nathan asked her if she was ready.

'As ready as I'll ever be,' she replied, her voice now a sleepy murmur.

He explained that he was going to use a basic hypnosis technique that had been tried and tested over the years and one that he found to be exceptionally good for the many different problems his patients suffered from. From smoking cessation to helping to alleviate deep physiological disorders.

'Not that you have any physiological disorders,' he said.

'Oh, I dunno about that,' Jennifer replied. 'But they'll keep for another day.'

Nathan smiled. 'Remind me to give you my business card later.'

'Let's do this,' she said.

'Okay.' He took a deep breath and exhaled slowly. He kept his voice calm and gentle as he began. 'I would like you to close your eyes, take a deep breath and hold it. Very good. Now breathe out slowly through your mouth. Expel all the air out of your lungs, relaxing as you do so. In again and then out again as you feel all the tension leaving your body. Now keep breathing slowly and deeply, in and out, in and out. And as you are doing so, I want you to imagine you are somewhere comforting. Somewhere peaceful. There is a gentle breeze blowing and you are relaxed and content. It is a beautiful day and you have nothing to do other than relax and enjoy the day. Take another deep breath and inhale all the pleasing scents around you. What do you feel? What are you experiencing now?'

'The breeze,' she murmured. 'I can feel it on my skin. It is warm and gentle. Like it's caressing me.'

'What can you smell?'

'Jasmine. And maybe honeysuckle. Yeah, I can smell honeysuckle.'

'Good. Do you like jasmine?'

'It's my favourite flower. But I like honeysuckle too.'

'Where are you?'

'I'm lying in bed. No. That's wrong. I'm lying on the sun lounger. Out on the patio. There are flowers all around me.'

'Can you still smell them?'

'Yes,' she said breathing in deeply again and a smile flitted across her face that softened her features. She felt relaxed and, if not happy, at the very least content.

'Is Ilan with you?'

'No. He's in the kitchen, I think. Well, he was in the kitchen. Now he's... I'm not sure where he is.' A frown creased her brows. *Where was Ilan? Hadn't he been here just a moment ago?*

'I want you to picture Ilan in your mind, Jennifer. He is nearby and you have to look for him.'

'I can't see him. Where is he? Why can't I see him?' A note of concern crept into her voice and she squirmed on the bed in an attempt to sit up.

'Okay. It's okay. Relax Jennifer. Just relax. Breathe deeply in and out. In and out. I want you to feel yourself relaxing as you exhale. Ilan is nearby and he is fine. He is waiting for you. You have no need to be concerned about him. He's okay. Just breath and relax.'

It took several minutes. She did exactly what Nathan told her to do. She breathed in and out, in and out. Eventually Jennifer felt the sense of peace and contentment return as she found herself surrounded by the flowers and the gentle breeze once more. She settled more comfortably into the soft mattress and her eyelids grew heavy again.

'Jennifer,' Nathan continued, his voice singsong and unhurried. 'I want you to close your eyes and count slowly backwards with me from ten. As you count down you will begin to fall asleep again and when you fall asleep, once again you will be lying on the sun lounger on your patio. All around you are gentle breezes and you are surrounded by the beautiful scents of your favourite flowers. Relax and enjoy the scents and the warm, gentle breeze and when you are ready, I want you sit up and look around you. Look around and see the door. It is in front of you. I want you to stand up and walk towards that door. And I want you to open that door.'

Nathan detected a slight frown on her forehead and her body tensed ever so slightly. He took her back a step.

'Don't worry, Jennifer. You are relaxed and you are comfortable. It is a beautiful day and I want you to relax and enjoy the sunshine and the warm, gentle breeze. Take another deep breath and inhale the jasmine and the honeysuckle. And another. There is nothing behind that door that you should be afraid of because Ilan will be behind that door. When you are ready, I want you to open the door and walk through it. Then you will be with Ilan. You will smile when you see him, and he will be smiling and happy. You will be talking to him and relaxing in his company as you sleep. You will talk to him and ask him questions about where he is and what he is doing.'

Nathan paused to allow Jennifer's mind time to absorb his suggestions. He would have preferred to keep up the momentum but, at the same time, he didn't wish to overload her. In normal circumstances, he would plant suggestions in a patient's mind one or two at a time, allowing them to take hold and work for the betterment of the patient over a period of several sessions.

But these weren't normal circumstances and Jennifer wasn't his patient. She wasn't there because she wanted to stop smoking or lose some weight. Nor was she lying on a bed, hooked up to various monitors, because she wanted to exorcise the demons an abusive childhood had left her with. Jennifer was here to carry out a mission. To aid them in, hopefully, averting an act of terror and he was there to ensure she did just that. And time was of the essence.

Saul Muller hovered nearby, and Nathan could tell by his body language that he wanted him to get on with it.

'Eight hours from now,' Nathan said as he picked up where he had left off. 'When you have finished your conversation with Ilan, I want you to walk back through the door. Back onto the patio with the gentle breeze and the beautiful flowers – the jasmine and the honeysuckle. And, once you walk back through that door you will waken up and you will remember everything you and Ilan spoke about. Are you ready to go to sleep now Jennifer?'

'Yes.'

'I'm going to start counting back from ten now, Jennifer. And you will count with me and fall asleep as you count. Do you understand?'

'Yes.'

'Okay. Let's begin. Ten,' Nathan whispered.

'Ten,' Jennifer repeated.

'Nine.'

'Nine.'

'Eight.'

'Eight,' Jennifer breathed.

And so on. Her voice grew softer as she counted down. When she reached three, her voice was nothing more than a murmur and she didn't respond when he whispered the next number.

'She's under,' Cohen told the others in the room.

'Now what?' Saul asked.

‘Now we wait. We monitor her and we wait until she awakens.’

‘Will she be okay?’ Nurit asked, concern made her voice catch in her throat.

‘She will be fine,’ Cohen assured her.

Chapter 13.

The door was there just like Nathan had said it would be, yet Jennifer found herself hesitant to turn the handle, open it and walk through. Even if Ilan was behind the door, a part of her felt uncomfortable taking that step forward. Because he might be there, but dead. Fear made Jennifer tremble, and it seemed so much easier to stay here on the patio and wait for Ilan to come out to her rather than go in.

Clouds that had been gathering on the horizon were now overhead. They blocked out the sun and the sky darkened. Big, fat raindrops, that threatened a deluge, fell from the clouds and splashed onto her head and her shoulders.

There was a flash of lightning and a crack of thunder and then the heavens opened. The wind strengthened and the rain lashed down in a torrent. It streamed around her feet as the water flowed in rivulets towards the storm drain in the far corner of the patio.

Still Jennifer hesitated. Afraid to turn the handle, open the door and walk in.

The sky began to darken even more. The lightning flashed and the thunder boomed and cracked like canon shots all around her. The rain – it had become a downpour – suddenly turned to hail. Golf ball sized chunks of ice fell from the sky and smashed all around her. Some struck Jennifer on her head. Some hit her back and shoulders. She crouched and shivered in the doorway as she tried to shield herself from the worst of the hailstones. But it was pointless. The wind blew the hail in her direction and it pounded her as it pummelled her back. She had no choice but to open the door and step inside.

The door was made of old oak. Heavy and unyielding. It appeared to be unlocked, yet it refused to open, the wood had swollen and was stuck within the frame. Jennifer turned the handle and, at the same time, slammed her shoulder against it to force it open. It resisted her attempts and she had to throw her shoulder against it several times before it gave way to grant her entry. She stepped through, closed the door behind her and left the noise of the storm muted on the other side.

Like a wet dog, Jennifer shook off the excess water and she slicked her hair flat against her scalp to wring at least some of the water out of it. Her T-shirt and jeans were drenched but there was nothing she could do about it. She slicked her hair a few more times and, in the dim light, glanced around.

She was in a large entrance porch. Cold, ancient tiles were under her feet and she could see a passageway that lead to a room, possibly a kitchen, but she couldn't be sure. The place seemed familiar, and that familiarity was enough to be frightening. But Jennifer couldn't figure out how, and from where, she knew it.

Her teeth chattered with the cold and the water still dripped from her, puddling around her feet on the tiles. An old-fashioned dresser was to her left with a mirror hanging on the wall nearby. Jennifer looked in the mirror. Her eyes were large and frightened, and her hair was plastered to her scalp. She ran a hand through it to slick off more of the wetness, then scrunched it into a semblance of her usual style as she began to walk further along the hall. Further into the darkness.

'I am the one who had to cut off your lovely hair and for that I must apologise.' A voice spoke from somewhere behind her.

Jennifer whirled around, searching for the owner of the voice. The surgeon who had operated on her had spoken those very same words. She squinted to see in the darkness but there was no one there.

Where am I? In Cyprus? Is this house near where we crashed on that dark side road? Is this a house? Why do I think I recognise it? Where is Ilan? He should be here. Or is he still in the car?

Had she climbed out of the car and had stumbled down

the middle of the road, looking for help, only to find this old house which seemed strangely familiar? She touched her head and her fingers traced the faint outline of the scar on her head from the accident and her operation years ago.

That was years ago, wasn't it?

She turned back and was about to step further along the hallway when she heard a movement behind her. Something that was almost, but not quite, a footstep caused Jennifer to turn around again.

'This was all your fault, you bitch.' This time it was a different voice that spoke. Not the surgeon. This was a female voice. And an angry one at that. 'You caused all of this.'

'What? I don't understand. What did I cause?'

'Take a look. Go on. Climb up those stairs and take a look through the door. Have a good look at all the damage you caused.'

There was no one there. Yet she had heard the movement and the voice. And Jennifer knew that voice. She would have known it anywhere, because it had invaded her dreams for so long. It was Lucy's voice. Lucy who had died when she had lived. She had gotten her life back, but Lucy had lost hers.

'Ahh, you haven't forgotten me. I was beginning to think you had. Or maybe you just shoved me to the back of your mind. Well out of the way where I couldn't upset your happy life. Well guess what? I'm still here.'

'What do you want?' Jennifer asked. She shivered, but not from the cold.

'I want you to see what you did. All the damage you are responsible for. The loneliness. The heartbreak. Go. Go and take a look. Up the stairs and into the bedroom on the right, along the landing. Go on. I want you to take a long, hard look and see for yourself the lives you have ruined. Then when you've seen that, I want you to come back down here and see how you left him. What you did to him.'

'Ilan? Is he here?'

‘Bollocks! Why on earth would your precious Ilan be here? Just go and look and see for yourself.’

More than anything, going up those stairs was the last thing Jennifer wanted. What she really wanted was to turn and run. Back out through the door and into the hail and the thunder and the lightning. She could shelter in the corner of the patio until the storm passed over. She could put up with being cold and wet because anything was better than being here inside this house, where her worst nightmare was coming back to haunt her.

But maybe she had to do this first. Maybe Ilan was somewhere beyond this nightmare scenario and she had to go through this, with all its terrors, to get to him. Maybe it was a test. A trial, or a rite of passage of some sort, and when she passed it, he would be there waiting for her.

Maybe.

Jennifer took a deep breath then exhaled slowly. She repeated the inhaling and exhaling process that Nathan had recommended until she felt herself relaxing. Not completely relaxed but calm enough to continue. Then she placed one foot on the bottom stair and slowly began to climb. Each step was hesitant – her foot on that first step felt heavy, almost turned to stone and her clammy hand gripped the banister as though her life depended on it. She forced her feet to take another step, then another, as she climbed the stairs.

Three of Lucy’s best photographs hung in frames on the wall to her right and as she climbed, she admired them. Lucy really had been a wonderful and talented photographer. The fact that some of her photos still sold for large amounts of money attested to this. Jennifer herself had one in the living room that she had purchased through an online auction for a hefty price. She often found it disturbing knowing that it was Lucy’s, but she loved its beautiful simplicity and she left it there as a reminder of the woman, and the circumstances of how she had come to know her. And as a tribute to her.

At the top of the stairs, she took a deep breath and wiped the sweat off her hand onto her jeans, surprised to find them completely dry now. As was the rest of her clothes, and her hair. It was as if the rain she had been caught in had never happened.

She stood still for a moment as her eyes grew accustomed to her surroundings then turned left along the landing. Her memories of the house hadn't failed her and even though she had never been inside it – she *still* wasn't *actually* inside it – she remembered every detail from her dreams.

More framed photos decorated the walls on the landing as she walked along it. Mostly Lucy's earlier work but they were still exceptionally good. Underneath the big window sat a small square table – one of those upcycled ones that Lucy had enjoyed making from old wooden pallets. It had been sanded and smoothed and stained in an antique dark oak colour that was still light enough to allow the natural grain of the wood to show through. On top of it a candle burned safely in a flat bowl. The flame flickered as if caught by a breeze, even though there was no breeze.

Probably because I'm in a house with a ghost downstairs. Or maybe I'm the ghost.

The smell of cinnamon wafted in the air around her. Jennifer wrinkled her nose. She wasn't particularly keen on the smell of cinnamon, but she remembered it was Lucy's favourite. Cinnamon and apple spice. Winter scents. Lucy had loved all things that pertained to winter. The cold and the frost. The snow outside on the ground and evenings spent curled up in front of a warm log fire, drinking a hot whiskey.

This was all wrong. She was in Lucy's dream when she should have been in Ilan's.

Beyond the table and the large window, she could see a door. It was ajar and the faint, warm gleam of a dim light spilled out through it. Jennifer walked towards it. The light drew her like a moth to a flame, and she gently pushed the door open to look in.

Two single beds greeted her. The light that had spilled out of the room came from a small lamp sitting on a dresser in the corner. It was a small night light with a lampshade decorated in cut-out half-moons and stars; the images were imposed on the walls and the ceiling. It was so obvious that this was a room belonging to a little girl. Or, in this case, two little girls. The pink princess wallpaper, the doll's house on a table against the far wall. The leggings and sparkly tops draped over a chair. The dolls and the teddy bears, and the boy band posters. The make-up, colourful mobile phone and iPad covers. All these things told her who the room belonged to before she even looked at the sleeping forms in the two twin beds side by side near the window. Amy and Chloe. Lucy's two young daughters.

Jennifer stood rooted to the spot as she watched the two girls while they slept. In their sleep they were safe in a world where there was no hurt or grief. No sorrow or loss. Their eyelids flickered and Jennifer knew they were dreaming.

Were they dreaming about their mother right now? Were their dreams happy and full of laughter as they inhabited, at least for a little while, a world in which their mother was still alive and with them? Did they laugh and play with her? Did she get them ready for school in the mornings and help them with their homework in the evenings? Play with them at weekends and during the holidays? Did she do all the things in their dreams that a mother was supposed to do in their lives? She hoped so.

'I'm so sorry,' she whispered to them and wiped away a tear that had trickled down her cheek. 'So very sorry.'

She watched them dream of happier times for another minute or two, then stepped back out of the room, treading softly so as not to disturb their slumber and their dreams.

Jennifer's feet dragged as she turned and walked down the stairs. Lucy was waiting for her in the kitchen.

'Now, go through there and have a look in the sitting room.' Lucy pointed to a room off the kitchen.

Jennifer did as she was told and walked through the kitchen to the room beyond. She remembered this room from her dreams. It was the small sitting room Lucy had nicknamed 'The Snug' because it was cosier than the larger, more formal sitting room.

The door was slightly ajar, and she could see flickering light coming from within it. This was the room with the dark curtains and the woodstove in the massive, stone fireplace. It had been Lucy's favourite room and she had often curled up on the sofa watching Netflix when Charlie wanted to watch football on the large-screen TV in the front room. Or it had been Lucy's favourite when she was alive, now it seemed that Charlie preferred this room. Maybe he felt closer to Lucy in this room.

Jennifer didn't want to look inside but some force compelled her to gently push the door open and step into the room.

Charlie had lit the fire. Naturally, for it was cold this evening. Wintertime in Yorkshire was a whole lot different from wintertime in Israel. Houses in Yorkshire in the winter, even with the heating on and a fire lit, sometimes struggled to warm up. It was certainly cold enough for a heavy duvet at night. A warm sweater and a coat, hat and scarf was always worn outdoors and sometimes a sweater was also needed indoors, even when the heating was switched on. It often snowed at this time of the year and, when it wasn't snowing, most days it rained, and the wind howled.

He was sitting by the stove in an old armchair, one that Lucy had bought in a charity shop and restored until it looked like new. His iPad was balanced on the arm of the chair and he held a glass of whiskey in his hand. Their old border collie lay asleep on the fireside rug, his head on the hearth. He didn't stir when Jennifer stepped into the room.

Charlie sipped at his whiskey and ignored the small screen as he stared at the glass-fronted stove. Jennifer wondered what he saw in the bright, flickering flames.
He had been scrolling through a website. Jennifer's curiosity

got the better of her and she stepped forward and peered over his shoulder to see what he was looking at. His face was in a side profile to her, but from the part she could see and the slump of his shoulders he looked older. And more downhearted. Like someone trapped in his grief, he was heartbroken and lonely. Unable to lift himself out of the swirling depths of sorrow, even three years on. She wanted to go to him, hug him and tell him to be happy for the sake of the girls. That Lucy would want him to move on. Would she? Jennifer had no idea, but it was probably something Charlie needed to hear. He probably did hear these very same words, from friends and family, and maybe on the surface he was happy. Maybe he woke up every morning and slipped on a mask of happiness and hid his true self from the world. He probably did. Life goes on. It had to. Maybe after all this time it was a little easier to forget about putting on that mask and, hopefully, there were some days when he hardly even noticed that he wasn't wearing it.

Maybe it was only now in the safety of the evening when the girls were tucked up in bed, sound asleep, that he took off his mask and grieved silently and alone for the wife he had lost.

Jennifer moved closer but stopped, and her heart pounded in her chest when he stirred. Had he heard her? Impossible. Felt her presence? Highly unlikely. She froze on the spot, ready to turn and flee, and watched as he drank the rest of the whiskey and set the glass down on the floor by his feet. He lifted the iPad and began to swipe through the contents of the website he had been looking at earlier.

Jennifer found her courage again and stepped closer until she was standing behind him and she could see the screen. It was a dating website. She didn't know whether to be pleased or sad for him. Pleased that he was at least trying to find someone but sad because he had to. She imagined the ad he would place – 'lonely widower with own business, big house and two young daughters seeks…'

She watched as he swiped from one profile to another,

pausing only when he saw photos of women who resembled Lucy. He seemed tempted to tap one, his finger hovering, but he hesitated then sighed and moved on to the next photo, and then the next, swiping faster as he dismissed each one. Jennifer silently encouraged him to pick one. Any one. Just for a date. Just for a chance to maybe smile and relax for an hour or two. *It doesn't need to lead to anything. It's not a betrayal of Lucy. It need only be a pint of beer and a bite to eat. Come on, Charlie. Pick one.*

But he sighed and set the iPad down and continued to stare into the fire.

Bearing witness to Charlie's grief tore through Jennifer's heart and she slipped, unnoticed, out of the room. She made her way back into the kitchen where Lucy was waiting for her.

Lucy was standing beside the large table, her arms folded in front of her. She had a smile on her face.

Good or bad? Hostile or friendly? Jennifer could not interpret the meaning in that smile.

'Grab a seat,' Lucy told her. With her arms still folded, she pulled out a chair with her foot and sat down at the table. She indicated with a nod of her head for Jennifer to take a seat opposite her.

Reluctantly, Jennifer pulled out one of the chairs and sat down across the table from this woman who was supposed to be dead. Yet, there she was and it was impossible not to stare at her. Lucy was wearing a pair of old, faded jeans and a dark green woollen sweater – the kind you'd wear around the house on a Saturday, if you were cleaning or decorating, or just lying on the sofa watching television and wishing it hadn't rained on your day off. One of the cuffs was snagged and looked as though it would unravel if it wasn't repaired. The jeans were frayed around the ankles and there was a rip on the left knee.

'I was wearing these clothes when I collapsed,' Lucy told her. She rested her elbows on the table and linked her hands together underneath her chin. 'I had planned on spending the day cleaning the house and bathing the dog but, instead, I dropped like a stone right over there by the kitchen sink. And, if I remember correctly, I was just about to fill up the kettle to make tea.'

'I thought you'd be wearing something more formal. Um, something…'

'Something I was buried in, you mean?'

'Well, yes. I suppose so.'

'I have no idea what they buried me in. Charlie probably picked out my best dress or maybe that dark grey trouser suit I owned. I hope not because I hated it. Funnily enough, it was the one I always wore when I had to go to a funeral, so he probably did choose it. Yuck.' Lucy paused and traced her fingertip along the line of a grain on the wooden table top. 'Yeah, I'd like to believe he picked something nice and made sure I was all dressed up and looking my best. Or maybe he was so grief-stricken he couldn't do it and Claire had the task of selecting something for him to give to the undertakers. Knowing her, I'm probably buried in a lacy negligee. Or a bikini.'

'So, how come I don't see you in er, that?'

'Because I'm not a ghost, Jennifer.'

'What are you then?' Jennifer asked, but she had a feeling she already knew the answer.

Lucy jutted out her chin and tilted her head as she thought about Jennifer's question.

'Definitely not a ghost,' she replied. 'Shame really because I'd be a fantastic ghost. I wouldn't go all poltergeist and throw stuff around, or switch the lights on and off or anything like that. I'd be friendly and helpful. The girls would love having me around to braid their hair or play with them. Or help them with their homework. And Charlie and I could do that sexy pottery-making thing with the wheel and the clay, like Patrick Swayze did with Demi Moore in the movie. But it isn't anything like that. I'm a manifestation that only exists in your dream. In your mind. What you perceive me to be is how I appear. Although I'm not sure how you came up with the torn jeans and this tatty old jumper that I should have thrown out years ago. Thanks for that!'

Lucy frowned as she looked at the woman in front of her. She spread her palms flat on the table.

Unable to speak, Jennifer stared at the woman across the table from her and wondered how her own mind, her own imagination, could have brought her to this moment.

'Do you want a glass of wine?' Lucy asked with a grin. 'How about a Caesar salad? Maybe that seriously weird waiter is around here somewhere.'

Jennifer swallowed hard. 'No. No, thanks.'

'So, what brings you to my neck of the woods then? Getting bored with Ilan? With Israel? Missing the British weather?'

'I'm not here, Lucy,' Jennifer told her. 'I'm still in Israel. In a dream.'

'So am I. In your dream, that is. Just like I said. How that happened I don't know. But since we're here, you and I might as well have a little chat.'

'About what?'

'Oh, whatever comes to mind. Are you sure you don't want a drink? I believe you like ice in your white wine now. There's plenty in the fridge and there's a bag of ice cubes in the freezer.'

'No thanks. I'm sure.'

Lucy shrugged her shoulders. She was more or less the same as Jennifer remembered. Her hair was still long and luxurious and it still had the red highlights that she had kept since the night of her first photography exhibition. Over the years it had become her signature look and Jennifer remembered how much Lucy had enjoyed the recognition.

She hasn't aged a bit in the time since she died. Well of course, she bloody hasn't. She's dead, you idiot.

Lucy seemed to have read her mind for she grinned, and she looked Jennifer up and down. 'You've lost some weight. Is Ilan keeping you fit and active with plenty of sex? By heck, he's good at it. I remember some of the sessions you and he had with extreme fondness. Mind you, Charlie and I were no amateurs in that department either. As you probably remember only too well.'

Jennifer felt herself blushing and Lucy grinned at her.

'Oh, don't be so coy. I know you well enough to know that you're not some simpering maiden. You enjoyed our sex life as much as I enjoyed yours. Once I got over the initial shock, that is. Of course, you still get to have fantastic sex with Ilan, whereas I haven't had it in a long, long time. Being dead doesn't half kill off your opportunities to get your leg over.'

'For fuck's sake drop it!' Jennifer had reached her limit. 'I lived and you died. I'm sorry that it happened. But you need to get over it.'

Lucy threw back her head and laughed. She couldn't stop and she laughed until the tears streamed down her cheeks and she had to hold onto her sides. After a few minutes, she calmed down, wiped the tears from her eyes with the sleeve of her sweater, and reached across the tabletop for Jennifer's hand.

Jennifer kept her hands clenched together in her lap. Lucy's reaction was so over the top it didn't make sense at all.

'Aww, I'm just messing with you,' Lucy said with a grin. 'Honestly, I bear you no ill will, Jennifer. I did at first, and you can't really blame me for that, but I am over it now. I've been dead for ages – three years now – and I guess you could say I'm over the worst of it. Seriously Jennifer, I'm glad you're here and we have this chance to speak. I'm glad you got to see my daughters. And Charlie. The girls are doing okay for the most part. Kids tend to be more resilient than we give them credit for. Yes, sure they miss me, but they're adapting and getting on with their little lives and I'm gradually becoming nothing more than a fading memory to them. But Charlie still misses me. Three years on and sometimes he still cries himself to sleep.'

Lucy paused, her face serious now, her arm remained

outstretched across the table, her hand palm up as though daring Jennifer to take it.

'Do you know, he's been scrolling through that dating website for ages, but he never goes any farther than that. Maybe he just hasn't plucked up the courage yet, but it seems to me he hasn't been able to move on. In a way I'm pleased, because it shows how much I meant to him. But he needs to move on now. I hope he will. I hope he finds someone who loves him as much as I did. And she needs to be someone who will love the girls as well. They'll need a mother figure when they get older. Someone who'll teach them about make-up and periods and boys and safe sex and what they want to be when they grow up. I worry about that part of their lives. Maybe Claire will step up for them if he doesn't find someone.'

Tears, of sorrow this time, welled in Lucy's eyes. She wiped them away on her sweater sleeve again and let out a sigh.

'I am so sorry, Lucy,' Jennifer said. She reached across the table towards Lucy's hand. Lucy stared at the outstretched arm, at the offer of an apology. She hesitated for a moment before placing her hand on top of Jennifer's.

Jennifer suppressed a shiver as she felt the coolness of the fingers touch her palm. It wasn't cold like dead flesh, but it wasn't warm either. Something about it felt – not quite human. Whatever it was, it was not living, breathing human skin and, more than anything, Jennifer wanted to pull her hand away. But she was afraid to do so, for fear that it would anger the woman sitting across the table from her.

Is this a dream or is she an actual ghost? Whatever she is, all of this is downright creepy.

Lucy smiled sweetly. 'I know it upsets you to see him still grieving for me. But I think I needed you to know all of this. Closure, I suppose. For both of us. Can we be friends now? Ha ha. Just kidding!'

Jennifer badly wanted a drink. She wasn't comfortable in Lucy's presence and she wasn't a hundred per cent sure

Lucy meant what she said. One minute she seemed genuinely pleased to see the woman who had haunted her dreams, and what she had said about Charlie and the girls, and how they should move on, seemed to be an honest reflection on how she felt. Then the next minute she was joking about the pair of them becoming friends.

Jennifer pulled her hand away, resisting the urge to wipe it on the leg of her jeans.

'A glass of wine would be nice right now.' Lucy echoed Jennifer's thoughts. 'So, what brings you here? What are you up to? I take it you really are in a dream. You haven't died or ended up in a coma again?'

'No. This is definitely a dream.' Jennifer said it more to convince herself than anything. 'You see, I'm working for the Mossad now and –'

'You're a spy? That is so cool. Did Ilan get you involved? Are you a sort of Jane Bond running around chasing terrorists and smuggling out nuclear reactor diagrams? Is it like Homeland?'

'No. I'm not a spy. They merely asked me to try and help them find him using what happened between you and me. He's missing. Has been for months now.'

'Has he defected? Oh, Ilan wouldn't go over to the dark side, would he?'

'No! At least they haven't mentioned anything like that. I think he's just stuck somewhere and can't make contact. Or he's dead.'

'Jennifer I'm so sorry. I hope that isn't the case and I hope you can find him. I really liked him. But I have to ask you – why are you here?' Lucy tilted her head and frowned.

'I honestly don't know. I was supposed to be searching for Ilan, but I ended up here. This is my first attempt.'

'Ahh,' Lucy nodded. 'Then it's possible you were thinking about what happened to us and that influenced your dream.'

'Maybe. Yeah. It's possible.'

'Here's a piece of good advice from beyond the grave.

Next time you dream, you should concentrate on thinking about Ilan. Mind you, I can understand why you were thinking of me instead of him when you consider the circumstances of how we got to know one another. Ya missed your old coma buddy, didn't you?'

Lucy grinned, leaned forward over the table, and punched Jennifer lightly on the upper arm. 'Seriously though, I hope it works out for you and you find that big, sexy hunk of yours. I mean that. The part about finding him. Okay, the sexy hunk part too'

Jennifer looked for insincerity in the other woman's voice but couldn't find any. Then all of a sudden, she felt movement all around her. A sort of shimmering shift that almost made her feel dizzy as the table seemed to fade before her eyes. She placed her hands flat on the tabletop to steady herself. She frowned.

'What's wrong?' Lucy asked.

'I'm not sure. I think I might be waking up.'

'We don't have much time then,' Lucy said. 'But before you go, I just want to say it's okay. I hated you for a long time, but I don't any more. I want you to find Ilan and be happy again. I mean it. Honestly.'

'Thank you.'

Lucy stood up. Jennifer remained seated at the table and watched as both Lucy and the house began to fade more quickly now. She slid back the chair and got to her feet. As she walked to the door, Lucy walked alongside her but she was barely visible now. Jennifer reached for the door knob then paused and turned back to Lucy.

'I wish it could have been different, and I mean that with all my heart, Lucy. I wish both of us could have recovered and went on to live our lives. Both our lives. You know, I would have contacted you. Met up with you, maybe. Friended you on Facebook or something. I think we could have been friends.'

'I would have done the same,' Lucy smiled and held out her arms. 'Come here.'

Jennifer willingly allowed herself to be embraced. The cold, not-quite-human sensation of Lucy's touch no longer bothered her. The two women held each other tightly and Jennifer marvelled at how Lucy still felt solid despite being almost completely invisible now.

'I hope you find him,' Lucy whispered in her ear. 'I hope you get him home safe and well and I hope you have a long and happy life together. Be well Jennifer. Be happy.'

'Thank you. Thank you so very much,' Jennifer said. She gave Lucy one last hug and a kiss on the cheek then she reached for the door handle.

Chapter 14.

Jennifer awakened slowly, with a stretch and a yawn, and, as she always did first thing in the morning, allowed herself a few moments of calm before she opened her eyes. When she did so, she glanced around at the confusing, unfamiliar surroundings. She frowned as she wondered where she was.

What's happened? Am I in a hospital? No. But I'm definitely somewhere similar.

She sat up and looked around her.

Ah, yes.

It came back to her now. She was in what they were calling the sleep room. Three, no four, tired but eager faces watched her as if they were awaiting great news.

'Good morning,' she told them.

She probably should have said something more earth-shattering or imparted some hitherto unknown secret of the universe, but she hadn't had her coffee yet.

Eyebrows raised now with unspoken questions, Saul, Nathan and the doctor watched her. The other guy whose name she couldn't remember concentrated on the laptop in front of him. Nurit stood in the background, out of the way, but her eyes were wide and she chewed her lip in nervous anticipation. She could see Nurit was as impatient to hear her news as the rest of them, and it was only that which kept her from winding them up a little. However, they would have to wait a few moments more.

'First I need to pee. Very badly. And I want to brush my teeth. I'll only be a minute,' Jennifer said as she slid out of the bed, grabbed her dressing gown that had been left over a spare chair the night before, and headed for the bathroom.

'Maybe someone could go and get me some coffee while you're waiting? That would be, you know, absolutely fantastic,' she said over her shoulder as she opened the bathroom door.

Jennifer walked back in looking and feeling a whole lot more awake than she had a few minutes ago. Nurit handed her a mug of coffee and she reached for it with a grateful smile. She blew on the steaming liquid gently, took a careful sip and then another. Once the caffeine hit her system she glanced around at the expectant faces of the people in the room. They were waiting for her to speak. To tell them all they needed to know. She hated the thought of disappointing them.

'It didn't work. I didn't have any dreams about Ilan. Or about anything for that matter. I'm really sorry,' Jennifer told them and watched their reactions. Saul ran his hand across his face and then folded his arms in front of him. He looked puzzled. Nathan Cohen shuffled his feet and seemed faintly embarrassed as though he was the one who had failed, not her.

'I am really sorry. I wanted it to work,' she said. Hopefully, they would believe her and leave her alone with her thoughts until they tried again tonight.

Four pairs of eyes bored into her and made her struggle not to squirm uncomfortably. Nurit looked heartbroken.

'Are you sure about that, Jennifer?' Saul asked, the puzzled frown still on his face.

'Yes. I didn't have a single dream.' The lie slipped easily from her lips.

Saul raised his eyebrows and pointed to the laptop sitting open on the desk at the workstation. The technician whose name was Ben, she suddenly remembered, turned it around to let her see the screen. On it was a graph of her brainwaves, the peaks and troughs of the lines charted Jennifer's increased brain activity while she slept. The laptop had made a liar of her. The timelines suggested she had spent a considerable time in REM sleep, and it was obvious she had been dreaming. The minimised screen at the bottom right was hooked to the cameras and clearly showed her eyes as she slept. Her eyeballs were moving underneath the lids.

Another clear indicator she had been dreaming and

more evidence of the lie.

'Okay. Yes. When I said I wasn't dreaming, I meant not about that. Not about Ilan. I'm sorry. I tried to think about him. I was thinking about him just before I fell asleep and I wanted more than anything for this to work. But it didn't. I'm sorry. Maybe it will work next time.'

'So, what did you dream about?' Saul asked.

'Oh, nothing worth mentioning.'

'We need to know the details.'

'You really don't,' Jennifer said. She did not want them to know it was Lucy she had dreamed about. 'It was nothing to do with Ilan. It was something else entirely. Not connected or relevant to this. It wasn't important.'

'It might not seem important to you Jennifer,' Saul told her. 'But it still could be relevant to this operation. It may seem insignificant and unimportant to you, but it could be useful.'

'Trust me, it isn't.'

'Jennifer,' Saul said. His voice was like that of a weary parent chastising a child who refused to behave. 'We are spending a considerable amount of money on this project. We need all of the information, whether it is relevant or not.'

Project? Is that all it is? Not a rescue mission but research and development? Okay, it's mostly a rescue mission. Of course, Ilan is important. They want him back because they need his intel but also because they want to save him. But there's definitely something else going on here. What they're doing here with me is important in its own right, regardless of who is rescued. And I have no choice but to go along with it. I have to work with them if I'm going to get him back.

Saul folded his arms in front of him and watched her as he waited. He made it perfectly clear that he was not going anywhere until he got some answers.

Jennifer sighed. She was not going to get out of this so easily and she knew she was going to have to tell them the truth. She couldn't meet their eyes, especially Nurit's, and she lowered her head and frowned as she studied the condition of her fingernails. They badly needed to be trimmed and filed. But going to her favourite nail bar for a manicure had been the last thing on her mind recently.

'I tried to concentrate on Ilan as I was going to sleep. I really did. Then I was in the place Doctor Cohen made me imagine – a place that was relaxing and comforting to me. I was out on the terrace at our old house in Cyprus and I could smell the jasmine and then, all of a sudden, it got cloudy and the wind picked up. There was a storm and it started raining. Really heavy rain with thunder and lightning. I knew I needed to get out of it and I could see a door, only it wasn't our old house. It was…another house and, I… was afraid to go through it. Then the rain turned to hail and the hailstones were huge. They hit my head and my back and they hurt. I knew I had no other choice but to go through the door. It was stuck at first, but I forced it open and, once inside, I sort of recognised the house. It was Lucy Wilson's house. She's the woman I exchanged dreams with. I recognised it because of the dreams.'

'Yes. We know who she is. Was. Carry on, please.'

'Well... I started looking around and then Lucy was there and she made me go upstairs and see her daughters. I didn't want to, but I went up anyway. I sort of felt compelled to go up. They – the girls – were asleep in their bedroom. Then, when I came back downstairs, she made me go into the sitting room and… and Charlie – that's her husband – was there. Sitting by the fire, drinking a whiskey. He looked so sad and lonely. I noticed he was looking at something on his iPad and he –'

'What was he looking at?' Saul's interested was sparked.

'Um, it was just a dating website. Nothing important to us. I guess he's moving on now,' Jennifer replied.

'There was nothing else?' Saul frowned.

'No,' she said.

'Was there anything relevant on the screen? Anything

relating to Ilan?'

'No. definitely not. It was just photos and profiles of some women.'

'Can you remember any of their names, or where they were located?'

'No. Sorry. I didn't really look at them all that closely.'

'Okay. Then what happened?' Saul asked.

'Lucy and I talked.'

'What did you talk about?'

'Look,' Jennifer said. 'I get that you need answers. I'm more than happy to give them to you if I can, but this dream wasn't about what we are trying to do. I dreamed that Lucy and I sat at her kitchen table and talked about her death and she told me she didn't hate me any longer. She said she no longer blamed me. We talked some more and she asked me why I was here, I mean there, with her in a dream. And I explained that Ilan was missing and that I was trying to find him. She wished me good luck and then I started to wake up. And that's all there was. I wish I could have found him but I couldn't. I think maybe she was on my mind because of all this,' she waved her arm, indicating the room and the equipment. 'And I didn't realise it and that's why I dreamed about her.'

Disappointed and angry at herself for falling at the first fence, Jennifer felt the tears sting her eyes until she detected the charged air of excitement in the room. Even Nurit seemed to take a keen interest in her every word as she stood in the background. Her role in this room was only one of moral support even though Jennifer's success or failure meant as much personally to her as it did to Jennifer.

'Please don't be downhearted Jennifer,' Saul smiled. 'This is very good.'

'Good? How is it good? I was miles off track.'

Saul reached for her hand and gave it a gentle squeeze. Jennifer found herself drawn to the older man. She liked him. There was an air of authority about him and a quiet intelligence that commanded respect above and beyond his age and his obvious seniority in the organisation. Yet, there was also a gentleness and a compassion in his eyes that appealed to her.

'It is good because it works, Jennifer. It's possible you found yourself in that particular dream setting because you needed closure from a part of your life that was, and still is, very painful to remember. You needed to settle the issues it raised that, unintentionally, you have held on to for so long and this was your mind's way of doing so. Now you can close that unfortunate chapter in your life and move on.'

'Do you really think so?' Jennifer asked and there was a tremble in her voice.

'Yes. I believe it is so,' he patted her hand and nodded. 'Stay positive. We will do what we can to assist you.'

Jennifer took a deep breath. 'So, what happens now?'

'Now, you should spend the day and the evening doing whatever you wish. As you have already been informed, we have excellent gym and spa facilities. There is a swimming pool and a cafeteria, and we also have a good library which includes an English language section. All we ask is that you don't relax too much and, of course, no afternoon naps. Try and keep yourself occupied so that you are reasonably tired by tonight and we will resume at nine forty-five this evening.'

With that the team powered down their laptops and equipment, gathered up the laptops and made their way out of the room.

Saul nodded an unspoken command to Nurit before he left and, much to Jennifer's amusement, she stood to attention and saluted as he left the room, closing the door behind him. Jennifer breathed a sigh of relief, glad to be alone with Nurit and no longer the centre of attention for a while.

'Do you want to get dressed and go get a quick coffee and a bite of breakfast before I go home to sleep for a couple of hours?' Nurit asked.

'Yes, please.'

Chapter 15 – Syria.

Jamal forced himself to internalise his fear and he set his face in, what he hoped was, a good imitation of calm neutrality as he walked towards the room situated deep within the compound. The compound used to be a village, but it had been abandoned and the occupants were long gone. They had dispersed to larger towns and cities and beyond or, more likely, they were buried in shallow, unmarked graves among the nearby hills. Those that had survived, fled to the cities searching for a better life. But when they got there, they found no better life awaited them and so they joined the throngs of refugees with their sights set elsewhere, to Europe and farther afield, in the hope of finding a newer, safer existence.

It was fitting that very soon this other group of refugees, his group, would walk in the same footsteps on their own journey. And like the original villagers, they would become invisible faces among the crowds that searched for a new life and a new hope. But *his* group were different in that they were going there to mix the false with the genuine, the perpetrators with the victims and they would remain there, hidden amongst the hungry, the weary and the broken. They would follow them to the cities and it was there, whether they were welcomed or not, that they would avenge their people.

As he walked through the dirt streets and avenues, past the small houses built from the clay of the surrounding land, Jamal imagined the lives the villagers had once lived. Although the buildings were of a basic structure, the people who once lived there had enjoyed running water and electricity. They had fridges and microwave ovens. They had internet access and sport on television. Rusty satellite dishes hung from the walls of some of the larger buildings and this told Jamal that the original occupants were able to watch Sky, with its news and dramas, football matches and movies, as well as BBC News and Al Jazeerah. They knew of the world outside, yet they chose to live here in this remote village until the day they were forced to leave.

A lot of the buildings had been well on their way to becoming rubble, blending into the earth once more, until Sayeed and his people moved in. They had left a lot of it to continue decaying and concentrated their efforts on reinforcing the outer buildings and repairing those in the centre of the village.

To the casual passer-by, the outer buildings remained the same – tumble-down and abandoned – but they had been carefully, and discretely, reinforced and now were homes to armed guards and lookouts. Jamal ignored them as he walked along and ducked out of the sunlight into darkened shadows that complimented his mood. His path seemed random as he turned left then right, then left again and he went deeper into what had once been the heart of the village. He passed the mosque without a glance. Behind it sat the remains of a school. He wondered where the kids who had attended had gone. Probably to a refugee centre somewhere. Or most likely dead.

He skirted the school yard and took another left turn down a narrow passageway until he came to a door. With his knuckles, he gave it three short raps and the door immediately opened inward. A young man, fear and reverence in his eyes, nodded in recognition and took a step back to allow Jamal to enter. Jamal inclined his head in acknowledgment and stepped inside, briefly blinded until his eyes became accustomed to the semi-darkness. A narrow passageway greeted him, the floor uneven, and he was careful of his step as he followed its path to the stairs that led down to their underground command centre.

The command centre did not resemble in any way, shape, or form, an abandoned village. They had arrived at the village in the dead of night, three nights ago, after a sudden decision by Sayeed to move location, and they had commenced work immediately. It had taken them less than twenty-four hours to set everything up – electricity, running water and, most importantly, satellite internet. Now, it resembled a high-tech operations room. For that's what it was – an extremely sophisticated and obviously expensive operations room.

There were no windows, but it was brightly lit and almost glaring. The brightness came from several overhead florescent tubes. They hung precariously from their wiring and were attached to the ceiling by heavy duty staples. The walls were papered with maps and diagrams. Plans and ideas. Along both opposite walls, banks of computers and monitors sat on rows of desks. All were manned by studious, frowning young men. Angry young men whose only goal was the completion of their appointed tasks in order to further their terrible ambitions. They kept their heads glued to the computer monitors in front of them as they concentrated on entering the details to the webpages on the screens. Each man had a stack of credit cards piled on the desk beside him. All fraudulent, all untraceable.

Jamal watched them for a moment. They were busy little bees, scurrying from web page to web page, entering names and address. Passport numbers and destinations. They checked flight departures and arrivals. Timetables of railways, ports and bus stations. All the places where Sayeed's little army would land. And from there, then they would go onwards to all the places where the infidels would gather. To their favourite watering holes. Their pubs and their clubs. Their schools and their sporting events. Their churches and their cinemas. All the places where they lived their everyday lives. And it was in these very places that they would die.

The plan was only three or four days from completion, five at the very most, and his team was awash with nervous energy and anticipation. He was finding it hard to keep them in check. Only stern words and the threat of execution brought to a halt their natural exuberance and they hung their heads in shame at his voice. He was not their friend. Nor was he their father-figure. But he was their teacher and they respected his authority and listened to what he had to say.

They were good boys, really. They just needed time to learn their lessons.

The operation was well-funded. Their backers were mostly Russian, not interested in their ideals but content to use them for their own ends – the destabilisation of Europe being their main interest and goal. Some of the funds also came from the United States. Their motives were not so clear. Sometimes it appeared that they simply liked to have their fingers in every pie and, as long as nothing happened on American soil, they didn't care what the 'ragheads' were up to. They would condemn it as an atrocious act, naturally, and when it became clear that the US was also a target, they would threaten invasion in retaliation and would promise a quick and sure justice. The Russians would pay lip service and agree wholeheartedly with the worldwide condemnation, but it was unlikely they would even bother making threats.

'Jamal!' Sayeed Qahtani's sharp voice interrupted his thoughts. He looked up and saw the younger man standing at the doorway of the small back room he had commandeered as an office. Sayeed waved to him, indicating he should join him. Jamal had no idea what he wanted and that frightened him more than anything.

Sayeed Qahtani was an enigma of a man, even to those who believed they knew him well. Not overly tall, he was shorter than Jamal by several inches and lighter skinned than most of his fellow Middle-Eastern countrymen. Born into a wealthy Saudi family thirty-two years ago he was the second youngest of his four siblings. His father was Saudi but his mother was Swedish which accounted for the lightness of his complexion. Two of his three brothers were involved in banking and the third was in IT. Little was known about his sister other than she was married with two children. His accent was Mid-Atlantic English with a slight emphasis on Americanisation, having been educated in universities firstly in the UK and then in the USA where he had studied English Literature and Business Management.

How he became radicalised no one knew and it was not

something he would ever discuss with anyone. Maybe he merely woke up one morning and decided that this was what he wanted to do with his life. Whatever the reason or the motive, he was a natural at it. Cold and calculating, with not an ounce of compassion in his body, he could, and did, kill without hesitation. Responsible for terrorist attacks in several European cities, one in Australia and another three in the United States, he was probably the current 'most wanted' man in the world. Yet he enjoyed Italian opera, could quote long passages from various Shakespeare plays, and he loved American and English sitcoms.

Jamal respected him and feared him in equal measure.

'Will you take tea with me, my brother?' Sayeed smiled as he lifted the kettle off the small stove. The office had all the comforts of home. A small refrigerator, a cooker and a sink took up the space near the window. A large, comfortable sofa that had seen better days was covered with cushions and took up the space in front of another wall. An elaborately ornate, hand-carved, low wooden table sat in front of the sofa and another armchair sat at right angles to it. The chair did not match the sofa but looked to be as old and almost as comfortable. All of the items in this small room had been scavenged from the nearby, abandoned houses.

To Jamal's left stood a desk and a wooden chair. On the desk was a laptop. It was switched on and he glanced briefly at the screen but whatever Sayeed had been looking at was minimised and the only thing on the screen was a generic wallpaper – a snow-covered Mount Everest.

Sayeed saw him looking and smiled. 'The Mother of all mountains, is it not?'

Jamal shrugged. 'I believe it is called by many names.'

'True,' Sayeed nodded as he poured tea into two glasses and carried them over to the table. He set them down on a brass tray, obviously not wishing to leave marks on the wood. Perhaps he was intending to return it to its rightful owner one day, if that owner could ever be found alive and well. 'Regardless of its name, it is beautiful and awe-inspiring. I have only seen it in pictures but I find it soothing and comforting.'

And why do you need comfort? The thought crept unbidden into Jamal's mind. But he kept this thought to himself and his face was impassive as he joined Sayeed at the small table. He took the chair and Sayeed took the sofa as he always did.

'I expected you earlier,' Sayeed said, and Jamal could hear the accusatory note in his voice.

'One of the trucks would not start. I was fixing it,' Jamal replied. 'It was nothing serious.'

'You are also a mechanic?' Sayeed asked.

'Allah gave me this skill. Is it not good that I can use it to serve Him?'

Sayeed merely nodded and took a small sip of his tea, but Jamal could see that the man was impressed.

'Our plans are on schedule?' Sayeed asked.

'Yes, my brother,' Jamal told him. 'The passports were delivered yesterday by our own courier. They have been checked and all are in order. All flights, ferries and train journeys are in the process of being pre-booked and the correct names and details have all been successfully entered. The same with the locations. They have been checked and double checked. All is in order. We have in total fifty… travellers.'

'The passports will pass muster?'

'Yes. The company who supply them are legitimate. The batch that had been stolen went unnoticed and it is highly unlikely this theft will be discovered until it is too late.'

Jamal had no idea what Sayeed's plans were. The man believed fervently, almost religiously, in compartmentalisation and had divided the people in his organisation into cells. Of course, this was standard operating procedure and there was nothing out of the ordinary about it. Terrorists the world over, since the beginning of modern terrorism, used this method of keeping the potential for infiltration and exposure of their plans from falling into the wrong hands. Everyone was expendable, but the operation was not and compartmentalisation was the safest way of protecting it. If one cell was compromised that was a sad loss, but they could never reveal other cells or anything more than their own small role in the operation.

Not that they considered themselves terrorists. They were freedom fighters. They were honourable men fighting a just and holy war. Sayeed believed this fervently, and he preached it frequently.

Just and holy it may be, but it would be useful to know some more details of what they were planning. Jamal would find out in due course, but it could be too late by that stage.

In the meantime, Jamal sipped the hot, sweet tea and watched Sayeed carefully. He wanted to ask him about the operation. He needed more details. Exact details. But if he asked, he could very likely arouse Sayeed's suspicions and would learn nothing. Sometimes the man was suspicious of everything and everyone to the point of paranoia. It made his job as operations manager a somewhat difficult task. If only he could explain this to the man seated before him. He had to try.

Sayeed looked at him and smiled. 'You have questions, my brother?'

Jamal shrugged. 'If I am to make this operation successful, I need –'

'Allah will decide if the mission succeeds or fails. But I have faith that He will make it a complete success.'

'Of course. I do not question that,' Jamal said. 'But it would assist me greatly in the logistics of our operation if I knew what it entailed.'

Sayeed took a deep breath and carefully set his glass of tea on the tray. He seemed to come to a decision and it seemed to Jamal that he had come to it reluctantly.

'I will tell you. But not yet. Tomorrow I may have another task for you to perform. After that you will know everything. If Allah wills it.'

With that, the man dismissed him from the small room that was now the control centre of their operation.

Chapter 16.

Jennifer carefully applied her lipstick, a shade of red that matched her dress, and stood up. The dress she was wearing was a new one. It was backless and had a plunging neckline and it clung to her like a second skin. She stood in front of the full-length mirror and turned to the left and then to the right glancing over her shoulder as she admired her reflection. Was she preening? Of course, she was preening. Who wouldn't preen in a dress like this? On a night like this?

Her hair probably should have been shoulder-length and worn in a Marilyn Munroe fifties style which would have been more suited to the dress. But she had worn her hair ash-blonde, short and spiked for so many years now and she never had the inclination to grow it or change the style. Except for that one time when she had almost... she chased the memories away. She was not going to think of that dark time in her life. Not tonight.

The diamond earrings that Ilan had surprised her with as an anniversary gift a few years ago sparkled as they caught the lights. On her left wrist she was wearing a Tibetan Mala bracelet, the dark red beads toned in nicely with the dress. It was simple and inexpensive yet there was an elegance to it that she loved. It had been her good luck charm for years. Would it work tonight? She hoped so.

One last twirl in front of the mirror. She looked good. Tall and slender. A body that would turn men's heads when she walked into a room. Fuckable was the word she was looking for. But there was only one man she wanted to look at her and think of her in that way. Only one man whose head she wanted to turn tonight. That man was her husband and she couldn't wait to see him again.

Jennifer looked herself up and down, nodded and smiled. *Not too bad for a woman rushing towards her mid-forties. Yeah, I can do this. Easy-peasy.*

With a dab of her favourite perfume on her wrists and behind her ears, she was ready. She lifted the small purse off the bed and placed her room key and lipstick in it. She checked that her credit cards were safely tucked inside the little zipped compartment, and headed out of the room. By now Ilan would be downstairs in the hotel bar waiting impatiently for her and probably drinking a whiskey sour.

Well, I'll definitely be worth the wait tonight. Eager anticipation put a spring in her step and a smile on her lips. She felt like dancing. Maybe he would take her dancing this evening.

In the elevator, she hummed a favourite melody and her hips swayed in time to the tune. She watched the numbers counting down and waited for the elevator doors to open just as Doctor Cohen – or Nathan as he insisted – had told her they would.

Three, two, one. The elevator pinged and Jennifer stepped through the doors as they opened onto a broad, richly carpeted expanse. In every direction there were comfortable leather chairs positioned around small tables – enough tables to ensure healthy profits, but not so many that it was overcrowded. Nearly every seat was occupied with people – couples sharing a romantic pre-dinner drink, business men and women relaxing after a busy day, others pulling tables and chairs together so they could drink and chat in a large group, maybe intending to have a few drinks before going on to a nightclub. It was just another normal night in a popular hotel in a big city.

To Jennifer's left was the reception area and when she turned her head to the left, she saw her destination – the hotel bar.

The deep pile of the carpet underfoot, the high ceilings with the magnificent chandeliers and the gilt mirrors all added to the opulence of the beautiful old building. Jennifer caught her reflection in one of the mirrors. She hesitated and her smile became a puzzled frown as the image wavered and seemed to change. She saw herself, not in a beautiful red dress with her earrings sparkling as they caught the light, but in a hospital bed. In a hospital room. Her eyes were closed and her face was pale and drawn almost invisible against the stark whiteness of the pillow beneath her head. Sensor pads were attached to her temples with their leads connected to machines and monitors.

That is all wrong. That is not where I am. I'm here. In this hotel. I'm dressed up to the nines and I'm about to meet my husband.

Then the image disappeared and Jennifer found herself back in the hotel again. She could feel the lush carpet under her feet and hear the noise of the crowd at the bar. It was a Saturday night. The alcohol was in full flow and the patrons were loud and cheerful almost to the point of rowdiness. Her red dress drew appraising looks as she walked past. A quick glance at herself in another mirror confirmed to Jennifer that she had left the image of her lying on a hospital bed far behind her and she was back in the dream once more. A couple of men, the alcohol having emboldened them, drunkenly called to her and invited her to join them.

'Come on honey,' they yelled. 'Come and have a good time with us. You know you won't regret it.'

She straightened her shoulders and held her head up high, and gave the crowd, the catcalling men in particular, a good look at what they could see but could not have. There was only one man in the whole building whose attention she craved tonight. And there he was. Sitting at the bar, where he sipped at his whiskey and made a point of ignoring her, refusing to turn around to see what all the fuss was about.

Brimming with the confidence that only her sure and certain faith in her sexuality could give her, Jennifer walked up to the bar and parked herself on the empty barstool beside her husband.

'What would you like to drink?' Ilan asked as he glanced her way and nodded as he caught the bartender's eye.

'Oh, I think I'll have what you're having,' Jennifer told him. She reached for his hand and linked her fingers with his as she looked at him. He was wearing a dark suit and a white shirt. The top button undone and, as was his habit whenever he could, he wore no tie. The suit seemed loose on him, as though he had lost some weight. Ilan had always kept himself in good shape by working out and swimming and jogging at every opportunity. But this came from stress and worry and fear: it was an *unhealthy* weight loss. She could also see that his hair was a little bit greyer than it used to be. As was his beard, which was fuller than she preferred.

For the first time since she had known him, Jennifer noticed the age in him. He was only nine years older than her, but right now he seemed to have aged at a faster pace. As if he was ill or something was sucking the life from him. He had a weariness about him that showed in the slump of his shoulders, the grim set of his mouth and the dark circles underneath his eyes. But, as he turned around, he squeezed her fingertips and smiled at her, the delight in his eyes at seeing her again was obvious. When he smiled at her a few of the years dropped away.

'Whiskey Sour? Are you sure?'

'Yeah. I don't feel like wine tonight, and a gin and tonic tastes so much nicer outdoors on a summer's evening. Well, to me it does,' she shrugged.

'It's good to see you, neshama,' Ilan said as he planted a kiss on her cheek. 'I've missed you very much.'

It was tempting to tell him that it was his fault they had been apart for so long, but the warmth of his voice took the edge off her feelings, and so Jennifer held her tongue as she concentrated on the two glasses of whiskey the bartender had placed in front of them. She lifted her glass and toasted him silently as she took a sip, swallowing the whiskey quickly.

She really didn't like whiskey prepared this way. Whiskey, whether Scotch or Irish, should only be drunk neat with ice or water in it. Or with hot water, cloves and a little sugar on a cold winter's night. These added ingredients – lemon juice, sugar syrup, egg white and whatever else they mixed into it just spoiled it in her opinion. But Ilan had developed a taste for it and it seemed right, under the circumstances, that she should join him in drinking his current favourite tipple.

'You look stunning tonight,' he told her. 'Is that a new dress?'

'Yes. Do you like it?'

'I do. But I would also like to see you not wearing it,' he said with a smile that needed no explanation.

Ahh, there was the Ilan she knew best and had loved for so long. She had missed him more than she ever realised. *Keep calm. You have a job to do first. Play the game and if all goes well all of this will become real.*

'Not in here, I hope.'

Ilan threw back his head and laughed.

Jennifer laughed along with him. Then her face grew serious as she looked at him. She longed to hold him. To take him to bed and make love to him and hold him close to her forever. To get him back into her arms and her life and never let him escape again.

'Then what would you like to do this evening, if you won't allow me to undress you?' Ilan asked.

'Maybe later,' she told him, but there was a look in her eye that said maybe was definitely.

'Perhaps I should just sit here and drink my whiskey sour all evening, since my mood will be sour if I can't undress you and make love to you.' Ilan raised an eyebrow.

'I didn't say you couldn't. I said – maybe later.'

'So, you want to torment me? Punish me for leaving you?'

'Now you are coming around to my way of thinking,' she said, giving him a leer.

'You are evil, my love.'

'Yep. That's me alright.'

They fell silent as they sipped at their drinks, both of them suddenly becoming aware that the conversation was unnaturally forced. The humour and the sexual suggestiveness seemed contrived, as if they were working from scripts and, like two bad actors, neither of them knew how to inject the correct emotion into the moment.

Conversations buzzed all around them as the crowd in the hotel bar began to relax and enjoy themselves even more as the evening wore on. To Jennifer it seemed that she and Ilan were trapped inside a bubble of tension and fear that they could never escape from. Yet, when she took Ilan's hand in hers and looked into his eyes, all of it was real. He was with her and they were the only two people in the room. In the hotel. On the planet.

What's wrong? Isn't this what I wanted? To find him and get the info from him that will bring him home? I have to get him to talk to me somehow.

But how does one get a man to talk when he does not want to talk? When he's afraid that something he says will be used against him in some way? Never Mr. Chatty at the best of times, Ilan was a professional and knew better than anyone when to keep silent. But it was her job to make him talk. To extract from him the information that they needed.

'I had a dream about you last night,' Ilan told her, his voice quiet and thoughtful.

Jennifer tilted her head back in surprise and looked at him. He was still holding her hand as though it was his lifeline. Perhaps it was. It was keeping them together for the moment. But the connection between then was fragile. It would take only the slightest hesitation on the part of either of them to break it and they would slip away from one another. Out of sight and out of reach. Maybe forever. Holding onto to one another seemed to strengthen the bond. As much as it was possible to strengthen it, considering the circumstances. Jennifer knew this, and she believed Ilan was also aware that everything could be lost in less than a heartbeat. She gave his hand a gentle, reassuring squeeze and leaned against him. Needing to feel the warmth of his body close to hers. Maybe they should have tried this in a bed somewhere.

'I've had a few about you recently,' she told him.

'This one was different,' Ilan frowned.

'How so?'

'It was very explicit.'

'Did you enjoy it?'

'Immensely.'

'Then why are you frowning?'

'Although I enjoyed it, I found it... somewhat disturbing. It was more than a dream. It was almost real but, while I enjoyed the sexual aspect of it, I could sense an underlying current of... hatred. No, that's too strong a word. Anger. Yes, I could sense anger.'

'Yours or mine?' Jennifer asked, not sure what his answer would be.

'That I don't know. You and I were not making love, Jennifer. We were fucking. Hard and fast. Neither of us cared if the other was in pain. It was pure animal lust. Sex in its most basic form. I'm not even sure if there was any emotion involved. That, in itself, was disturbing.'

'But we've done it hard and fast before. We've both been so horny that we didn't care what we were doing. Why did you feel this was different?'

Ilan looked down at her hand in his and sighed. The weight of the world was upon his shoulders. Literally. And it was almost too much to bear. He took another mouthful of whiskey and held up his glass to get the bartender's attention once more.

'Talk to me, Ilan.'

'It's hard to explain, neshama,' he began slowly. 'It didn't feel like a dream. It was more a... memory and there was a sadness and an anger in you. In both of us. I cannot explain why. This is how it appeared to me. The sex was great, don't get me wrong, I can assure you that it was great. As always. But there was something missing. The love was no longer there. It was as if we had… lost one another and we could not find our way back to being the couple we were. At the end of the dream, you were sad and you admonished me for leaving you. You said this as you walked away from me. In the end it was you who left me. I mean in the dream.'

He looked closely at her. 'At the end, I felt you were leaving me. That I had lost you.'

'That will never happen, Ilan. I love you as much today as I have ever loved you. I won't leave you. In a dream or in real life.'

'I know that,' he replied. 'It just seemed so real to me.'

'Don't I know it,' Jennifer muttered.

'Of course, you are an expert on dreams, yes?'

'Well, I'm not really what you'd call an expert. But you know my history and you know that when I was… ill… I was caught up in some fairly realistic dreams, to the extent that when I came home from hospital, I didn't know what was real and what was not for a long, long time. But this is different. With you away for so long, with us being apart for so long, it's only natural that you'd dream of me in such a way. I've had a few fairly explicit dreams about you myself, you know.'

Is it time to play the ace card up my sleeve? No, not yet. I need to reel him in some more before I cut to the chase. First of all, I need to tell him how I got here and why I'm here. Then if he doesn't believe me, I'll whip out my ace card and just hope it works.

'In fact, this is a dream right now,' she said as she took a deep breath. Another whiskey would have made this so much easier but it was probably not the best idea under the circumstances. A clear head was more important.

'I don't understand,' Ilan frowned.

'It seems like you and I are sitting here in this hotel bar. But it's a dream. In reality, you are missing somewhere in Syria and I'm fast asleep in a room in Mossad headquarters, hooked up to monitors and dreaming about you. About all of this.' Jennifer waved her arm in a sweeping gesture, indicating the bar and their plush surroundings. 'I'm here because your bosses want to find you and bring you home. And of course, so do I.'

Ilan stared at her as if she was crazy, or had grown horns. Or both. Under his gaze Jennifer grew uncomfortable.

Suddenly her dress was too tight. Too revealing. The sparkling earrings she loved so much and the bright red lipstick now made her look like a high-priced whore. She couldn't decipher the look in his eyes. Was it disgust? Fear? What? How could she not know? How could she not be able to read his thoughts and emotions? This was the man she had woken up beside almost every morning for the best part of thirteen years. The man she hoped to wake up beside for the next thirteen. Times two. Times three. And hopefully for many more years after that.

'Are you out of your mind? This is insane!'

'No, Ilan. I am very serious. When they lost contact with you, they showed up on the doorstep and asked me if I would try and help them. They knew all about me, about what I went through with Lucy after the accident,' Jennifer glared at him, about to question him on *that* subject, but she knew that this was neither the time nor the place to go into how the Mossad knew so much about her history. 'They told me they wanted to try something similar to find out what is happening with you. I know you are working undercover with a terrorist group and that they are planning something. Something big. They need to stop it. And I need you to give me the details to help them stop it. And get you home again.'

Jennifer held her breath. She had what, she hoped, was a sincere expression on her face. Ilan must believe her. If he didn't then all was lost. *Come on. It's me. You know it's me. You know what I'm telling you is true.*

Ilan's eyes were black and angry, his brow furrowed in a frown. He gripped her arm and she tried to pull away as she squirmed under his look. He was hurting her now.

'I don't know who the fuck you are,' Ilan whispered as he leaned closer to her face. His voice was a low, menacing growl. 'But if you think I am going to believe a word of this rubbish, this shit, just because you resemble my wife, you can think again.'

'You're hurting me. Stop it,' she said loudly. A little too loudly perhaps, for a few faces nearby turned towards them.

But Ilan didn't stop. Still holding her by the upper arm, he yanked her to her feet. The bartender stared open-mouthed, tempted to intervene, but unable to decide on a course of action. Ilan threw a handful of banknotes in his direction – plenty enough to cover the cost of their drinks and him the kind of tip he had only ever dreamed about. The man grabbed the notes, took one glance at Ilan's angry face and, with a shrug, decided doing nothing was the sensible thing to do.

Ignoring the looks from the two or three patrons who had overheard Jennifer's words, Ilan pulled her tightly to him in an embrace that was definitely not a loving embrace. Still holding her arm in a tight, very painful grip he made for the front door. One man started to get up, to come to her rescue. Jennifer smiled at her would-be rescuer and shrugged her shoulders in a 'this is just a little game we enjoy' kind of way that caused him to hesitate. A glare from Ilan, followed by something that was not quite a snarl but close enough, swayed his decision in favour of sitting down again.

In a matter of seconds, they were out of the hotel and onto the street.

It'll be okay. He's just surprised by what I said. He probably doesn't want to talk in the bar where we could be overheard. Jennifer took a deep breath, and a brief moment to look up and admire the lovely old building – the sandstone and the ornate design spoiled only by the scaffolding on one side of it. Obviously, some renovation work was being carried out to give the old hotel a bit of an exterior face lift.

Then she was yanked away in the direction of the main road. Where was he taking her? Worried now by his demeanour, Jennifer tried to resist. She pried at the fingers of the hand that was gripping her arm and pulled back in an attempt to slow him down.

'Stop, Ilan. Please,' she begged but he ignored her and continued dragging her along the footpath. She tried to keep from stumbling and looked around, realising now that she needed help. The streets were empty. Not a single person walked past them or towards them. She glanced around her, twisting her head from side to side. The city streets couldn't be this empty. Where was everyone?

Ilan turned right and, still holding her arm, pulled her down a dark alley. He slammed her against the wall and pressed his body against her. There was nothing sexual in his actions. He was merely restraining her. He pressed his whole body against hers so she couldn't even raise her knee to slam into where it would hurt him the most.

'Who the fuck are you?' Ilan demanded.

'Let go of me, you bastard.' Jennifer bared her teeth in a grimace of anger and pain and heartbreak. This was not how she'd imagined the night would turn out. Then her eyes opened wide in shock as she felt something hard and unyielding pressed against her ribcage. He had produced a gun and was threatening her with it. She couldn't believe this was happening. But it was. Tears sprang into her eyes.

'Start talking or I will shoot you,' Ilan said and she didn't doubt his word for a minute.

'Let go of me first.'

He tilted his head, his face up close to hers. Too close, but the wall behind her prevented her from backing away from him. All Jennifer could manage was a pathetic squirming motion against him and this sickened her to her stomach. This was her husband. Her lover. Her best friend. How many times had she squirmed against his body, both naked and fully clothed, in passion and in fun? But this? This ruined all of it. She would never be able to erase this from her memory.

Ilan's eyes were angry and full of menace. They burned with hatred and disgust and, for the first time since the Mossad had contacted her, Jennifer felt real fear. If Ilan shot her now and she died right here in this dark and dingy alleyway, would she waken up? Or would she die in her sleep? Or worse – not die but not waken up either? The gun was still against her ribcage and his forearm was now pressed on her throat. A little more pressure and he would choke the life out of her.

He'll either strangle me or shoot me. Or both. Fuck. He's a highly trained Mossad officer and I'm a former interior designer who walks dogs for a living. He can pick any one of a hundred different ways to kill me and I won't be able to do a thing about it. I won't stand a chance unless I can talk him down.

All these thoughts raced through her mind in less time that it would have taken Ilan to pull the trigger and end her life then and there. Jennifer knew she had to somehow convince him she was indeed who she said she was.

'Wait. Listen. Listen to me, Ilan. Just stop and take a moment and listen to me.' Her voice was hard and firm. She didn't scream at him but she didn't whisper either. 'Just let me explain. Please.'

'Start talking,' Ilan's head rocked back so he could see her face more clearly as he thought about her suggestion. 'Explain yourself and maybe, just maybe, I won't kill you. First, you tell me who you are and who you are working for.'

He released the pressure slightly on her throat but kept the gun where it was.

Jennifer took a deep breath. It was a relief to no longer feel his arm against her throat. There was some pain but she could live with it. Her eyes met his and it broke her heart that she could not see even a tiny shred of the love that usually shone in them.

'I'm me. I'm Jennifer,' she said as she echoed the word that she had said to him in the hospital over three years ago.

'Impossible,' he said. The angry look was still in his eyes.

'I'm serious, Ilan,' Jennifer took another deep breath and allowed her body to relax against him. She placed her hand lightly on his shoulder, tempted to stroke his cheek with her fingertips but afraid she would overdo it and arouse his suspicions even more. 'Let me explain everything, please.'

He was still tense, still very much on alert but something in his gaze seemed to soften and he watched her carefully as he considered her request.

Finally, he nodded.

'Your bosses came to the house when they lost contact with you and they asked me to help them find you,' Jennifer said. 'They knew all about what happened to me in Cyprus, and that's something you and I will need to have a little discussion about. But not here and not now. It'll keep. But we will definitely need to talk about it.'

'Get to the point,' Ilan snarled.

'They told me that they wanted to try a form of remote viewing with me. Well, actually a combination of remote viewing and lucid dreaming. To try and recreate a version of the dreams I had when I was in the coma. But this time they were going to hypnotise me and use um... suggestive something or other to –'

'It's called suggestive therapy.'

'Yes! That's what they called it. They suggested I think about you before I fell asleep. To visualise you. Really concentrate on you. Then I would dream about you and, in the dream, I would be able to talk to you in an attempt to find out where you are and what is happening to you.'

'When did this start?'

'The day before yesterday. This is my second attempt at it. The first time I was all over the place and I couldn't find you at all. I'm not sure why, but I ended up… well, somewhere else. But this time it's worked because here I am.'

'Here you are indeed,' he said. He caught her lower jaw in his hand and tilted her face up to his. For a second Jennifer thought he was going to kiss her.

'Now tell me why I should believe a word you are saying?'

'Because I *am* telling you the truth. If I was someone else trying to get you to talk, how the hell do I know about the coma I was in?'

'Someone could have accessed your medical files,' Ilan said. But he didn't sound confident in his assumption.

Jennifer could tell he was wavering, thinking about what she had told him. He was on the brink of believing her and all he needed was a little push. 'There's one thing I can say that will make you believe me.'

'What?'

Jennifer put her arms around his neck and reached up to him. She whispered their safe words into his ear. It was a short phrase they had agreed on many years ago and neither of them had ever said it aloud in the presence of any other person. Ilan's body went rigid with shock when he heard Jennifer utter the words. He knew them well. He knew that Jennifer was the only other person in the world who knew them. With the gun still in one hand, he caught her by the wrists and pulled her arms away from his neck. Still holding them he looked into her eyes and saw the sincerity in them.

'How is this possible?'

'I told you. This is a dream. This is me in a dream looking for you. Trying to save your life.'

'It is hard to believe.'

'But not impossible,' she insisted.

'Keep talking.'

'You know that it is possible. You know I've done this before. I'll admit I never did it by choice but I did prove it was possible. And with a little help from a very nice hypnotherapist called Nathan Cohen, I have managed to do it again.'

'It is really you?' He was still not a hundred percent convinced.

'Yes.'

'Did we, did you dream about me before you began this experiment?'

'It's a rescue mission, not an experiment and yes, I did dream about you the night before we started. Why?'

'Because I wasn't lying when I said earlier that I had the most explicit dream about you.'

Jennifer frowned as more memories of the dream she had experienced came back to her. It had been explicit. How did that happen? Okay, she had been thinking about Ilan before she went to bed but she did that every night. There had been nothing different about her thoughts that evening. She certainly hadn't been fantasising about sex with him. If anything, her thoughts had been more negative towards him for putting her in such a position. So, why had she dreamed something so sexual and intense about him? And, more importantly, they seemed to have shared the same dream. No answers came to her. None that made sense anyway.

'Mine was explicit too,' she admitted.

'But this was before you began the hypnosis, yes?'

'Yes. But I don't know how or why it happened. Look, Ilan. It's not important right now. What is important is that you believe me and believe me when I say that I'm here to help you. Do you?'

'Yes,' Ilan said and his voice was barely a whisper as his body relaxed and he leaned towards her, his forehead against hers. The relief on his face was obvious but his eyes were still wary, still untrusting… but wavering.

He took a deep breath and seemed to come to a decision. He slipped the pistol he was holding back into his pocket and his hands caressed her neck where earlier they had threatened to choke her; his fingertips gently stroked her skin. 'Yes, neshama, I believe you.'

Oh, thank heavens!

'I've missed you so much, Ilan,' she told him. 'Please come home to me.'

'I can't,' he shook his head. 'You know that. You know I have to see this through.'

'But you might die.'

'That's a risk I have to take.'

'If I told you that I –'

'Wait.' Ilan held up his hand in a warning for her to be silent. Startled, he glanced around as though he had heard something.

'What is it?' Jennifer asked.

'Did you hear that?'

'No. I didn't hear anything. There's nothing to hear.'

'I have to go,' he said.

'No. Ilan, wait. Please. This is very important.'

'What?'

'They need details. They desperately need to know your location so they can find you. They need co-ordinates, if you have them. And they need to know what is being planned.'

'I don't know what is being planned. I have my suspicions but I need more time to confirm it. Tell them that. Tell them that I am okay, but I need more time. And tell Saul Mueller that maybe we *should* retire and go fishing.'

'What?' Jennifer frowned and stared at her husband. *Fishing? He's talking about fishing at a time like this?*

'Just tell him. He will understand,' Ilan said.

'Okay, I will. But what about your location? They need to know where you are?'

Ilan stared at her for a moment. He knew why they were asking. What they would do if all else failed. But he couldn't tell her this.

'I don't know,' he said, his desire to live a little longer made him stall for time. 'I will try and find out. But for now, I must go.'

'Another moment, please. Hold me in your arms.'

Ilan rested his forehead against hers and breathed in her scent. He could feel the warmth emanating from her body as his arms slipped around her waist and he pulled her close to him. Then he stepped back and cradled her face in his hands. He studied her face and memorised the blueness of her eyes and his finger lightly traced the tiny scar beneath her left eyebrow – a souvenir, she had told him, from her tomboy childhood when she fell off a dirt bike. Then he traced the faint laughter lines that crinkled at the edges of her eyes when she smiled, and finally he ran his thumb over the lips he loved to kiss. Jennifer caught his thumb gently in her teeth.

He sighed and stepped away from her.

'I'm sorry. I cannot stay any longer. I love you,

neshama. With all of my heart and soul. If nothing else, remember that,' he said as he turned and, in a flash, he was running back along the alleyway towards the main street.

Jennifer couldn't let him disappear. What had he heard? Whatever it was, it had frightened him. She tried to run after him but it was impossible to keep up in her high heels. What wouldn't she give to be wearing jeans and tatty old trainers right now? By the time she got to the street he was gone and it was still as deserted as it had been earlier.

Dejected, Jennifer walked back to the hotel and into the bar. Parking herself on the only available barstool, she caught the bartender's eye and ordered another whiskey sour. She told both of the men, and the one woman, who tried to hit on her, to take a hike.

Chapter 17.

Jennifer raised her glass to her lips and drained the contents, disappointed that things had not gone as well as she had hoped with Ilan. It wasn't all doom and gloom, though. With some persuasion, he eventually stopped threatening to kill her and admitted that he believed her. Their next meeting would be easier. Still, it would have been nice to have gotten all the information she needed in one go and they could begin the process of getting him home safe and well.

Maybe tonight. We won't have to go through all that rigmarole of convincing each other we are who we say we are. We can just get down to the nitty gritty of where he is and get it over with.

Although tempted by another drink, Jennifer left the hotel bar and walked to the elevator. The doors opened as she approached. She stepped through them and found herself back in the room. She sat up on the bed, threw back the sheet and swung her legs out.

'I got him,' she said with a triumphant smile. 'He's alive and I managed to convince him I was who I said I was. Mind you, that took a bit of work but I got there in the end.'

'Tell me?' Saul stepped forward, holding out a bathrobe and helping her into it. He was making it obvious that he wasn't prepared to wait until she had taken a shower and had her coffee. That was okay with her this time.

Someone handed Jennifer a coffee while she was relating the details of her dream to Saul and for that she was grateful. She gave Saul an account of everything that had transpired. Well, almost everything. She left out the conversation about the sexy dream Ilan and she had shared. This was something she needed to think about, long and hard. The fact that she had been able to get into Ilan's dream without the use of hypnosis was something that both puzzled and disturbed her in equal measure. Telling the Mossad about it wasn't a good idea at present, in her opinion. *No, they definitely don't need to know about that!*

'And,' she continued, taking another quick sip of her coffee. 'Once he realised, I was telling him the truth he put his gun away and let go of my throat. Well, he'd already let go of my throat by that stage or else I couldn't have talked to him, but you know what I mean.'

'Did he tell you anything at all about the mission?' Saul asked.

'No. We didn't get that far.'

'His location? Did he tell you his location?'

'No.'

'Did he say what the group is planning?'

'He doesn't know yet. He told me to tell you that he is still trying to find out.'

'And that was *all* he told you?'

'Yes.' Jennifer glared at him. As far as she was concerned, they had made a big leap forward. Ilan was alive and he would soon be able to tell her where he was and what was happening.

Saul's face hardened at her words. He didn't seem at all pleased by her admission. He looked away from her and then he took a deep, exasperated breath. 'So, what exactly did you and Ilan talk about, Jennifer?'

'Well, apart from what he said before he did a runner, mostly it was me trying to convince him I was real. Oh, and he muttered something about you and him going fishing,' Jennifer shrugged. 'What's that all about?'

Saul's face registered a moment of shock but then seemed to brighten at her comment, although he didn't remark on it. 'Where did this conversation take place?'

'Well, it began in a bar in a hotel. I didn't plan any of that. It was just where I happened to appear in the dream when I walked through the door. He was waiting for me and we had a couple of drinks and began to chat. When I told him why I was there, he got angry. And I mean, really angry. He caught me by the arm and dragged me out into the street and down a dark alleyway around the corner from the hotel.'

'Did you engage in any sexual activity with Ilan in your

dream?'

'I beg your pardon?' Jennifer stared at him.

'We observed that your heart rate increased significantly at one stage.'

'He stuck a gun in my ribs and he had his hand around my throat. You can bet your ass my heart rate increased significantly! And I can assure you there was absolutely nothing sexual about it!'

'How did you convince him that it was really you?'

'I told him the phrase that we agreed on years ago.'

'And that worked?' He seemed surprised.

'Yes, of course.'

Saul thought for a moment then looked at her closely. 'What is the phrase?'

'I don't think that is any of your business,' Jennifer told him sharply.

He nodded, slowly acknowledging that not only was it none of his business, it was not relevant. His unspoken apology, if that was what it was, did not exactly win Jennifer over, and she continued to glare at him.

'Did you manage to discuss anything else about who he is with. Any names?' He quickly steered the conversation in the right direction again.

'No. Nothing like that. Like I said, he was dubious at first – more than dubious, he didn't believe me at all – but once I convinced him I was genuine he was relieved that I was there. He accepted that I was able to be in a dream with him. I don't know if he knew he was dreaming too. He didn't say anything to suggest that. He was pleased I was there and I got the impression he would have talked more but,' she scratched her head. She badly wanted a shower. 'He seemed to hear something. He glanced around and he was listening. He wasn't happy. It was like he was frightened. Then he told me he loved me and took off like a bat out of hell. I tried to go after him, but he got onto the main street and just disappeared. Just like that, he was gone.'

'When you talk about the hotel you met Ilan in, and the

street outside, do you know where this is located? What city or town it could be?'

Jennifer shook her head. 'No. Sorry. It wasn't anywhere I recognised.'

'Did it look European? Middle Eastern? Asian?' Saul asked.

'I'm sorry. I didn't recognise it at all.'

'Did you not ask Ilan where he was?'

'Of course, I did. He either didn't know or didn't want to tell me,' Jennifer said. She took a deep breath. She was tired of this – interrogation. For that's what it was, an interrogation. It wasn't getting them anywhere and all they were doing was going around and around in circles. She wanted Saul to stop. To leave her alone to think and to get through the day. By herself.

'Look. I'm sorry. I know you want me to give you all the answers, but I don't have them. Did you expect me to just wake up and be able to write down a set of map co-ordinates and tell you – here he is, go and rescue him? I don't think it works that way. In fact, I know it doesn't.'

'Jennifer, I'm sorry. Please accept my apologies. You are correct in what you say. I can only tell you that I am a very impatient man. I was expecting results immediately when I should have realised that something such as this is an unknown. We need to let it play out in its own time.'

'Apology accepted. I want results too, but I do feel I have made some progress. Maybe tonight I will be able to get more.'

'Okay then. I will leave you to do whatever you want for the rest of the day and I will see you tonight.'

'Where is Nurit?' Jennifer asked, suddenly realising that her step-daughter hadn't been in the room when she woke up.

'She is off duty and probably at home sleeping. She will be back on shift tonight. Do you need her for anything?'

'Nope. I just wondered where she was. Could someone please let her know that I made contact with her father.'

'Of course. I will do so myself.'

With that Saul stood up and patted her on the shoulder before leaving her alone with her thoughts and the realisation that she was famished.

Chapter 18.

Back in the penthouse – the nickname she had given to the small living unit they had placed her in – Jennifer laid out her clothes for the day and got into the shower. As she stood under the steady stream, she relished the simple pleasure of the hot water cascading over her body. Her throat felt a bit constricted but she was sure that it was merely her imagination. The same with her ribs. Sore… yet not sore. More like a remembrance of pain in a part of the body that had now healed. Yet, before she stepped into the shower, she found herself standing in front of the mirror checking for bruises and was relieved when she didn't find any.

Remembering how she had admired herself in the mirror in the dream, Jennifer laughed at the memory of the red dress she had worn. It was so not her. Since her early teens she had always been a jeans and vest top kind of girl, only dressing up when the occasion demanded it. The same was true of her today, and her wardrobe at home contained only two dresses and one skirt. Her posh clothes as she called them. But that dress! No wonder she had been propositioned by members of both sexes. It was a magnet for anyone looking for a one-night stand. Especially in a hotel bar. Without even thinking about it, in her dream, she had been trying to go for a sexy spy look, but ended up looking like a high-class call girl. That part had been fun in a way. The rest of the dream had not.

Ilan's behaviour and attitude had frightened Jennifer a lot more than she cared to admit. He had pulled a gun on her and threatened to shoot her. He had also almost strangled her. It was an aspect of him she had never known and she realised now that there was a whole part of her husband's life that was unknown to her. *Well, not unknown. I knew some of what he did and I've watched a lot of spy movies. It was just something I never thought too much about. But, bloody hell, it's frightening!*

As she shampooed her hair, Jennifer's fingers touched

the old scar from her brain surgery and thought about the dream. This one had been much more controlled. The first one – the one involving Lucy – she had no control over and she wondered if perhaps a part of her had needed to seek out Lucy. For closure most likely. But last night's dream had gone according to plan. She was able to meet Ilan as she had been instructed to do. Well, it had gone *mostly* to plan. She hadn't been able to get all the information she needed but it was a step in the right direction.

And, as she wondered about it, it occurred to her that she had discovered something in her mind, maybe something caused by the damage to her brain, that made what she was doing possible. The thought that she might not require Doctor Cohen's services to put her into a dream state wherein she could control her dreams amazed her.

Lucid dreaming – the awareness that one is dreaming, and even in some cases the ability to control the subject matter of the dream – was something both she and Lucy dreamed they had read about when trying to understand what was happening to them. And it was something she read a book or two on when she was convalescing. But all her research told her that this ability took a lot of practice. It didn't happen naturally. At least she had never read about it occurring naturally. Could a brain injury activate some previously inert part of the brain, increasing the REM stage of sleep but also allowing control over what a person dreamed about? Possibly. It was an intriguing notion.

Jennifer permitted these thoughts to swirl around in her mind like the water swirling down the shower drain at her feet. They kept her from thinking about her feelings for Ilan. That was a place she didn't want to go to for a while. His reaction to her and her reaction to him had created too many conflicting thoughts and emotions that she was unable to sort out at present. They would definitely have to go on the back burner for now.

She pressed her palms flat against the wall of the shower and stood under the water as it washed away her fears. The release felt cathartic and allowed her to pull herself together and strengthen her resolve to rescue her husband. She refused to allow the negativity to cloud her emotions. All she had to do was get him to tell her where he was, then the Mossad would bring him home and they would pick up where they left off eight months ago. Once he was home, she would feel different towards him. She was certain they would be okay. In time.

A pile of fresh towels had been left in the small cupboard beside the bathroom. Jennifer stepped out of the shower and wrapped herself in the biggest, softest one she could find. How would she spend the rest of the day? *Well, I'm starving so I suppose I could start by getting something to eat.*

That was next on today's to-do list. A hearty breakfast, eaten at a leisurely pace, and washed down with about a litre of coffee. That should kill at least an hour, maybe an hour and a half if she drank the coffee very, very slowly. But she had a lot more hours to kill before the evening when the whole thing would begin all over again. How was she going to manage it? An hour or so in the swimming pool and sauna would have passed the time and she kicked herself for not bringing a swimsuit. But how could she have known? *I could borrow one, I suppose.* But the thought didn't appeal to her much.

The jeans and T-shirt she had spread out on the bed had been her first choice of clothing for the day but, as she dressed, it was obvious they weren't going to be warm enough. The whole building, as far as she was aware, was heated, but it didn't seem to be cranked up all that much. It was cool enough to make her shiver in only the T-shirt. Goose pimples had already formed on her arms and she looked inside her bag for a long-sleeved top. There was nothing suitable other than the sweater she had thrown in at the last minute. It probably wasn't enough but it would have to do. She would make out a list of things she needed for Nurit to pick up for her. As she put it on, she picked up her key card, ID and the paperback book she had brought with her, and went to get some breakfast.

This early in the morning the cafeteria resembled a ghost town. Other than two members of staff, the only customers were three young guys – in their early twenties or possibly younger. All three were dressed in army uniforms and they sat huddled at a corner table. Two of them looked decidedly hungover and all three were laughing and joking, nudging each other and groaning as the memories of the night before came back to them. The one who wasn't hungover, he had most likely been the designated driver – or maybe he just didn't drink alcohol – was the one telling his colleagues what had transpired the night before. But other than herself, the party animals in the corner and the two guys behind the food counter, the place was deserted. And that suited Jennifer perfectly. It meant she had peace and quiet to enjoy her breakfast of fresh fruit followed by croissants and scrambled eggs, washed down with orange juice. Then a couple of chapters of the book she was currently reading, along with a few more cups of freshly brewed coffee, and she could pass the time for at least part of the morning.

She took her time. She lingered over the coffee, read for a while and then watched as people gradually wandered in. Most were in uniform but quite a few were dressed in civilian clothes. They were made up of all ages and both genders, and they went straight to the food area, grabbing trays and cutlery, pouring glasses of orange juice and placing their orders. The food, unlike most work canteens, was excellent. Jennifer didn't blame them for piling their plates high with dishes such as shakshuka – eggs poached in a paprika-spiced tomato sauce – cheese omelettes, salads, fruit and pastries, or various smoked fish.

As the morning staff workers began to fill up the seats and tables, all of them hungry and in a chatty mood, the noise level began to rise. Jennifer missed the peace and quiet she had enjoyed earlier. She closed her book and decided it was time for her to leave. Time to figure out what she was going to do for the remainder of the day and then the evening.

But she lingered on, reluctant to leave despite the noise and the crowds. She got another cup of coffee and found a different seat near the window, one that overlooked the swimming pool. One lonely mermaid was ploughing up and down the left-hand lane, her head down and an air of determination in her movements. As Jennifer watched the swimmer, she counted eleven lengths in the short time since she sat down with her coffee.

As she watched the swimmer, Jennifer's thoughts, as usual, found their way back to Ilan. She remembered what a nervous swimmer she had been until Ilan encouraged her not to fear the water, either in it or on it. It had taken a while, and more than a few moments of sheer panic when she vowed never to dip a toe into the sea ever again, but she got there in the end. He had been an excellent teacher and gradually built up her confidence until it became second nature to her. She considered snorkelling to be the greatest thing ever until one day he taught her to scuba dive. It was then they jokingly decided she must have activated some latent fish or dolphin DNA in her genetic make-up.

Maybe she *should* borrow a swimsuit. It would be nice to feel the sensation of water again. To get lost in the rhythm and just allow her mind to clear as she swam up and down the length of the pool.

'Mind if I join you?' Nathan Cohen appeared before her, interrupting her thoughts as he pulled out a chair and sat down opposite without waiting for her answer.

Lost for words, and a little startled, Jennifer could only nod and point to the chair even though he had already sat down in front of her. He was holding a spoon in one hand

and two cartons of yogurt in the other and he quickly peeled the lid off a carton of strawberry flavoured yogurt. Jennifer watched with a certain amount of amusement as he licked the tin foil lid, not realising that most of it was now caught in his moustache. He spooned his way through the pot of yogurt like he was starving. Jennifer tried not to grin as she watched more and more covering the moustache. It looked like pink shaving cream. When he finished, he set the pot and the spoon down on the table, sat back and smiled at her. It was a big yogurt smile. Jennifer pointed to her lip and made a brushing motion. He got it in one and grabbed his paper napkin and hastily wiped away the excess yogurt from around his mouth. To be such a brilliant psychotherapist and hypnotist, Doctor Cohen's appearance still reminded Jennifer of someone who worked with his hands for a living. A farmer or a construction worker, maybe. He was big and muscular with large, rough hands and that gave more credence to his outdoor look. His face was deeply tanned and laughter lines creased the skin around his eyes.

'You have a bit of an English accent. Where are you from?' Jennifer asked.

'Originally from London. I grew up there but I immigrated here fifteen years ago.'

They chatted for about five minutes on the differences between the United Kingdom and Israel, mainly the climate and the cost of living. Both of them quickly concluded that Israel was the better of the two places to make a home.

'So, tell me Doctor Cohen, why did you become a hypnotist?' Jennifer asked as she kept a straight face and tried her best to look interested. She wasn't all that interested, but if it passed the time for a little while longer, she was happy to sit and chat with him.

'I've already said that you should call me Nathan, please. Doctor Cohen is way too formal and I feel uncomfortable using it other than on my emails and business cards,' he said with a grin.

'Okay. Nathan. What made you become a hypnotist?'

‘I’m not a hypnotist. I specialise in hypnotherapy,’ he said as he took a deep breath and stared her straight in the eyes. Almost as if he was daring her to contradict him.

Jennifer couldn’t help but notice the defensive tone in his voice. ‘I’m sorry. So, what is the difference between hypnosis and hypnotherapy? I’m afraid I don’t know all that much about it.’

‘Most people don’t,’ Nathan told her. ‘Hypnosis is a process while hypnotherapy is a form of psychotherapy that uses hypnosis. That’s it in a nutshell.’

‘There’s gotta be more to it than that, surely?’ Jennifer asked. ‘How does it work? I mean how do you hypnotise someone? How did you hypnotise me? And other than what I’m doing, what is it used for?’

Nathan sat up straight in his seat, the second pot of yogurt forgotten. He was taken aback by Jennifer’s volley of questions and he looked surprised and more than a little bit frightened.

‘Well…’ he paused for a moment to gather his thoughts and chose his words. ‘For a start we don’t use watches or shiny jewels. That’s just a distraction technique. It’s all to do with having a calm and steady voice so that a person in a state of hypnosis, that’s you, usually experiences a sense of deep relaxation. Their attention is narrowed and they are focused on appropriate suggestions that are made by their therapist. That’s me.’

‘Go on,’ Jennifer said. She was more interested than she thought she would be.

‘When you are under hypnosis, you’re not in a deep sleep, more of a trance-like state and you are still in control of your own thoughts and actions but a new level of awareness is opened up to you. A good way to describe it is that your rational conscious state is now closed off and you have more access to your subconscious mind. When this occurs, I can… well, take control is too strong a way of describing it… it’s more a case of me being able to push you in a certain direction. In your case, I can tell you what to dream. I mean, I can't tell you *exactly* what I want you to dream about, but I can point you in the direction that we want you to go. By using the door, I am telling you to open your mind and step through into the world that your dream is creating. What you do when you get there is up to you and your subconscious.'

Nathan opened the second pot of yogurt, peach flavour this time, and spooned a small amount into his mouth.

Jennifer glanced around at the nearby tables and leaned forward. Her tone was conspiratorial. 'How does it work on me? I understand it's nothing to do with remote viewing, but I still don't know exactly what it is.'

'Well, it is and it isn't,' he said, also leaning forward and becoming a part of the conspiratorial aspect of their conversation. 'Remote viewing might be real and it might not. But basically, it's when a person is able to describe something that is inaccessible to the normal senses. It has never actually been proven and has been described as a psychic phenomenon but in some cases, I believe, it is a learned skill that helps someone harness his or her innate, underlying abilities. Like hypnosis, it is a method of accessing the subconscious. Which is what we are doing in your case.'

'But didn't Saul say it wasn't remote viewing?'

'That is correct,' he said. 'What we are doing in your situation is more akin to what's known as lucid dreaming.'

'Okay, I've heard of that,' Jennifer said as she fiddled with a few crumbs of croissant on her plate. 'And I've read quite a bit about it. But I'm not sure I completely understand what it means, or what it entails.'

'Well, your situation is a lot more like lucid dreaming than it is about remote viewing.' Nathan finished the yogurt and glanced at his watch. 'I'm sorry. I really don't have much time. I have a meeting in an hour and I need to prepare some files for it.'

'Stay a few minutes longer,' Jennifer said. 'I want to learn more about it.'

‘It’s a learning curve for all of us, Jennifer. What we are attempting, to the best of my knowledge, has never been tried before. Or if it has, then there are no official records of it. Certainly, there is nothing available to the public. What you read on the internet is mostly speculation and –’

‘Yeah, I get that. But what am I doing when I go to sleep at night? How am I doing it?’

Nathan sighed. ‘Lucid dreaming is when someone knows they are dreaming and they have control over what happens within that dream. Control over the characters they are interacting with, what happens within that dream and even *where* they are in the dream. Like the hotel bar you found yourself in. Or when you were in the dead Englishwoman’s home.’

‘Lucy. Her name was Lucy.’

‘Sorry. Yes, of course. Lucy.’

‘So, if this is all just a dream that I’m able to control, how is Ilan able to know that I’m really there to help him?’

‘That’s the part we can’t figure out, Jennifer. We don’t think he is aware but the fact that you can interact with him, and obtain information from him, is enough. He may, on waking up, remember dreaming about you but that is all.’

Jennifer’s eyes narrowed as a seed of suspicion crept uninvited into her thoughts. ‘Did Ilan know I was going to do this? Was it all planned before he even went on this operation?’

‘I’m sorry. That is way above my security clearance. I have no idea what he is even doing, or where he is, let alone if he planned this contingency should something go wrong.’

Ilan was expecting me in the hotel. The sneaky fucker. This was all planned by him. He knew the whole time that I’d come racing to rescue him if I was offered the chance. He never doubted me for a second. He’s known about this ability, or whatever it is, from the moment I woke up in that hospital and I told him all about the dreams I had. And he’s kept it up his sleeve in case he ever needed it. I’ll bloody well kill him when I see him again. I probably should be proud of his faith in me. But, still...

'Jennifer? Hey, Jennifer. Are you okay?'

She blinked and looked around her, suddenly unsure of where she was and why she was there. Nathan's face was the picture of concern and she raised an eyebrow.

'What?' she asked.

'Are you okay? The look on your face was a bit strange. What's wrong?' Nathan frowned at her.

'Um, nothing. I was just thinking that I... well, I'm not sure really. It doesn't matter. I guess I'm just overthinking things.'

It was obvious he didn't believe her but Jennifer had no intention of telling him what was on her mind. It was something she needed to work out for herself and something she needed to think long and hard about. But now was not the time.

Nathan had a fair idea what Jennifer was thinking. He realised she was putting two and two together and he realised he had probably said too much. Not that he had compromised the operation or anything. They had merely decided it was better that she didn't know all the facts at this stage.

'I really have to go now, Jennifer,' he said as he produced an e-cigarette from his pocket.

Jennifer studied the device in his hand. This one was a strange looking device, not at all like the slim pen-shaped one she bought Ilan as a present and a means to stop him smoking. This one looked like a miniature soldering iron. He waved it in the air in front of them.

'I want a few minutes to have a vape outside before I prepare for my meeting. I need my morning nicotine fix,' he said and smiled at her as he stood up to leave. 'I will see you this evening. Yes?'

'Yes, of course. Nine-thirty in my bedroom. It's a date,' Jennifer smiled.

As she watched him place his cup and yogurt cartons on the plastic tray and step away from the table, her mind was racing. But she knew what he had said was something she would have to forget about for the present. Deal with it later, she told herself. Her first priority was to get Ilan home safe and well. That was her goal. Her mission. She would deal with this other, more worrying, aspect of it later.

Nathan Cohen turned back and faced Jennifer again. 'This thing we're doing? You know you're a natural at it, don't you?'

Chapter 19.

'Bring in the prisoner,' Sayeed commanded. His voice was strong and determined and his eyes narrowed suspiciously as he scanned the faces of the people gathered around him.

Each and every one of them felt fear and discomfort under his gaze and they lowered their heads, unable to make eye contact. Doing so might draw too much unwanted attention their way and the suspicious, angry gaze of their leader lighting on any one of them was not something they desired. He commanded respect, there was no doubt about that. But he also commanded great fear.

Jamal felt his stomach begin to churn as the door opened and two of the guards dragged a bedraggled, bloody shape into the large room. A collective gasp echoed around the room as the guards dropped it onto the floor in front of Sayeed and Jamal. Sayeed peered down at it and smiled. Jamal didn't know which was worse – the pitiful creature slumped on the floor or the expression of pleasure on Sayeed's face.

To call it a man was a misconception. It had been a man once. An ordinary man who had a life and people who loved him and were probably right now wondering where he was and whether or not he was safe and well. But what lay on the floor now could barely be described as human. It was still human on a cellular level, but that little spark of humanity that remained was barely distinguishable amid the agony and the blood. Yet this lump of flesh and bone, blood and pain, still had a beating heart, a soul and a mind. It was still a living thing and even in its dying state it fought to live. The natural human instinct to survive even when there was no hope forced it to raise itself upwards, in a pathetic attempt to stand, to prove to those that stood and watched, that he was a man and that he was alive.

He almost made it. There were a few moments when it seemed he would get to his feet and stand in front of them, tall and proud. But he couldn't. He fell to the ground once more and collapsed in a tangled heap, broken and beaten, and flanked by the two sneering guards who had brought him in.

Sayeed beckoned to the guards. They each took an arm and lifted the prisoner to his feet, forcing him to stand on soles that were raw and bloody. Jamal stepped forward and cast an appraising eye over this naked, bloody figure that had once been a man. As he quickly took stock of the injuries that had been wrought upon him, he could see that the prisoner was suffering and close to death.

Both legs were broken, the kneecaps shattered beyond repair. Similar damage had been done to the elbows. The shoulders had been dislocated – the arms in place only because of the tenuous hold of skin and sinew. Bruises and lacerations covered the torso and Jamal could see several broken ribs piercing the flesh.

The face was an unrecognisable, bloody pulp. Misshapen and broken. One eye was swollen shut but the other, still partially open, stared up at him. In it, he could see the agony and the fear. And the plea for mercy.

'Has he told us anything?' Jamal asked to no one in particular.

None of the guards or the young men gathered in the room answered him.

'Has he told us anything?' Jamal repeated. His voice was louder this time.

'Other than his name, rank and serial number nothing,' Sayeed answered. 'We know he is an Israeli and he is a spy. But that is all. We have… questioned him intensely, as you can see, but he has not told us anything that can be of use to us.'

'What do you plan to do with him?' Jamal asked.

'Interrogate him for a while longer,' Sayeed said. He shrugged, but there was glee in his eyes at the prospect. The implications were clear.

Jamal pulled out his gun and shot the prisoner in the head. The bullet struck just above the eye that mere moments ago had silently pleaded for mercy. The prisoner's dying wish had been granted.

The guards jumped in surprise at the sound of the gunfire and dropped the prisoner. They bent to pick him up again.

'Leave him!' Sayeed roared. They dropped him immediately as Sayeed turned his face to Jamal, the unspoken question passing between him and his second-in-command.

'Days of interrogation and torture and we have learned nothing from him,' Jamal explained, returning Sayeed's angry stare. 'He was of no further use to us and, judging by his injuries, it is unlikely he will ever talk. Continuing to torture him further would be a waste of time.'

'Do you have compassion for this man, my brother? For this Israeli spy?'

'Of course not. I merely see that to continue would be an exercise in futility. We have better things to do than concern ourselves with this… dog.' Jamal spat out the words.

And like an injured dog, I have put it out of its misery.

He steadied himself against Sayeed's penetrating stare and waited while the younger man mulled it over. His decision to shoot the prisoner had been made in a split-second, but now he wondered what the consequence of that decision would be. Sayeed didn't enjoy his authority being undermined. How would he react? Jamal realised he was going to find out very soon when Sayeed ordered everyone back to work and told the guards to 'clean that mess away' as he put it. Jamal was about to leave with everyone else.

'No,' Sayeed said, and his voice was steel. 'You will come with me.'

Chapter 20.

'Something's wrong. Wake her up? Now!' Saul's voice was raised in alarm, despite his outwardly calm demeanour.

'I can't,' Nathan said. 'If I try to waken her now it could be dangerous. She has to do it herself. She has to walk back through the door out of the dream and waken up naturally.'

'You have to do something! Look at her!'

Jennifer was still asleep but she thrashed from side to side on the bed as though possessed. Her head slammed from left to right on the pillow and her eyes, under the lids, were moving frantically back and forth. She whimpered and moaned and cried out words over and over again that were unintelligible to everyone in the room. It was obvious she was in the grip of a terrible nightmare.

The monitors were still attached to her body and the alarms screamed in response to her movements and her body's response to whatever trauma she was experiencing.

'Turn off those fucking alarms!' Saul yelled.

Everyone in the room froze. No one could put their hand on their heart and say they had ever heard Saul Mueller swear before.

'Now!'

Someone flicked a switch and the alarms fell silent. The only sound that filled their ears was that of Jennifer's distraught weeping as she slept. She was still in REM sleep and still dreaming. That was obvious because of the movements of her eyes, still tightly shut, and the frantic thrashing she was doing as she lay on the bed.

Her distress was painful to watch and Saul's eyes locked onto Nathan's in a silent plea to help her.

'There is nothing I can do,' Nathan said. 'If I try to waken her up, the psychological damage could be severe. Possibly even fatal. I just don't know what might happen and I can't take the risk. She has to waken up herself.'

'Could? Might? Is that all you have?' Saul glared at the

younger man. 'I was told you were the best in your field. That is why I recruited you.'

'I am the best,' Nathan replied, defending himself and thinking furiously at the same time. If only he could come up with something. Anything. 'But this is a whole different ball game. No one has ever tried this before – sending someone into their mind, their dreams, on a mission such as this.'

'Think, man. You were able to put her under easily enough and send her where we wanted her to go. It can't be that hard to get her back again.'

'Sir. Her heart rate is severely elevated. Adrenaline levels are off the charts.' Ben, the technician, informed him.

Saul turned to the monitors to see for himself. He stared at them for a moment, as if by his mind alone he could set them back to their normal levels again.

They watched helplessly as tears streamed down Jennifer's face from under her tightly closed eyes. They splashed onto the pillow beneath her head. Whatever she was seeing in her dream it was causing her obvious distress. Nathan took her hand lightly in his and wracked his brains for a solution. He needed to come up with something very quickly.

He went through the process in his mind. The varying steps and techniques he used with his patients. He remembered when Jennifer asked him if this was totally safe. He had told her it was.

'I won't have to spend the rest of my life lying on this bed squawking like a chicken?' she had jokingly asked him.

'Of course not,' he had replied and explained to her what he had termed the 'door' technique he taught his patients to use in order to waken themselves up. That conversation had taken place before they began the first session. They had come a long way together in such a short time and he had marvelled at this natural ability that Jennifer possessed. But how could it help her? He went over the process again in his mind from start to finish.

The door! Of course! Hadn't he promised her he would

leave the door open for her? Jennifer had made a joke of it – about how polite he was holding the door for a lady. But, joking aside, he had told her that the door was always her way back.

'Where is Nurit?' he asked Saul. 'She needs to be here.'

Saul picked up the phone on the desk and dialled an extension number. He spoke quietly into the phone and then put it down again. He turned to Nathan with a questioning look on his face.

'I need Nurit to talk to her. She has to tell Jennifer to come through the door.' Nathan explained.

'She's on her way,' Saul told him. 'But why can't you do it?'

'It's better if it is a voice that she is familiar and comfortable with. It's similar to the loved ones of coma patients talking to them. An encouraging voice in their ear often has a considerable and positive impact on the speed of their recovery. Jennifer has more chance of responding to the voice of someone she knows well rather than yours or mine.'

'Nurit will be here in a couple of minutes.'

Just as he spoke the door opened and a bleary-eyed Nurit walked in. It was obvious she had been trying to catch up on some sleep. Her eyes were heavy and the imprint of her hand was across her right cheek. Her uniform was crumpled and she self-consciously tried to smooth out the wrinkles.

Saul waved her forward. He shooed Nathan out of his seat and invited Nurit to sit down. With a confused frown on her face, Nurit did as she was told. She stole a glance at her stepmother's face.

'What's wrong with her?' she asked.

'We think she is caught up in a nightmare,' Saul told her. 'Nathan will tell you what we need you to do.'

In a hushed voice, Nathan quickly explained the situation and how she could help. 'Speak softly. Try using a gentle sing-song voice, like I'm doing now, and keep talking about the door. Keep telling her to come back through it.'

Nurit nodded and chewed her bottom lip thoughtfully as she listened to the instructions the hypnotherapist gave her. When he told her to begin, she swivelled the seat around to face the bed and took Jennifer's hand in both of hers. Jennifer, in her sleep, tried to pull her hand away but Nurit held on.

She leaned forward and, as she followed Nathan's words to the letter, began to talk to her stepmother in a gentle tone.

'Jennifer. It's me. Nurit. Why don't you waken up? We have stuff… things to do today. Open the door and come through it. Please, Jennifer.' It was as if she was talking to a sleepy child – as though reading a bedtime story – her voice lulling the weary toddler off to sleep. Was that the effect they wanted? Surely, they were trying to waken Jennifer not lull her off to sleep again. But Nathan had explained that they were attempting to plant a suggestion in Jennifer's mind while she slept. It appeared obvious that, due to the continuing nightmare she was experiencing, she had forgotten all about the wake-up trigger – the door. A vocal reminder coming from a gentle, familiar voice would penetrate her sub-conscious and allow her to waken up more easily, and more safely, than a more brutal noise, such as an alarm clock or someone shaking her and yelling at her.

Nathan stood beside her ready to whisper suggestions in her ear should she run out of things to say. He could sense that Saul was growing ever more impatient and he squeezed Nurit's shoulder.

'You're doing great,' Nathan said. 'Don't forget about the door.'

Nurit took a deep breath and continued her one-sided conversation with the woman lying on the bed.

'Hey Jennifer. I hope you can hear me. I'm not sure where you are right now, but I think you should open the door and come on in. I have wine.' She glanced at Nathan; her brow furrowed with a questioning expression. Was this the correct approach? Nathan nodded and gave her a thumbs up.

'The door is open. We can have a glass or two of wine together. I have it chilled, but I can add ice if you want. I've been waiting for you and I –'

'Keep mentioning the door,' Nathan whispered in her ear. 'You have to emphasise it and keep telling her to come through it.'

'The front door is open, Jennifer. You just have to step through it. I'll pour you a glass of wine and we can go through the door out onto the patio and sit there if you like. We can drink wine and chat. And the cats are out there too. They're waiting for you to come through the door and say hello to them.'

But Jennifer didn't appear to hear anything. Her head thrashed from side to side and her weeping had turned to heartbroken sobs.

'Keep going,' Nathan said. He made a circling motion with his finger.

Nurit nodded. *Cats and wine. That'll waken her up. For sure.*

'Come on in Jennifer,' Nurit said. She kept her voice soft but firm. 'The door is open. I have some new photos of the kids on my phone. Do you want to see them? Okay, I know you prefer photos of the cats to my kids. Hey, we're friends on Facebook and I've seen what you post on your page! All those cat memes and cute kitten photos and videos you like to post. Just come through the door, Jennifer and look at my photos of my kids and I promise there'll be one or two of Sooty in among them.'

Nurit paused. Was Jennifer slightly calmer? She appeared to be. She looked to Nathan for confirmation. He nodded.

'I think it's working. Keep going,' he whispered.

'I'm holding the door open for you, Jennifer. Just walk through it and we'll drink wine until the sun goes down. Come through the door, Jennifer. It's not locked. It's already open. Just walk through the door. Please.'

Chapter 21.

With a resounding crack, the gun went off. As it echoed around the large room, Jennifer jumped in shock and clamped her hands over her mouth to keep from screaming aloud. From her position, the man who had pulled out the gun and fired was partially turned away from her and she couldn't see his face clearly, but she knew he was tall and seemed to have a beard and grey hair. Long, straggly grey hair. She didn't get a chance to take note of what he was wearing because it all happened so quickly.

There were others in the room. Two men stood in front of the tall man and between them there was a prisoner. He had been badly beaten. Tortured by the look of it. She couldn't be sure but…

'I think the prisoner was Ilan,' she said as fresh tears spilled from her eyes. 'And the tall man with the grey hair pulled out a gun and shot him in the head.'

A moan escaped Nurit's lips and she stood there, rooted to the spot, her eyes wide with the unbelievable horror of the knowledge that her father was dead. Suddenly everyone was in shock as the realisation of what Jennifer had said hit them. The atmosphere in the room became thick and heavy as the sense of loss and failure descended like a shroud around them. Saul, his own shock and grief hidden behind the mask of his calm features, ushered everyone out, leaving Jennifer and Nurit alone for a short while.

The two women looked at one another. Nurit's face crumpled and tears fell from her eyes. In a couple of steps, Jennifer was beside the younger woman and she pulled her into her embrace. They held on to each other for a long time as both of them cried their hearts out. And, as they sobbed, their bodies shook, almost in unison. As she held her step-daughter close to her, her arms tightly around Nurit's back, Jennifer could hardly tell if the violent shaking was coming from her own body or Nurit's. As the seconds ticked by, they continued to hold each other, neither of them wanting to let go, as the realisation of all they had lost sunk in.

Eventually Nurit pulled away. She fumbled in her pocket for a tissue. Finding none, she wiped her eyes on her sleeve. Her grief was all-encompassing but she knew she had to put it away for a while and become a soldier once more. They had to find the terrorists and stop them so her father's death would not be in vain. She said this to Jennifer.

'I know. I know. I just need a few minutes.' Jennifer closed her eyes and took a deep breath. She tried to stop her tears from falling but they were relentless, like heavy rain. 'Give me ten minutes and tell them to come in again.'

Nurit put her arms around Jennifer again and held her tightly.

'They won't let this go unpunished,' she whispered. Her voice, like her heart, was raw with pain, and tears began to spill from her eyes once more. 'They will get those who killed him, Jennifer. They'll find them and they will be punished. And when they do, we can grieve for him properly.'

Jennifer nodded. She really didn't care if they were punished or not. Ilan was dead and nothing would bring him back. She extricated herself from Nurit's arms, leaving the younger woman standing there, alone with her pain, and made her way to the bathroom to wash her face. In the mirror she stared at her reflection. Her eyes were red and swollen.

I look a mess. So what?

She slowly dressed in jeans and an old sweat shirt of Ilan's that was too big for her. As she put it on, a wave of realisation swept over her: this was the closest she would ever be to him again. That thought almost brought her to her knees but she fought against the pain and the heartache as Nurit's words came back to her.

Nurit is correct. They should be punished. It's what he would have wanted.

As she made her way out of the bathroom, Jennifer silently promised Ilan's memory that she would do all she could to avenge his death.

Fifteen minutes later they crowded into her small apartment and shrunk it even further with their presence. Nathan was perched on the armchair. Saul was standing by the window and Nurit was alone on the sofa. Bina had made a pot of coffee and she distributed a cup of the steaming liquid to everyone. Jennifer acknowledged both the coffee and Bina's silent nod of sympathy with a tight smile and sat down on the sofa close to Nurit, grateful for the younger woman's presence beside her.

Nurit had stopped crying and her eyes were dry but she had a haunted look about her. Nathan's downcast eyes and depressed demeanour hinted that he felt as though he was the one who had failed them, and Bina was trying, but failing, to be motherly. Saul had buried his own emotions deeply with in him and was as efficient and boss-like as ever.

'I am so sorry, Jennifer. This was not the ending we had hoped for,' he told her. 'And as much as I hate intruding on your grief, we need to hear the details from you about what occurred in your dream. The sooner we get this over, the sooner you can go home.'

My dream? God, I wish it was only a dream.

'Whenever you are ready, Jennifer,' Saul said.

Jennifer took a sip of coffee and set the cup down on the small table in front of her. She leaned back, pulled the sleeves of Ilan's sweatshirt down over her hands and folded her arms in front of her. She wasn't a psychologist but she knew it was a classic defensive posture.

'Yeah, I know.'

It took an hour and a half but, in between bouts of tears, futile anger and silent grief, Jennifer managed to tell them the whole story. How she found herself in a small, deserted village. And how she'd walked around, searching and exploring until she stopped outside one building in particular.

'It looked a bit like a combination of a village hall and a large house,' she said. 'The door was open and I walked in.'

‘Go on,’ Saul’s voice was gentle. She supposed he was also grieving. He had known Ilan for many years and considered him a friend as well as a colleague. At least that was what he had told her and she had no reason to doubt him.

‘There was a long corridor with various rooms on both sides, you know, like a hotel corridor,’ Jennifer continued. ‘But the place was dilapidated and looked disused. All the doors were open. I peeked into one room and there were maps on the wall, and computer terminals. It was like an operations room. One big map of Europe had red pins stuck in most of the capital cities – London, Paris, Berlin, Madrid. But not just the capitals. Major cities too. Belfast. Glasgow. Liverpool. Frankfurt. Barcelona. Nice. All the big cities. The same for the one of the United States and Canada. Pins were stuck in Washington DC, New York, Los Angeles, Las Vegas. Toronto and Montreal. Vancouver too. There wasn’t a map for Asia or India or Africa. Or even Australia. It was just Europe and North America. There was nothing for South America either.’

‘What else did you see in this room, Jennifer?’ Saul asked.

‘I’m not sure, but I think there was a table with a stack of passports on it. And a pile of papers. Maybe travel documents? You know, e-tickets? I’m not sure. I only looked in through the door. I didn’t go into the room.’

‘What did you do next?’

‘I walked on down the hall and I stopped at another room with a glass panel in the door. There was a keypad on the doorframe and the glass was covered in this white stuff. Like it had been smeared with that stuff you use to keep people from looking in. I couldn’t see much but I was able to make out what looked like a large glass box. Really big. Floor to ceiling. There were metal tables around the sides of the room and I could see test tubes and stuff like that on them. I tried the handle but it wouldn’t open. I don’t know why but I got the impression this was a lab of some kind. Yeah, it definitely looked like a laboratory.’

'Why do you think that?'

'Honestly, I don't know. But seeing the stuff in the room, and the way it was laid out, made me think of a lab of some kind. Plus, the door was heavy. Solid. There seemed to be a rubber, or something like rubber, seal around the edges of it. But I can't be sure. Like I said, that was the impression I got.'

'Go on.'

'I kept on walking and there was another door in front of me. I opened it and it led out into a small courtyard. Like... if you can imagine the backs of four houses that meet in a square and this courtyard was at the heart of the houses. A communal area. It had big flower pots with dead plants in them and there was a small fountain but no water. There were stone seats – benches. It made me think of a place where families would gather in the evenings to socialise. Three other doors led off the yard and one of them was slightly open. I walked in through this door and... that's when I found myself in... *that room*. The room where... where *it* happened.'

Jennifer stopped, unable to continue as her eyes filled with tears once again. She wiped them away and took a deep, shuddering breath that became a sob.

'Do you want to take a break?' Saul asked. 'Or would you like a glass of water, perhaps?'

I want to go home. I want a real drink. Not water or coffee but a real drink. Wine or gin. Or whiskey. And I want to be far away from here and I want to drink until I pass out. Maybe then it won't hurt so much.

'No. I want to too continue. Please.'

'Are you sure about this, Jennifer?' Saul said as he looked at her. He wasn't convinced about her state of mind. 'Maybe a break would be a good idea?'

'No. Let's get it over and done with,' she said.

Right now, Jennifer knew she could focus on what had happened in her dream and pretend that's all it was. A dream. If it was a dream then she could do her best to ignore the fact that Ilan was dead. A break was the last thing she needed or wanted. It would only leave her time to think. And she couldn't allow herself to do that because that would destroy her completely.

They went over every detail of Jennifer's dream. Again, and again. They insisted she begin from the moment she closed her eyes and walked through the door that took her into the café. It was a Greek café, almost identical to one she had frequented a number of times with Ilan back when they still lived in Cyprus. It had been one of their favourites. Why she found herself there this time she had no idea. Maybe it was the remembrance of happier times that made it easier to connect with Ilan, she did not know. She did not care either. They could have met in a café on the dark side of the moon for all she cared, as long as it worked.

This time, however, it didn't. She was seated at the corner table – the one they always preferred when it was available – and had ordered a gin and tonic, sipping at it while she waited for him. She glanced at her watch a few times and frowned as the minutes dragged on while she watched for him coming through the door. He was late, and that was not like him. But he would appear. Jennifer was confident of that and so she waited patiently, ordering another drink and ignoring the sympathetic smile from the waiter. The look behind his smile told her that it was a shame such a beautiful woman had been stood up and if she was still there when he finished his shift… well, she didn't have to be alone all night.

Piss off. She smiled politely at him, gave him a slight shake of her head and took another sip of her drink.

Ilan was very late. Something must be wrong. A note of concern crept into Jennifer's mind as she checked her watch once more. Her glass was empty and another drink no longer appealed to her, so she decided to wait for him outside.

'It was stuffy and I needed some fresh air,' she

explained. 'I paid for my drinks and walked out through the front door and that's when I found myself in the village.'

Saul asked her to describe the village once more. He questioned her on what she could see until she was able to tell him every small detail. How many buildings could she see on her left? How many on her right? Were they tall? Regular-looking houses or apartment-type square blocks? Did any of them resemble stores, or cafes? Business premises? How many? What colours were the walls? Could she see what kind of material was on the roof of each building? Could she see anything beyond the village? Hills? Mountains? Roads, maybe? Which direction did they come from?

Jennifer scoured her memory and answered his questions as best as she could. It was surprising to both herself and Saul as to how much she could recall. The more he questioned her, the more it seemed she was back in the dream, once again walking through the near-deserted, tumble-down village. She noticed a look in Saul's eyes when she answered his questions with such clarity, and she wondered what exactly he thought about all of this. And about her. And why did it matter now?

Finally, they came to the part where she entered the courtyard. Once again Saul questioned her over and over again. He needed the size as best as she could estimate. How many seats were there? What type of buildings overlooked it? How tall are they, Jennifer?

Details. Details. Details. He asked for details and she gave them to him.

Then all of a sudden, he stopped asking her questions. He stood up and began to pace the room. Not the easiest thing in the world to do since it was a smallish room and pretty crowded with furniture and people at the moment. Deep in thought, Saul side-stepped the obstacles and continued to pace, and Jennifer wondered what he was thinking. Or planning.

In mid-stride he stopped and turned to face Jennifer. He

tilted his head quizzically as though studying her.

'What about the people in the room where you say they executed Ilan?' he asked.

Executed? Those bastards murdered him in cold blood.

'What about them?'

'How many were there? Can you describe any of them? How many were armed? What kind of weapons did they carry? The man who shot Ilan? Did he use a hand gun? Can you describe it, and him?' Saul rattled off a string of questions that would have impressed a quiz show host.

'Fuck's sake! Slow down!' Jennifer's hands curled into angry fists as she glared at him.

For a moment Saul nearly chewed her out for her insubordination. But then he remembered who she was and why she was there.

'My deepest apologies, Jennifer,' he said, spreading his hands in a placating gesture that he was not convinced was successful. 'All the questions came into my mind at once and, believe me, they are important.'

'Yeah, okay. But maybe one question at a time, please.'

'I'm sorry. Yes. One question at a time. So, tell me about the room, Jennifer?'

'It was a large room,' she began. She hesitated because this was the part she did not want to remember. 'When I say large, I mean it was a lot bigger than a living room. More like a school room, maybe. It didn't have any furniture and there was only one window at the back. It had two doors – the one I came through and one on the opposite wall.'

'Was there anything in the room? Or on the walls?'

'I don't think so,' Jennifer said. She paused and concentrated on the memory. 'No. They were an off-white colour and there was definitely nothing on them that I could see.'

'How many people were gathered in the room?'

'Maybe twenty-five. Maybe thirty. I can't be sure.'

'Can you describe them?'

'All men. Youngish – they varied between late teens

and mid-twenties. Some of them looked frightened. Some looked angry and full of hatred. They were dressed... okay this is weird. They were dressed in western clothes. You know, denim jeans and T-shirts. Baseball caps. Hoodies. That sort of stuff. Oh, and they were all clean-shaven and I'm not being racist when I say this, but none of them looked Arabic because of what they were wearing.'

'Were they armed?'

'No. They weren't. But a few men standing around the edges of the crowd were.'

'What sort of weapons were they carrying?'

'Sorry, I don't know. Rifles, I think. Maybe semi-automatics. One or two had handguns tucked into their belts but I don't know what type.'

Jennifer closed her eyes. She was exhausted and, surprisingly, hungry and she wanted this to be over. She raised her head and took a deep breath.

'Can we take a break? Please?'

'It is imperative that we get as much detail as we can,' Saul told her.

'I know that. And I *will* give you everything. But I need a break. Please,' she implored.

Jennifer watched Saul as he mulled it over, keeping her fingers crossed as she waited for him to decide. If he told her that he wanted to continue she would refuse. Nurit was sitting nearby with her head hung low and her distress was obvious. Both of them needed to get out of there for a while. If Saul said no, she would refuse to answer any more of his questions.

'You are correct. We should all take a break and meet back here in an hour. Some time out will be good for all of us,' he said, much to her surprise.

Saul grabbed his jacket from the back of the chair and put it on. He nodded to Nathan and Bina; his instructions clear. They followed him out of the room, leaving Jennifer alone with Nurit once more.

The two women looked at one another. Nurit's eyes

filled with tears again and she fought to keep them from spilling over. She failed.

'I'm sorry,' she said as Jennifer offered her the box of tissues she had found in the bathroom. Nurit, took one and blew her nose with it. 'I just can't believe he's gone. When I was growing up, I knew he was my father even though I was raised by my aunt and uncle. And because of that, I had two brothers and a sister. Although they were my cousins, I thought of them as siblings and I had a great childhood. I was happy living with them. And in some ways, I saw him more as my uncle, even though I knew he was my dad. But I was so proud of him and what he did. He was my hero. But I was always afraid that I would lose him. That's why I love the fact that Reuben is a traffic cop. He books people for speeding and unauthorised parking. A nice safe career that brings him home after every shift and I don't expect him to be away from me for more than a day at the most. My kids won't have to wonder where their father is every day. Or if he's coming home. Every time my father went away, I said goodbye to him, as if it was the last time that I would ever see him. It was horrible when I was a child but worse when I got older and I knew *what* he worked at and *why* he was going away.'

She buried her face in her hands and hid herself from the reality of it. Jennifer put her arms around her and held her tightly. The two women stood together in that position for a long time, silently mourning the loss of a husband and a father.

Chapter 22.

Jamal imagined he could hear the staccato hammering of his heart in his chest as he followed Sayeed into the room that served them as an office. His gun was tucked inside his shirt and he debated drawing it and killing the man in front of him in a pre-emptive attempt to save his own life. Not that he stood a chance of success. A gunshot – another gunshot – would mean half a dozen guards rushing into the room. The sight of their leader dead on the floor and him standing over the body, a smoking gun in his hand, would seal his fate in a heartbeat.

'You did well, Jamal,' Sayeed said as he closed the door behind him.

Did I? I shot dead a prisoner in cold blood. A man who once had a life and people who loved him. I murdered him.

'But I have to ask you why?'

Sayeed had turned to face Jamal and his face was hard to read. Accusatory? Suspicious? Impressed? Jamal could not begin to define the man's expression. He shrugged his shoulders. He knew he must tread carefully, and select his words equally as carefully.

'There was nothing further to be learned from him,' he said. 'Permitting him to live would have been a waste of time and resources. He was redundant and I saw no reason to waste any more time on him.'

'My men could have worked him over some more,' Sayeed replied. 'It would have been good training for some of them, particularly the younger ones. They could have used him to… perfect their techniques.'

'If I have done wrong, I apologise, my brother. I have only your best interests, and that of our cause at heart.' Jamal inclined his head in a placating gesture. 'If it is Allah's will.'

'Inshallah. That is a very apt choice of words, my brother,' Sayeed chuckled.

Jamal's head snapped up and he stared at the man in front of him. 'I do not understand.'

'Because 'Allah's Will' is the name I have given to our Jihad. I thought of it only this afternoon. It is fitting, do you not think?'

Jamal could only nod in agreement. The smile on Sayeed's face was terrifying. *But what is it? This Jihad? What is it that he has planned? I know he's planning something. But I need the details.*

'You have the wisdom of your years Jamal and I am a mere child standing here before you. In truth, I do not know you. You were a stranger to me until you joined us, yet I trust you. Perhaps you are my conscience, perhaps not. But I have faith in your determination to advance our cause and I believe you have been sent to me by Allah, praise and glory be to Him…'

'Praise and glory be to Him,' Jamal responded with another slight bow of his head.

Sayeed nodded, a curious smile on his face. He opened a desk drawer and took out a large key. 'Now, come with me. I believe it is time you see for yourself what 'Allah's Will' entails.'

Jamal assisted Sayeed as he pushed the heavy bookcase away from the back wall of the room. Judging from its weight and the number of books on the shelves – their covers now faded with age and shrouded in a fine layer of dust – the previous occupant had been an avid reader. For a moment the bookcase swayed forward and it threatened to topple and spill its contents onto the two men but Jamal put his hand against the front, pressed backwards and steadied it while it made up its mind to remain upright a while longer.

There was an ancient wooden door behind the bookcase. Ancient in all respects except for the shiny new handle and heavy-duty lock. Sayeed inserted the key into the lock and opened the door. He motioned for Jamal to enter ahead of him.

Jamal hesitated. *Was this a trick?* He couldn't know. It was possible Sayeed was still intending to punish him for killing the prisoner and usurping his authority. If that was

Sayeed's plan, there was nothing he could do about it. He stepped forward through the door. It didn't slam shut behind him and he let his breath out slowly and his tense muscles relaxed a fraction.

They had stepped into a small room. It was not a cell, though it could be used as one. There were no windows to escape through other than one large window on the far wall. But escape would be impossible because the window was made from thick, reinforced glass which appeared to be new and recently installed. The small room itself was unfurnished apart from a desk and a chair and there was a black sheet, just over a metre square in size, pinned to the wall with a camera mounted on a tripod in front of it. The desk was strewn with papers, reports and files.

It was the window that drew Jamal's attention. *This has been a long time in the planning. Longer than we've been here.*

'This is X129D. Allah's Will.' Sayeed stood beside the window and made a grand, sweeping gesture as he invited Jamal to take a closer look. There was pride in his voice.

'What is it?' Jamal asked. He peered through the glass that faced him. Beyond it he could see a laboratory. His heart thudded in his chest and he felt the cold fear of suspicion settle on his shoulders. Through the glass, he could see several people – men, he presumed – their gender was impossible to determine but it was unlikely any of them were women. They were dressed from head to toe in yellow bio-hazard suits and the black gloves and the black rubber boots that they were wearing were sealed to the suits with heavy duty tape. Their features behind the visors were hidden as they worked. Their movements and mannerisms relayed a confident professionalism and a dedication to their work that was probably as fanatical as it was professional and dedicated.

Laptops and small desk-top refrigerators, bottles and glass jars were spread out, in a neat and organised fashion, across the tops of the metal tables that were fitted to the walls. Jamal scanned the area and counted five laboratory table-top centrifuges. Near the work stations on a small metal table, he saw a box that looked, at first, to be an incubator. The kind that premature infants were placed into. But this was not something a baby would ever be found in. Two pairs of extended rubber gloves hung from attachments on either side of the box. Air inlets and outlets were on either end and a detachable sealed opening covered the top. The kind that could be placed in position and the opening slid across to allow items to be placed into the box, like a miniature airlock.

Several rows of cages, stacked on top of each other and situated against one of the walls, held white rats. They scurried back and forth within the confines of their small prisons as though searching for the way out. But there was no escape from this hell.

Jamal noticed a metal door to his right, a window that had been obscured in a white film and a heavily reinforced door that was surrounded by an airtight rubber seal. There was a keypad mechanism to enter and exit. He called up a layout of the village in his mind. This room was off the corridor that led to the courtyard.

Beyond the studious, yellow-suited workers, a large box-shaped construction made either of glass or heavy-duty Perspex dominated the far corner. It had an airlock door and heavy-duty air extraction piping leading out of it into the wall high up near the ceiling. The construction itself was about two metres wide and rose to height of approximately three metres falling about half a metre short of the ceiling. There was a door-sized airlock at the front and an air inlet pipe ran from a hose that came out of the wall along the floor and into the box. From his knowledge of the layout, the pipes ran out in the direction of the hills behind the village.

Inside this box was a single sleeping cot and a bucket for a toilet. There was no one currently inside the glass prison.

'What is this?' Jamal asked. His voice was low and his

wide-open, awe-struck eyes and his eyebrows, raised in wonder to emphasise his question, were a mask that hid his anger and his fear. It was obvious to him that this operation had been planned and activated many months ago. Sayeed had always intended moving them to this location for the final stages.

'Allah's Will is a bioengineered variant of pneumonic plague. The letter D denotes the fourth variation. As you may already know, pneumonic plague is currently very rare. It is caused when Yersinia pestis bacteria infect the lungs and cause pneumonia. Pneumonic plague spreads from person to person and causes symptoms such as fever, weakness and pneumonia in the initial stages and, if not treated early, leads to respiratory failure, shock and death.' Sayeed lectured as though teaching a class.

Jamal turned away from the glass window and fixed his eyes on the younger man. His stare became an angry frown. He tore his gaze away and briefly looked down at the papers on the desk. Handwritten notes and phrases covered the pages. Some lines were scored out and amendments jotted in the margins. The hand writing was Sayeed's. He had seen it enough times to recognise it. A quick scan of the words told him the man beside him was in the process of writing a speech. Such was his arrogance.

Jamal slammed his fist down on the table, disturbing the papers that were strewn over it. He turned back to the glass window, taking it all in.

'You did this?' Jamal demanded. 'All that money? All the months of planning and readying our soldiers? For *this*? For *pneumonic plague?*'

Sayeed nodded.

'Why bother?' Jamal asked. 'The mortality rate of pneumonic plague is known to be relatively low in the west. It can be cured with strong antibiotics?'

'You are quite correct,' Sayeed's voice was calm and his accent wavered between American and British as he continued his lecture. 'But, as I said, this is a bio-engineered variant. In its natural state, the mortality rate is minimal with treatment. But if untreated the mortality rate is between ninety and one hundred percent. To ensure this we have developed an antibiotic resistant strain. The D variant. Which I have called Allah's Will.'

'Has it been tested?' Jamal asked. He already knew the answer. The glass containment box with the sleeping cot inside told him the answer.

'Yes. And our results have been excellent. Although we haven't quite finished the testing.' Sayeed's accent headed west across the Atlantic again then travelled a distance down the eastern coast of the United States before changing its mind and returning once more to the shores of England. 'The usual incubation period is two to four days from infection to becoming symptomatic, sometimes up to one day, but we are working to extend this to ensure maximum exposure in order to increase the R rate, and we –'

'You can do this?' Jamal asked, doubt written over his face.

'We are almost there, my brother. With Allah's blessing we will succeed.'

'Why the plague?'

'Pneumonic plague,' Sayeed corrected him and his voice held onto its English accent. 'Our variant will render antibiotics worthless against it. The extended incubation period will ensure a larger number of people will be exposed and infected. It will spread with ease from person to person long before quarantine measures have been implemented. It will cause symptoms such as fever, weakness and pneumonia in the early stages and, without any viable antibiotic treatment, it will lead to respiratory failure, shock and the death of thousands – hundreds of thousands – of infidels.'

Jamal nodded and kept his face impassive amidst the horror of what he had just learned. *I thought they were suicide bombers. Bad enough. But this?* He relaxed his shoulders and tilted his head in a non-threatening posture, as he allowed his body language to remain neutral. Sayeed was sharp. He could pick up on any real, or imagined, threat and his reaction, when it came, would be swift and deadly.

'Why did you choose this?' he asked.

'Is it not perfect?' Sayeed asked. He spread his arms in an all-encompassing sweep, taking in the laboratory, the small room and Jamal.

'It is. But why this in particular?' Jamal asked.

'For many centuries the plague has been intentionally used as a weapon,' Sayeed said. He had found his Mid-Atlantic lecturer's voice again. 'After the Tartar's transformation of plague victims into bioweapons with catapults in thirteen forty-six, the Japanese, during World War II, developed plague into a biological weapons agent. The simple design of the bomb was a ceramic container filled with plague-infested fleas and flour. Once the container reached the ground and broke, the flour attracted rats, which in turn attracted the fleas thus spreading the disease via the rats. The Japanese tested the weapon by dropping plague-infected fleas over populated areas in China and Manchuria in World War II. During the nineteen eighties, Soviet scientists successfully produced large quantities of antibiotic-resistant plague organisms suitable for weapons. We obtained stock from that strain of bacteria from a... let's say a very good friend in the former Soviet Union who is very sympathetic to our cause, and X129D – 'Allah's Will'– is a derivative of that stock.'

Jamal paced the confines of the small room and gathered his thoughts before he spoke. He stopped and turned his gaze to the window again – at the laboratory and all he could see, and imagine, beyond it. It was imperative that he ask the right questions now. He thought some more and paced some more before turning once again to Sayeed. 'How many jihadis are we going to infect?'

'All fifty of our soldiers will die for Allah.'

'They are the delivery method?'

'Yes. They will be infected before they leave this location. This is why we needed to increase the incubation and infection times. They will be shipped, mostly by plane to various cities in the United States and Europe. It is a convenient method as we all know how airplane air-conditioning can spread something such as this. From there they will travel as much as they can, via trains, taxis and ferries. As well as our soldiers, the passengers on their planes will also become infected and it will spread exponentially as those passengers alight in airport terminals, board trains and buses and taxis. They will drink coffee in cafes and alcohol in bars. They will walk along crowded streets and stop to talk to friends and acquaintances. They will enter shops and along with the money they hand over – whether cash or credit card – they will pass along this death that they are carrying. They will go to work and spread the infection among those they meet in their day. They will return home to their loved ones, infecting them and they, in turn, will infect those they meet at schools and supermarkets. It will spread beyond the control of the authorities before they even know it is there. Once they become ill and visit their doctors, or go to a hospital, it will be too late. They will ask for antibiotics and they will take them, hoping for a recovery. But they will find their pills and potions useless. Then they will die. Slowly and in great pain. The same way many of our brothers have died over the years.'

Jamal tapped his fingertips on the top of the desk as he read a few lines of the words written on the papers. Sayeed's great speech. It was basically what he had just said aloud, but with more flowery language. The sort of language a general would use to stir his troops into a battle frenzy before sending them out to die for the cause.

'Sayeed, are you certain this will succeed?'

'I am. Even if a small percentage are stopped and detained, they will already have spread the infection. This will not fail.' His words, like his written speech, brimmed with the confidence only the truly fanatical could conjure.

'And the timeline?' Jamal asked.

'We hope… we intend to have our troops on the

ground, and delivering the infection, well before the infidels begin the celebration of their Christmas holidays.'

Chapter 23.

Jennifer ignored the tap on the door and, with her arms folded tightly in front of her, she leaned against the wall and continued to look out of the window. It was sunny and the sky was cloudless. It was good weather for December and it would be cool in the shade, maybe even cold enough for a coat, but in the sunshine, it would feel pleasantly warm.

Grey, cloudy skies and rain would have been more suitable on this particular day.

She wondered if it would snow this winter. There had been light snow last year, or was that the previous year? She frowned, unable to remember. Why couldn't she remember? *Does it really fucking matter now whether it snowed last year or the year before?*

Ilan hated snow. He hated being cold. He bitched and complained more and more as the leaves started to fall, the days became shorter and the temperatures took a downward turn.

Yet he took her skiing in France one winter. The reason he gave for booking the trip made no sense to her whatsoever. 'Because I want to go skiing with you.' He had told her with a shrug. She gave him a shrug back, agreed with him that it could be fun, and proceeded to spend a small fortune on warm clothes for both of them.

The trip had been fun. Of course, he had bitched and complained about the cold, she never thought that he wouldn't. But the skiing had been good. It was something she had never tried before and he was an excellent teacher, despite his hatred of the cold conditions. It turned out to be a holiday that, surprisingly, both of them had enjoyed immensely.

The memories of those two weeks made her smile. Another gentle tap on the door made it achingly clear to Jennifer why she had only memories left now. She continued to ignore it and remained standing by the window, staring out at the blue sky as she kept up her silent vigil.

She shivered, despite the fact that the heating system was working more than efficiently, and thought about what she should do. She knew what she would *like* to do – go home, get drunk and hide from the world. Forever. But the knock at the door was telling her that this was impossible for the moment.

She puffed out her cheeks and blew gently onto the glass pane, momentarily blotting out the view. With her fingertip, she traced the outline of a heart on the fogged-up windowpane. Then she put a jagged line down the centre of it. It was a broken heart now. Just like hers.

It will be Christmas soon. And I haven't bought him anything yet… No! Don't think about that. I hope Reuben is giving Possum and Holly some love and attention and not just feeding them and cleaning out the litter trays. I should call Dad. Mum too, probably. And tell them what? Nope. Nothing to tell them. Not right now. I couldn't do it. Dad thought the world of him… it was a man and a car thing. I feel sick. I'm hungry too. So how come I feel sick? Am I coming down with a bug? Have I got the 'flu? Or does grief make you physically sick? Ilan always made me hot drinks or chicken soup when I was ill. Who's gonna do that now? No! I'm not going there! Not yet.

These random thoughts spun around and around in her head and made no sense at all. Jennifer didn't care. She would sing, dance, scream and daydream, force her thoughts to run riot in any direction they wanted to go, just so long as they didn't go in that one particular direction. She had to keep that thought well tucked away until there came a time when she would be able to deal with it.

Having decided knocking on the door wasn't going to work, Bina opened it and stuck her head around the door, a sympathetic smile on her face.

'There's been a change of plan, Jennifer,' she said. 'Saul asked me to come and fetch you.'

Who? What? Then she remembered. *Oh, right. We haven't finished the debrief.*

'Yeah. Okay. Can you give me a minute?' Jennifer replied. She used her sleeve to wipe away the broken heart on the window.

'Are you okay?' Bina was still trying to be motherly. 'Is there anything I can do?'

Build a time machine and take me back about eight months so I can lock Ilan up in the basement and refuse to let him out 'til he promises not to go on this operation? Can you do that? No? Somehow, I didn't think so.

'I'm fine,' Jennifer said as she wiped her palms on her jeans. She badly needed a shower and a change of clothes, but it could wait. 'Let's get this over with.'

Following Bina out of her little apartment seemed like the most stupid idea Jennifer had ever come up with. She was so tempted to turn on her heels, run back to pack up her meagre belongings and demand someone call her a taxi to take her back home, because the last place on earth she wanted to go to was that fucking room again. What had they christened it? Oh, yeah – the 'sleep room'. *Sleep room my arse. It's the place where all your nightmares come true.*

But, to her surprise, Bina turned left along the corridor until they came to the elevator doors. Jennifer followed her dutifully, not even interested enough to ask where they were going. She was numb. Even her natural curiosity couldn't be piqued and she was content enough to follow her.

In the elevator – they were going down – Jennifer sensed that Bina wanted to say something. *Please don't. I don't need sympathy and platitudes.* Every now and then Bina would open and close her mouth, on the brink of saying something important, or profound, or maybe just about the weather or the slow progress of the elevator. Then she would change her mind and say nothing at all.

Jennifer felt an insane bubble of laughter building within her and threaten to spill over and burst out in a fit of giggles. Which would be wholly inappropriate at this juncture. *My husband has just died, for fuck's sake!* Saying it, even to herself, was like pouring a bucket of water over a flame and the threatening laughter subsided immediately.

The elevator took them all the way to the ground floor. As they exited and turned right down another long corridor, Jennifer dutifully and silently walked along beside Bina. Most people they met, smiled and nodded at Bina and a few spoke a word or two of greeting but no one spoke to her.

Feeling paranoid was ridiculous because Bina worked here and she didn't. Only a small, isolated handful of people knew who she was, and even fewer knew what she was doing. But Jennifer couldn't shake off the feeling that they were ignoring her simply because they were too embarrassed to acknowledge her new role as the widow of their fallen hero. It made her feel uncomfortable as she walked along the corridor, as if there was a sign hanging above her head. One that told everyone she had failed to save her husband. Their hero.

They came to a door with a sign that read 'Yetsiat Cherum'. Jennifer knew it translated as 'Emergency Exit' and she frowned in confusion as Bina used her keycard to open it and they walked through. *Where were they going? And why does an emergency exit door need a keycard?* The staircase led downwards – six steps to the next level. But instead of going down beyond the first landing to what was, presumably, the actual exit out of the building, Bina stopped at another door. This one had both a keypad and a swipe feature and the sign on this door said 'Ein Knissa' which she knew meant no admittance. That didn't stop Bina though. She swiped her card, entered a four-digit number and the door clicked open.

As the two women walked through the door, Jennifer gazed around her. The secured door was only pretending to be a fire escape exit. A large command and control room was hidden behind it.

There were no windows. The light came from recessed fittings in the high ceiling and around the walls. Apart from one wall. This light came from banks of large monitors.

Facing the wall with the monitors there were three tiered rows of desks that took up most of the floor. All of them had computer terminals and phones and they were manned by military personnel. It put Jennifer a little in mind of NASA's Mission Control room. She had seen it many times over the years in movies or on news footage and this was definitely similar. Her curiosity was piqued as she stepped into the room. *What was going on? And what do they need me for?*

Saul was chatting to one of the people in military garb who was seated in front of a desk on the top tier. He spotted Jennifer and beckoned for her to join him.

Bina patted her on the shoulder and told Jennifer that she would see her later. 'Maybe we can have a coffee together,' she suggested.

'Yeah. Sure. Why not?' Jennifer replied.

Bina gave her a faint smile that hinted at sympathy then made for the exit door and Jennifer found herself wondering what Bina's role was in this place. The woman was small in stature and seemed to be in her mid to late sixties – grey-haired, and motherly to a degree. She also had an air of quiet authority about her and had the attitude of a woman who believed in getting things done with no fuss. *Maybe a PA? Or an office manager of some sort. Yeah, definitely in an administration role. But important, too.* She wore a wedding ring – a simple gold band – and Jennifer toyed with the idea that she might be Saul's wife.

Jennifer cautiously walked over to him. *Please don't do the sympathy thing.* Sympathy was the last thing in the world she needed or wanted right now. It appeared to be the last thing on his mind too for he pulled out a chair and motioned for her to sit down.

'Thank you for doing this, Jennifer,' he said. 'Hopefully we won't take up much more of your time.' There was no acknowledgement of her grief. Or of the loss of such a valued operative as Ilan. He was probably saving it for the eulogy.

'Okay,' she said as she made herself comfortable in the

chair and pulled it closer to the desk. At the same time, she pulled it slightly away from the man standing beside her. She glanced at the monitor in front of her. It showed a grainy black and white satellite image. To her left and right were screens showing similar images and they corresponded with the images on the larger screens on the far wall.

'What do you need me to do?' she asked, still unsure of the reason they had asked her into this room.

But before Saul could explain what he wanted from her; the door opened. Saul looked up and immediately straightened up, not quite to attention – but close enough – as the Prime Minister walked in.

He was wearing a dark blue suit and matching tie, and his face was solemn as he approached Jennifer and Saul. She made to stand up but he motioned her to remain seated and reached for her hand.

'I am honoured to finally meet you, Mrs. Ben-Levi. But it is a shame that it is under such tragic circumstances.'

Jennifer could only nod. She knew that if she spoke, she would start crying again.

He seemed to realise that she was on the brink of tears and he squeezed her hand gently. 'Ilan was a great man. We are all proud of him and his great service, over the years, to Israel. I have met him on many occasions, formally and informally, and I am honoured to have known him. His loss is a sad day for both his country, and for me. For all of us. If there is anything that I can do for you, please let me know.'

You could start by apologising for authorising this stupid mission that got him killed.

Jennifer met his eyes, expecting the normal – devoid of all empathy – blank look of a politician, but all she saw was genuine sympathy and sadness. He seemed to be silently acknowledging a personal loss as well as a professional one.

'I didn't vote for you,' she told him.

'That's okay,' he said with a smile. 'You would be surprised how many people tell me that.'

'I probably will next time.'

'Thank you.' He nodded. 'But I'm not on the campaign trail now. I'm here to tell you how much I appreciate what you have lost and extend my deepest sympathies to you and Ilan's family.'

'It doesn't help much, but I appreciate what you've said. Thank you.'

'I believe you have more work to do with Saul. I'm not sure exactly what it involves but Saul has told me that it is of great importance, so I will let you carry on. Once again, I am so sorry for your loss.'

With another gentle squeeze of Jennifer's hand, the Prime Minister nodded to Saul then turned on his heels and walked out of the room.

Not sure what she was feeling, Jennifer blinked a couple of times and turned to Saul. 'That was really *him*?'

'It was.'

'He looks older in real life,' Jennifer said as she shook her head, partly in amazement and partly to clear her thoughts. 'So, where were we?'

Saul pressed a couple of keys on the keyboard in front of her and the large screen came to life.

'These are satellite images of the area in Syria close to where Ilan was working,' he said as he pointed to the screen. 'There are old, abandoned villages in this region and it's possible they had converted one of them into their compound and moved there.'

'And I'm guessing you want me to try and identify which village from my dream?'

'Yes.'

'Okay. I'll have a look but I'm not sure if I'll be able to recognise anything. Other than the little courtyard I didn't really see any of the outside.'

'I understand,' Saul replied. He grabbed an empty chair from the adjoining table, pulled it over and sat down beside her. He pointed to the keyboard and explained to Jennifer how to scroll through the various images. 'And if you need to zoom in or out use this key.'

‘Are these real time images?’ Jennifer asked as she stole a glance at the man sitting beside her. ‘It’s just ... I’m not sure I can look at them, if I might see Ilan’s body lying somewhere. I mean…’

‘They’re not in real time, Jennifer. These images were taken over eighteen hours ago. We are just asking you to try and identify the area,’ Saul replied.

Jennifer detected a note of impatience in his voice. Another quick glance at him confirmed his mood and she noticed how tired he looked. His eyes were red-rimmed and black shadows surrounded them. His hair was dishevelled and, judging by the stubble on his face, he hadn’t shaved in a day or two. His age was hard to determine. Mid to late fifties, definitely. Early sixties? Possibly. There was also a sadness around him that seemed to have settled with an old familiarity onto his shoulders. Whether it had always been there or it was his reaction to the events that had unfolded these past few hours, Jennifer couldn’t tell. As for her own sadness, she kept that locked up tightly within her. It belonged to her, and her alone, and she had no desire to share it with anyone.

Her fingers found the keyboard and she called up the first image. There were thirty-seven in total and, while she wanted to get this over and done with, she wanted to do it thoroughly and properly, so she took her time and allowed her eyes to become accustomed to the graininess of the images. She studied the first image slowly and carefully and tried to remember, as best as she could, the courtyard she had walked through in her dream. But it was not in this village.

Nor was it in the second image that Jennifer carefully scrutinised. Or the third or the fourth. The fifth looked slightly familiar and she zoomed in on this photo and studied it intently as she tried to compare it to the memory of the village she had seen in her dream. After a few minutes she shook her head and discarded it. She heard Saul sighing beside her, but she ignored him and selected another image.

And so, it went on. Jennifer scrolled carefully through

the images, discarding most of them, occasionally going back to have a second look at one or two before carrying on. She tried to put herself back into the dream, visualising her surroundings as she walked down the corridor where she saw the laboratory-type room, then going through the door at the end and stepping out into the square.

It was night time. The courtyard was in semi-darkness – lit only by the half-moon in the clear, cloudless sky. This was an aspect of the dream Jennifer hadn't remembered. Or was her memory playing tricks on her? No, it had definitely been night time. She tried to remember walking across the courtyard to the door on the opposite side, but this was where she stalled. It was like coming up against a mental brick wall. Through that door was the room where she had witnessed Ilan's murder. She simply couldn't go through that again, no matter how hard she tried.

Jennifer shook her head to clear away the image that crept unbidden into her mind and tried to concentrate on the one on the screen in front of her. But it was no use. She kept going back to the room where the two men who seemed to be in charge were standing in front of a gathered group. Before them was Ilan – broken and bloody. Then the taller of the two men pulled out a gun and…

Hot tears stung her eyes. They blurred her vision as they threatened to spill over. She couldn't look at the screen anymore and concentrated instead on the keyboard in front of her. It was all she could do to stop herself from slamming her fist down on it.

I need to stop thinking. I need to just do my job. Finish it and get out of here.

Wisely, Saul did not speak. He offered Jennifer no words of comfort, perhaps knowing that to do so would destroy her.

He must have signalled to someone because two cups of coffee were placed in front of them. Jennifer took hers gratefully. It was strong and black, the way she preferred it and she was glad of the momentary distraction. She blew gently on the hot liquid to cool it, still keeping her eyes away from the screen.

'Do you want to take a short break, Jennifer?' Saul asked.

Jennifer couldn't help but wonder if the suggested break was for her benefit or for his. It could merely be the lighting that gave him a deathly pallor, but it was the expression on his face and in his eyes that told the true story. He looked exhausted and ill. Worse than he had looked earlier.

'I'm okay,' she said. 'But I can take a break if you want one.'

Saul hesitated for a moment, considering it, then shook his head. 'No. It is better to continue.'

Jennifer nodded in agreement. She drank the remains of her coffee, tilted her head from side to side a few times to work the stiffness out of her neck and shoulders, and turned her gaze to the screen once more.

Less than an hour later, after having gone over the satellite images several times, Jennifer could only find six that came close to the area she remembered in her dream. And even they weren't completely identical to the dream, so she couldn't say with any certainty that even one of them was the village in question. It was the best she could do and she apologised to Saul for not being able to help him.

'You did well, my dear. Please do not apologise for anything. What you have given us will help.'

'How?'

'Thanks to you we can eliminate the areas where we can say with a good degree of certainty that they are not in. We know they moved location but we have been unable to locate their new compound. This helps us a great deal.'

'But you still don't know where they are?' Jennifer frowned.

'This narrows our search down considerably and it is only a matter of time until we locate them.'

'So, you don't need me anymore? I can go now? I want to find Nurit and see how she is.'

'Nurit has been sent home,' Saul said. 'She was placed on compassionate leave and has gone home to be with her family.'

And what about me? Ilan was my husband. My family. Don't I count? Don't I get compassionate leave?

'And I've just lost my husband. I would like to go home now and grieve for him.'

'I appreciate that, Jennifer but…' Saul hesitated, embarrassed and uncomfortable all of a sudden. His head dropped and he concentrated on the empty coffee cup in front of him, unable to look her in the eye. To ask more of her.

'But what?'

'We need just a little more of your time. To look at some photos. Mug shots, I suppose you would call them. Maybe you would recognise some of the people you saw in your dream?'

'Seriously?' Jennifer stared at him. Disbelief etched in her frown.

'We think it is worth a shot.'

'Are you looking for someone in particular?' Jennifer asked.

'Yes.' Saul admitted somewhat reluctantly.

'Who?'

'I prefer not to say. It could skew your judgement.'

Jennifer rested her elbow on the desk and wearily rubbed her eyelids as she considered his request. When she thought about it, it made sense. She had gotten a good look at one of the two men involved. They seemed to be the ringleaders and maybe she could identify him from a photo. The other man, the one with the gun who had shot Ilan... *don't go there...* his back had been to her and she never got a look at his face. The best description she could give of him, the only description, was that he was tall and had long, scruffy, grey hair. But the other man? *Yeah, I'd know him again.*

'Let's do it,' she said with a sigh.

Chapter 24.

In his frustration, Jamal paced back and forth and stepped out the boundaries of his small room, from one wall to the other. He felt trapped. Contained. His anger impotent. He wasn't locked in; the door had a handle that he could open and walk through any time he chose to do so. But to all intents and purposes he was a prisoner. A prisoner of his own rage and impotence, and he could see no way to escape.

He slammed his fist into the wall. The skin on his knuckles broke against the hard stone and the pain was good. It kept him from howling out his anger and frustration. He focused his mind on that pain and, like a wounded animal, he licked away the blood. Cleansing the wound.

Killing the Israeli spy had been an impulsive act and one that could have gotten him killed. It should have gotten him killed. If the roles had been reversed and Sayeed had fired the shot that ended the prisoner's life, Jamal would not have hesitated. Yet Sayeed had not only permitted the public affront to his authority, he appreciated it.

That act of impetuousness led to Sayeed taking him more deeply into his confidence and Jamal finally learned the true nature of their planned attack. Their Jihad. The word itself meant struggle but, in the that context it was used today, it meant a holy war. But this. This was not a holy war. If anything, it was... unholy. Jamal ran his fingers through his long, straggly hair as he paced. He knew in his heart he was a dead man walking. Once they – the infected – left on their journeys of death, Sayeed would ensure there was no one left as a witness to his deeds. He would move on to somewhere safe in the knowledge that his plan had been successful and there was nothing he, Jamal, could do to prevent it.

His agitation grew as he considered his next move. *Could I...? No. I wouldn't stand a chance. But what if...*

His thoughts walked alongside him while he paced. They mirrored his steps as he walked the dimensions of the small room. They switched direction each time he covered the length to one wall and they walked with him as he turned back again.

What if I had explosives? Then maybe... no, I haven't found explosives anywhere in the compound. I can get guns, but how many could I take down before they take me down? Not enough. But I have to try. I have to think of something. Do something. But what?

Jamal scratched his beard as he pondered his situation. A beard that was tangled and filthy from the dust that surrounded the compound. Dust that was blown on the wind and found its way in through the cracks in the walls and the broken windows of the buildings in this long-ago abandoned village. It was everywhere. On his clothes. In his hair. In his eyes. In his mouth. It settled over him like a second skin. *What would I give right now to stand under a steaming, hot shower and wash away this filth? To use soap and shower gel and shampoo? To shave again? And cut my hair? Become human again? To feel the warmth of the water and the scent of her... Don't go there! That way leads to heartbreak and madness!*

He needed to get out of this room. Out of this prison that was of his own making. He needed air and space around him. He needed a cigarette. *Where had that thought come from? I haven't wanted a smoke in months. Haven't thought about a nicotine fix in a long time. Maybe I could bum one from a guard?*

If only for something to do, Jamal stepped outside. He took a deep breath and savoured the crisp, clear winter air as he walked along the narrow streets. Past the crumbled buildings that told a lie to cover up what was behind their crumbling façade.

Once out of the confines of the room, Jamal felt his head beginning to clear. He spotted one of the guards – a youth name Ali. Jamal knew Ali smoked and he always had a pack hidden about his person.

'Do you have a spare cigarette, brother?'

Ali recovered from his slouch against the wall and stood

to attention. Jamal made a gesture with his hand, telling him to relax and once more asked for a cigarette.

Reluctantly, Ali reached inside his jacket and, for a second, Jamal thought he was going to produce a firearm. But no, he held a crumpled pack in his hand. He fumbled and almost spilled the contents on the ground but managed to pull one out and handed it to the man standing in front of him. Jamal thanked him and then asked him for a light. From the same inside pocket, the guard produced a battered Zippo lighter.

'I stole this from a dead American soldier,' Ali told him with a grin.

Or you bought it on eBay, most likely.

Jamal put the end of the untipped cigarette in his mouth and cupped his hand around it as he lit it. He inhaled the harsh smoke deep into his lungs, held it for a moment, then exhaled slowly. Within a few seconds the nicotine hit his nervous system and he felt the familiar sensations as his brain released the adrenaline. He took another deep drag, closed his eyes and enjoyed the momentary high he had not felt since... *Don't go there!*

'Thank you, my brother.'

Ali nervously offered him the rest of the pack.

'I will take only one. For later,' he said as he removed another cigarette from the packet.

'Keep the lighter,' Ali said. 'I have two more. From dead American soldiers.'

Jamal inclined his head in a gesture of thanks and examined the old lighter before tucking it away in his own pocket. *I stole this from a soon-to-be-dead Jihadi.* A story to tell his grandchildren one day, perhaps? *Don't go there!*

Jamal thanked him again. He took another drag on the cigarette and walked away.

He meandered aimlessly through the ruined village. Most of it was familiar to him but not all of it. Now, his legs carried him on a previously untrodden journey, but his thoughts were vicious circles, trapped by solid, unyielding barricades. The freedom that his footsteps enjoyed did not free his mind.

Finally, he stopped at a low wall on the farthest edge of the village. Beyond the wall the land opened up and his eyes followed the ground to the hills on the horizon. The sun was low in the sky. Jamal shivered and wrapped his old coat more tightly around him to ward off the chill of the wind. He stood motionless. Even as the sun set for the day, his eyes remained rooted to the spot on the faraway hills where it had vanished. *What was beyond those hills? Freedom?* He placed his hands, palms down on the top of the wall. *What if I just climbed over this wall and started walking towards those hills? I could walk until I was free. Become someone else. Leave behind everything. Could I do that?*

But it was all he would be leaving behind that told him he could not walk away. He could never climb over this wall.

It would be dark in a few moments – night came quickly here – and soon only a few streaks of light would remain in the evening sky. Jamal welcomed that darkness. It hid the world around him from his sight but it could not erase the memory of what he had seen earlier that day. And all that he had learned.

There is nothing I can do. And this could be one of the few nights on earth left to me.

With that realisation, an air of acceptance and regret settled heavily onto his shoulders. There were so many regrets. So much he would be leaving behind. So much left unsaid.

In the welcoming darkness he closed his eyes. If only he could go back to the compound within the ruined village and fall asleep to escape the horror that surrounded him. But he doubted sleep would come to him tonight. He bowed his head and said a silent farewell to the life he had known and the man he had once been before walking slowly back to the compound, and the room that was now a prison cell.

Chapter 25.

The conversation in the car had consisted of no more than a dozen or so words on the short journey through Tel Aviv to her home. That suited Jennifer perfectly. She had no desire to strike up a conversation with her driver, someone she did not know, and it seemed he had no desire to talk either. Other than to remind her to fasten her seatbelt and ask her if she needed to stop anywhere along the way.

'Just take me home,' she told him.

It's my house now. Not ours. It isn't a home anymore. Not without you. The thought occurred to her as she leaned her head against the window and watched the city passing by with each kilometre. The weather was grey and miserable. A few drops of rain fell on the windscreen and the heavy sky threatened more. Still, it was good to get out of that building where, from the moment she had entered it, she had felt like a prisoner. How many days ago? Three? Four? Or was it five? No, not that many. Definitely three. Maybe four. It had been so easy to lose track of time in there.

Jennifer didn't look back as she closed the car door and walked the few steps to the gate. She already had her keys in her hand and she quickly unlocked the gate, stepped through it and felt a sense of relief that this part of her ordeal was over.

It had been a long and mentally agonising day. She had worked with Saul for another two hours, taking only a thirty-minute lunch break for a quick sandwich and a coffee. Then he took her to another room, sat her down at a table, and proceeded to have her look through dozens of large file folders that contained photographs of various known, and unknown, terrorists.

Jennifer looked at him in surprise and asked why they weren't stored on hard drives. 'It seems a bit old-fashioned having actual photographs in a folder.'

'They are all on hard drives. These are back-ups,' Saul

said. 'I thought you might want a break from staring at a screen.'

'Yeah, my eyes are stinging a bit. Thank you,' she said as she opened the first folder. There were four photographs to a page and Jennifer began the slow, painstaking task of looking carefully at each image.

When they resumed after the short lunch break, Jennifer found several possibilities and pointed them out to Saul. But she couldn't say with one hundred percent confidence that any one of them was the man she had seen in her dream. Saul took these photos out of the folder and placed them to the side.

About half way through the folders she turned a page and stopped. The memory of her dream came flooding back, and along with that memory came the horror of what she had witnessed. A small gasp escape from between her pursed lips.

'What is it? Do you recognise someone?' Saul asked, a note of excitement in his voice.

'This one,' Jennifer said as she pulled the page with the photograph out of its laminated sleeve and looked again at it. That smile. She remembered it when he had been looking at Ilan. Just before the other guy shot him. Then a fleeting anger had crossed his face when the other man – the tall man with the long hair and straggly, grey beard – had shot Ilan, but it disappeared as quickly as it had appeared. Replaced by the smile once more. The smile on the face of the man in the photograph sent a shiver down her spine. Jennifer wanted to look away but she couldn't. 'I think this was the man I saw.'

'Are you sure?' Saul asked.

'Yes. I'm sure. This was the man in the room when Ilan was murdered. That's him.'

Saul let out a long, slow breath as Jennifer handed the photograph to him.

'Who is he?'

'His name is not important. He has been on our watch list for a while now but we had nothing on him that would validate capturing... arresting him.'

A priceless bit of honesty there, Saul. Maybe if you'd just lifted him anyway, we wouldn't all be in this mess now?

'I don't get how merely knowing who he is helps you find him?'

'I cannot go into the details, but believe me Jennifer, it helps. It helps us a great deal.'

It was obvious to Jennifer that Saul was never going to tell her anything more. She was out of the loop now. A civilian. An intruder.

Well, okay then. If that's how it's going to be, okay then. I can live without it.

She stood up and turned to face the man before her. Her captor. 'If there's nothing else I'd like to go home now. Get on with my life. Or what's left of it.'

Saul stood up too. 'Jennifer, we cannot thank you enough, I cannot thank you enough, for what you have done. Putting yourself in this position showed a courage that –'

Jennifer raised her hand to silence him. 'Drop it, Saul. Just drop it. I don't need any of this. I don't need to hear your thanks or your glowing praise. I don't need you to stand there and tell me how helpful I've been in the 'fight against terror' because I really don't think I have been all that helpful. My husband is dead and you are nowhere near catching those who killed him. Or stopping their terrorist plot, whatever that may be. Or even if there is a terrorist plot. Who knows? I certainly don't. And you know what I think Saul? I think all of this – the sleep room, the hypnosis, all of it – was just a chance, an excuse, to really see how good I am at this.'

She ran out of steam and stopped. The silence between them hung in the air.

Saul opened and closed his mouth a few times. Was he on the brink of telling her she was wrong? Maybe? Possibly? Jennifer watched him and waited. But he couldn't meet her eyes. He couldn't look her in the face and deny what she had said. His silence told her some of what she said was true – especially the part about it being a way to judge what he was now calling her 'remarkable ability'. And she hated him for it.

'Can you organise someone to take me home, please?' Jennifer said.

'Yes. Of course. I will do that right away,' Saul said. He took his phone out of his pocket and dialled a number. 'Be at the front gate in twenty minutes. A run within Tel Aviv. One passenger.'

And that was it. Jennifer's short career in the Mossad was over and done with. She went back to her little apartment that now resembled a prison cell – albeit a well-furnished, comfortable one, but a prison cell nonetheless – and packed up her few items of clothing and toiletries, including the two bottles of wine which had been returned to her. She unscrewed the cap on the bottle she had opened when she arrived and sniffed it cautiously. She was tempted to swig a mouthful but she was doubtful about it so instead, she poured the contents down the wash hand basin and dumped the bottle in the waste bin. The other, she carefully packed inside her clothes. It took all of ten minutes and she was ready to get out of the room, and the building.

At the main door – the one she had walked in through a lifetime ago – she handed back her ID card and lanyard and, for the first time in what seemed like ages, stepped out into the fresh air. A car pulled up in front of her immediately and she opened the back door, threw her holdall onto the seat and slammed the door shut. She opened the front passenger door and got into the car, not caring if Saul, or Bina, or Nathan, or the whole bloody lot of them were standing on the steps, waving goodbye to her. They weren't and that was good because she didn't want to see any of them ever again.

Now she was back home and all she could do was stand inside the gate for a moment and stare at the house that was no longer the home she shared with Ilan. It was hers alone now. Her car was parked in the paved driveway where she had left it. The space beside it was where Ilan always parked his car. But it was empty now. For a brief second Jennifer allowed herself to pretend the car wasn't there because Ilan was at work and would be home soon. Then she realised that she had spent the last couple of days in the building where he worked. She had walked the same corridors that he had. Ate in the same canteen. Maybe even sat at the same table. *So close to you and yet I still couldn't find you. I'm so sorry, my darling.*

Jennifer closed her eyes and then an image of his old BMW came into her mind. The old, black convertible he loved that was always breaking down and spent most of its days in the driveway of their home in Cyprus.

'It's a classic,' he would tell her when she complained about it sitting there rotting slowly and cluttering up their nice driveway. She smiled at the memory. Hold onto those ones, she told herself. Throw away the bad ones and keep the good memories. She had plenty of them. Enough to sustain her over the coming years. But right now, they were as painful as they were pleasant.

Tears welled in her eyes. They threatened to spill over and she knew that once she began crying, she would never stop. Not for a long, long while. But she was made of tougher material than that and she wiped them away before they could gain a hold of her.

Possum and Holly came forward to greet her as she opened the door. They meowed softly, hesitantly, giving her wide-eyed, reproachful stares for leaving them for so long. She placed her bag on the chair and crouched down in front of them.

'It's okay kitties. Mummy is home now. She had to go away for a few days to try and find Daddy, but she's home now. And she won't go away again.'

They didn't believe her and it took two pouches of their favourite cat food to win them over. Even as they were eating, they still eyed her with suspicious glances every now and then.

The house was cold and had a dreariness to it that was nothing to do with the fact that it had been unlived in for the past few days. Jennifer no longer felt the rush of homeliness she would feel every time she walked in the front door. Knowing Ilan was gone made the house no longer a home. The home she had shared with him.

Where was home now? Could she put her hand on her broken heart and say with all honesty that it was this house in Tel Aviv? She didn't know. *I could leave Israel.* Talia would re-house the cats and Reuben had a cousin who was in real estate. The house would easily fetch a good price in today's market. She would phone him in a few days to get the cousin's phone number.

So where would I go? Cyprus? No, not there.

The memories she had of living in Cyprus were good, but that last night when they had to flee cancelled out all the happy memories. No. Cyprus was out of the question. And as much as she would like to see her father again, the thought of moving back to the UK was definitely off the table. *Maybe I could go to Australia for a while and see Mum.*

Since her parents' divorce a year ago, her mother had moved there, found a toy-boy and was currently running a beach bar with him in a little place north of Cairns. They seemed to be happy together. Her mother was enjoying herself immensely – reliving her youth again with parties on the beach in the evenings, her days spent working the bar, chatting and flirting with the regular patrons, and her free time was spent swimming and surfing. She had sent Jennifer some photos a while back. There she was standing on the beach with the ocean behind her, smiling and squinting in the sun. All tanned and sporting curly blonde hair, looking for all the world like a beach bum, and looking at least twenty years younger.

Her dad hadn't let a little thing like a divorce slow him down either. He'd bought a forty-year-old MK2 Escort, restored it to racing specifications and went rallying in it – competing every few weekends in the historic classes. He had a new partner too. A woman who was only a few years younger than him and also a car fanatic, so they were well matched. At least they were of similar age, unlike her mum and whatshisname? Brian or Wayne? Or something. Darren, possibly. He was in his late fifties. Not really a toy-boy, but still a few years younger than her mother, and he looked as though he had been born attached to a surfboard. But both of her parents were enjoying their new relationships and had even stopped hating one another, which was a relief to both Jennifer and her brother.

Yeah, it would be nice to see Mum again.

But these were thoughts and plans for another day. Right now, she needed food and wine. And she needed to sort herself out first.

The first thing Jennifer did was switch on the central heating and pull the blinds closed against the darkness of the evening. It had fallen quickly, as it did at this time of year, and she felt isolated and alone. She hurried into the utility room and switched on the security lights. They worked on sensors and would light up the instant something or someone crossed their detection beams. At first Jennifer had hated them. They would come on at the slightest thing, frightening the life out of her, until Ilan adjusted the sensitivity to prevent anything smaller than a dog or cat activating them. After a while she began to accept the lights, along with the alarm system he had installed, as a necessary part of their lives. And it became a comfort to both of them.

The last thing she did was key in the four-digit number to set the alarm system and, with it and the lights, her solitary fortress was secure for the evening.

The heating system was beginning to warm the house, dispelling the chilly, unlived in feeling that had caused Jennifer to shiver when she walked in through the door.

Feeling more comfortable now, she turned her attention to feeding herself before settling down for the evening. *Practice for the rest of my life, I suppose. Not that I haven't had plenty of practice this past eight months. But it's permanent now.*

The realisation hit her and a sob escaped her. But, before it could get a hold of her, she forced the thought away and concentrated on only the next few minutes and making herself something to eat.

No. I need a glass of wine first. If there is any.

It seemed as if she had been away for ages and she couldn't remember when she last went grocery shopping, or what she had bought. But she usually kept a bottle of wine chilling in the back of the fridge.

The horseshoe wine rack that she had bought on the internet held six bottles of red wine. It had been a silly, impetuous purchase that ended up costing her more in shipping than the actual purchase. But she loved it. It looked great sitting there in the corner although it didn't seem to have brought her the good luck horseshoes were *supposed* to bring.

But right now, she wanted *white* wine. She opened the fridge door and found, to her surprise, that it was fully stocked with fresh fruit and vegetables and three casseroles that she only had to heat up. There were also several desserts, six pots of yogurt, a plate of cold meats and four bottles of chardonnay. By the looks of it, someone had left the food either today or yesterday. Saul, maybe? Well, not him in person, but he probably had sent someone.

But how did they get in? And how creepy is that?

With a frown, she took out one of the wine bottles and reached up to the cupboard for a glass. It was then she spotted the note on the kitchen counter. It was from Reuben.

'Hi Jennifer,' the note read. 'Cats are fine but missing you. I figured you wouldn't be thinking of groceries so I stocked up the fridge with food and wine. Nurit is staying at home today. She has taken her father's death hard. As you'd expect. She has to go back into work tomorrow, but if there is anything you need, let me know.' He had signed it then added a postscript. 'I'm so sorry about Ilan. Nurit is heartbroken and we know you are too. He was a great man.'

Yeah, a great man who left us. He just had to go off and save the world, without a thought for us here at home.

She scrunched up the note and threw it at Possum who loved nothing better than chasing a scrunched-up piece of paper across the tiled floor. He leapt on it and batted it a few times, then crouched down to attack it. Holly sauntered into the kitchen to see what he was playing with, but she didn't join in. She considered herself too important and well-bred to be chasing a mouse made from paper.

Unable to make up her mind what to eat, now that she had a selection of food to choose from, Jennifer cracked open the wine and poured out a large glass. She took a small sip, then another one, and relished the coolness and the delicate flavour. She gathered up the accumulated mail from where Reuben had left it, tucked it under her arm and carried her glass and the bottle into the living room. She dumped the mail onto the coffee table and placed the wine bottle within easy reach.

She picked up the television remote and began surfing up and down through the channels, stopping only when something sparked her interest. Both the BBC and SKY news was all about the mess Britain had gotten itself into over Brexit and there were no other programmes worth watching so Jennifer selected a box set she had downloaded a few weeks ago, but it was about an undercover agent searching for a terrorist. *Oh, I'm definitely not going to be watching that one for a while!*

Nothing appealed to her, so she found an easy listening music channel, something bland, and turned the volume down until it became background noise. It was something to take away the unbearable silence.

Tucking her legs underneath her, Jennifer pulled the throw from off the back of the sofa, draped it over her and took her phone out of her pocket. Holly leapt up onto the sofa beside her and settled down on the warmth of the throw. Possum was still in the kitchen hunting and killing his piece of paper.

She scrolled through the phone. There were a couple of missed calls and numerous texts and WhatsApp messages, mostly from Ilan's sisters and other close family members who had been informed that he was missing and presumed dead. Nothing official had been released and only Nurit and herself knew the truth. But the rest of the family were assuming the worst and most of the messages were of sympathy – sorry for your loss – or – if you need anything, call.

Sorry for your loss is a horrible statement. Makes it sound like I can't find one of my earrings or something. Makes it seem trivial. When I've really lost everything. My best friend. My lover. The man who shared my bed every night. Well, most nights. The man who loved sex like it was his favourite pastime. The man who taught me chess and who got really upset when I beat him and then refused to play against me ever again when I beat him twice in a row. The man who cleans out the cat litter for me and keeps me warm and safe and happy.

Bereavement is another fucking shitty word. 'You've suffered a bereavement,' They say. No. I suffer when I have a migraine because I drank too much. That's suffering. Or when I stub my toe on the furniture. That sharp pain that makes you scream and swear aloud. Now, that's suffering. This is different. This makes you numb. And you don't scream and shout and swear. You just sit there wondering what happened. To 'suffer a bereavement' makes it sound like I'll get over it. There's no getting over this. This is for keeps. This is it.

Jennifer poured another glass of wine and realised that at some stage she would have to think about her future. She would also have to organise his funeral. *I don't know the first thing about planning a funeral – Jewish or otherwise. How do you have a funeral when there's no body to bury?* Then she remembered he wasn't actually confirmed as dead and, other than herself, only Nurit and Saul's small team knew what had transpired in her dream. *Reuben knows too, obviously or he wouldn't have left me the note and, besides, Nurit would have had to tell him because of the state she was in. But as for the rest of Ilan's family, would they eventually be told the exact nature of how we know he's dead? Would they be told I saw him murdered in a dream? Obviously, they'll be told something at some stage. But they'd hardly just accept it on the strength of a dream I had. I can't see that happening.*

It was something she would have to deal with at some stage. And planning his funeral was also something she would have to deal with. But for now, she was going to sit on her sofa and drink wine and eventually she would climb into bed. *Hopefully I'll be drunk enough to fall asleep.*

Chapter 26.

A room dedicated to military operations is usually the place from where a battle would be commanded and controlled, not where it was waged. But before he even entered the room, Saul Mueller knew he would most likely have the mother of all battles on his hands. He put his exhaustion to one side, opened the door and walked in with his shoulders squared, steel in his eyes and all guns blazing. He was ready to state his case.

Despite his build and his outdoorsy, tough guy appearance, Nathan Cohen was nervous. He let out a long, slow breath and tried not to let his anxiety show as he entered behind Saul. According to Saul, it would be his testimony – his reports and the information within them – that would swing the decision. Nathan hated the thought of that amount of responsibility sitting firmly on his shoulders. It was a heavy weight to bear because he was a psychotherapist, not a military advisor. As a result, he had brought along with him all of his research literature and notes pertaining to what he was now calling, at least to himself – 'Sleep Travel'. The Mossad probably had another name for it – Operation Rip Van Winkle or Operation Sleeping Beauty, or something similar. But he liked 'Sleep Travel' the most.

His notes were in an old-style leather school satchel slung over his left shoulder. The satchel was old and battered, with some of the stitching beginning to come away around the seams. The faded lettering on the front bore the initials NC. Most people believed they were his initials but the bag had belonged to his father, also called Nathan, long before he had ever laid claim to it.

His laptop, containing all of the video sessions with Jennifer Ben-Levi, was in a case slung over his right shoulder. Nathan wanted to believe that it was the combined weight of these two bags that made his shoulders stoop, but he knew it wasn't.

About half of the seats in the room were empty and

Nathan was ushered to a chair at the massive round conference table. Saul had already claimed his seat nearby. He nodded briefly to Doctor Miriam Melandri, their resident psychiatrist. Doctor Melandri had been involved with this project from the beginning. Sceptical when first offered the position, her interest was sparked once it had been explained to her and she had leapt at the opportunity to be a part of something never tried before. Saul had brought her on board in a purely analytical role and, although she had never met Jennifer, Miriam had spent a lot of time reading and assessing Jennifer's history – from her medical reports pertaining to her accident, brain injury and subsequent coma, and her recovery and rehabilitation. Of particular interest to Miriam were the notes and recordings of Jennifer's therapy sessions and, it was through these, she was able to compile her own assessment of the woman in question. She had studied with interest the videos and transcripts of the sleep sessions. She was present today, not only to report on her findings, but to give evidence of Jennifer's, and the experiment's, credibility.

Along with Nathan and Saul, she was a vital part of the trio that made up 'Team Jennifer' and both Nathan and Saul hoped that her valuable input would sway any decisions taken in their favour.

Several men and four women filed in and everyone took their seats. Saul stood up to begin but was waved to sit down again. It was not a formal conference. They were even dressed casually. Two pots of coffee, a jug of water, cups, tumblers, plates and napkins, along with trays piled high with pastries sat like centrepieces in the middle of the table. One or two helped themselves to a couple of pastries and coffee but most of them settled for a glass of water.

Saul cleared his throat and was about to begin speaking when a door at the rear opened and a familiar figure walked into the room. Everyone in the room stood up, but the Prime Minister motioned them to sit down again. He was, like those already gathered, dressed casually – trousers and a dark blue jacket over a light blue polo shirt. He removed the jacket, draped it over the back of the chair he had pulled out and then glanced around at the people sitting at the table.

'Let's begin,' he said as he sat down and helped himself to a glass of water.

Saul cleared his throat once more. Addressing his words to the Prime Minister directly, but also for everyone in the room, he began with a brief summary of the subject – Jennifer Ben-Levi, nee Scott. Her age, her career, her political views, such as they were. He told the people gathered before him that Jennifer, a British national living in Cyprus, met Ilan Ben-Levi in a bar in the Cyprus town of... he checked his paperwork for the name of the town which always escaped him. 'They began a relationship, fell in love and later married.'

Saul continued with his brief summary of Jennifer and her relationship with Ilan.

'Is this woman who she says she is?' someone asked.

'Yes. Considering Ilan's seniority, she was thoroughly vetted when Ilan notified us of his intentions to pursue the relationship and she has been assessed at regular intervals since. There was nothing to indicate she was anything, or anyone, other than who she claimed to be,' Saul replied. The question did not come as a surprise to him. 'Of course, we can never be one hundred percent certain, but we found nothing in her history that gave us cause to doubt her. Their relationship was allowed to continue and within a few years they married and they have been together, happily it would seem, ever since. They have no children and that, I was told by Ilan, was a mutual decision.'

There were a few nods of agreement but Saul also noted one or two frowns as he continued with his summary. He took a deep breath and told them of the events leading up to the circumstances in which Ilan and Jennifer had to flee their home in Cyprus. The resulting car accident and Jennifer's subsequent head injury. And there he paused and took a sip of water. He was about to step into uncharted waters and he knew this was the part where they would either believe him or laugh him out of the room and send him home with a box set of The X-Files.

'This is where it becomes... interesting,' he said and plunged in. 'We have all heard fanciful stories of what people experience, or believe they experience, when they are in comas or near to death. We have all seen the bottom feeder tabloid headlines – 'Woman In Coma Travels To Mars!' or 'Unconscious Man Remembers Where He Left Lost lottery Ticket!' but this is not a fanciful tabloid headline.'

For the most part, Saul read interest on the faces of the people in front of him, but on one or two, including that of the Prime Minister, he saw scepticism and mild amusement. *Yes, the X-Files are waiting for me.*

'Jennifer Scott was placed in a medically induced coma after her brain surgery. She awakened nine days later and informed her husband that during that time she experienced one of those life-flashing-before-your-eyes experiences, but – and this is the part that we are most interested in – it wasn't *her* life that flashed before her eyes. She relived the life of *another person* – a woman known as Lucy Wilson. English. Former primary school teacher turned landscape and wedding photographer. Married with two children. It transpired that Mrs. Wilson suffered a head injury near her home in Yorkshire, England within a few hours of Jennifer's accident. And Jennifer believed that their consciousnesses became connected, or entwined, in some way. She believed that this other woman was living her life at the same time.'

Saul paused and took another sip of water, not daring to look at any of the faces before him.

'Ilan was naturally disbelieving, but Jennifer was adamant this had occurred to her. She insisted they travel to the United Kingdom and then he could see for himself that what she had told him was all true. They did indeed find the woman's grave and the date of her death was the day Jennifer awakened from her coma. Obviously, a simple name and a date on a gravestone wasn't enough to convince Ilan, but

Jennifer was nothing if not persistent. Then they drove past a remote farmhouse that Jennifer had – on their car journey to Yorkshire from London – described in great detail and she told Ilan that Lucy had lived there with her husband and two daughters. Discreet enquiries on a local level confirmed that this woman had indeed lived the life Jennifer experienced in her mind.'

'A coincidence, surely? Or she knew this Wilson woman and merely dreamed about her?'

'On the surface, Gavi, that seemed to be the most plausible explanation. But we looked into both women and could find no link between them whatsoever.'

'So, how does this relate to the situation in Syria?' the Prime Minister asked.

'If you don't mind sir, I will get to that in a moment,' Saul replied.

The Prime Minister indicated with a nod of his head for Saul to continue.

Saul gathered his thoughts once again. 'Ilan informed me about what had occurred to Jennifer as he was concerned about her and any possibly likelihood that she had been used to gain access to him. His concerns were confirmed to be unfounded. He also suggested that maybe this occurrence could be looked into for future reference but he did not want, under *any* circumstances, his wife involved in any way. Basically, he wanted it noted but not acted upon. This, I agreed to.'

When there were no questions, Saul took a moment and debated whether or not to continue or to allow them to learn more of Jennifer's character and state of mind. He decided on the latter and introduced Miriam to them.

A little startled, Miriam Melandri looked up sharply, surprised to be centre stage so early in the proceedings. She half stood up, thought better of it and sat back down again. Her notes were on her iPad within reach, but she knew she did not need them. The near perfect photographic memory she was blessed with was all she required. That, and a drink of water.

Miriam self-consciously cleared her throat and poured water into a tumbler. She took a couple of sips and began to tell them of her findings regarding Jennifer Ben-Levi. She explained that she had not met or spoken to Jennifer, but had extensive access to her medical records and of course, the transcripts and video and audio recordings of the sessions. The conclusion she had come to, she informed the panel, was that the subject was a mentally well balanced, intelligent woman. The subject was not lying when she told her husband what she had experienced in her unconscious state. During her recovery period, Jennifer did suffer from mild PTSD in that she had trouble sleeping, possibly because she was afraid that she would not wake up. And of course, the combination of the physical trauma caused by the accident and the trauma of having to flee her home and relocate to a different country, affected her greatly for a time.

'This was eventually alleviated by several therapy sessions and, to quote Jennifer herself, 'whiskey and sleeping pills helped'. Her recovery was within the normal time period for her injury and it was complete. She now lives a normal, happy life with her husband. Or rather she did until he became operational again approximately eight months ago.'

'How do you think Ilan leaving affected her?'

'It affected her no more or no less that it affects any woman who is married to someone like Ilan. She feels anger, a sense of abandonment, worry and loneliness – the same as any wife would in similar circumstances. Her emotions are perhaps more pronounced, in that she is a stranger in a strange land with less of a support system than other women would have. But she loves her husband and knew this possibility could arise, despite Ilan's protests that he had quit operational work.'

'How do you think she has adapted to living in Israel?'

'She has adapted very well considering the traumatic circumstances of why they moved here. She has learned the language. She is in employment, uh, working at an animal rescue centre. I know she was quite a successful interior designer when she lived in Cyprus but, other than some work for friends and family, she has not carried on with her career. I believe this was her own decision.'

'Is her relationship with her husband a good one?'

'As far as I am aware yes, but I really have little or no knowledge of her personal life so I cannot comment on it.'

'What do you know of lucid dreaming and remote viewing?'

'I have heard the terms lucid dreaming and remote viewing, but I have little or no knowledge of either subject.'

'Even as a psychiatrist?'

'Yes. These are not the kind of subjects that I have had occasion to deal with in my professional life.'

'And outside of your professional life?'

Miriam shrugged her shoulders. 'Well, I was a big fan of The X-Files back in the day.'

This comment was met with muted laughter and Saul glared at her.

They decided then to take a thirty-minute break. Nathan escaped to the carpark where he could top up his nicotine levels and Miriam caught up with Saul in the corridor outside.

'How is Giovanni?' Saul asked.

'As far as I know he's good. Haven't spoken to him in a day or two,' Miriam replied with a pout. 'Haven't seen him in a lot longer than that. Marry a doctor my mother told me. I did that and she was delighted. Unfortunately, I married the wrong kind of doctor!' Her Italian husband was a researcher and was working on an Antarctic base. He had been there for over three months now and her only contact with him was by e-mail and video-phone.

'I guess I shouldn't have made that last comment in there,' she said.

'It didn't help, Miriam,' he told her. 'Why did you say it?'

'I'm sorry. It was out of me before I could stop it. You should know that when it comes to para-psychological phenomena we psychiatrists are the most sceptical. Worse even than physicists when it comes to anything even remotely supernatural and –'

'This is not supernatural,' Saul replied.

'I didn't say it was. I'm just giving you an example of what we are like. Think about it, Saul. Think about the human capacity for self-deception and finding, what they consider to be, rational explanations for coincidences.'

'So, you don't believe Jennifer is capable of lucid dreaming, or even remote viewing?'

'I didn't say that, Saul. I have a healthy level of scepticism but that doesn't mean I'm not open to exploring possibilities and even changing my mind if evidence that proves something is put before me.'

'Yet you made the X-Files comment?'

'I know. My big mouth as usual. You know me. And, once again, I am so sorry.'

'Don't worry about it. I've thought I was in the middle of a sci-fi movie a few times since we started this.'

'Are they finished with me? I have another meeting shortly.'

'Go. We'll contact you if we need you.'

Knowing that if he had been in her shoes, he probably would have made the same quip, Saul watched her walk away, glancing at her watch as she did so. Miriam was a good shrink and a good friend and he bore her no ill will, even if her comment hadn't helped his cause. *They are probably all thinking it anyway. Miriam just reinforced it. But she's totally correct about her big mouth.*

He didn't need food. He knew he should go and get something, but he was too nervous to eat. Instead, he found himself outside in the cold air, relishing the temporary sense of freedom it brought. He spotted Nathan leaning against a guardrail and walked over to him.

'Is that as good as the real thing?' he asked as he

pointed to the object Nathan was holding in his hand.

'This?' Nathan studied his e-cigarette. He smiled at it almost lovingly, held it to his lips and took a long slow drag on it. He exhaled and disappeared from sight, lost in a white cloud that smelled like cherries. He reappeared and looked at Saul standing beside him. 'This is better than the real thing. A million times better.'

'Why?' Saul asked. He couldn't see the point of it. You either smoked or you didn't. Right now, he wished he still did.

'Well, for a start it's been reckoned to be about ninety-five per cent safer. It doesn't stink the way real cigarettes do. Unless you use some weird flavour and, believe me, there are some weird flavours out there. And if you're addicted to nicotine you still get your hit without the risk of lung cancer and all the other related illnesses. Oh, and it's cheaper.'

Saul didn't look convinced. 'Why not just quit?'

'Tried to. Many times. And I always started again. Mainly because I enjoyed smoking. I loved to smoke but I was terrified of dying from it. This is something I dreamed about ever since I took my first cigarette as a teenager. A safer way to smoke.'

'Do you ever miss having a cigarette?'

'No. Not at all. Not since I bought this baby.'

'My wife made me quit. She practically threatened me at gunpoint,' Saul said miserably. 'I've been off them twelve years now. At times like this I want to start again.'

'Do you want to try this? I keep a spare one, fully charged, in the car. You can have it if you like.'

Saul wavered as he considered the offer. It was tempting, but he didn't want to start again. If he tried the e-cigarette, he could end up buying a pack of his favourite brand of real cigarettes on the way home. Then he would have to face his wife.

'No. I'm good. Thank you,' he said.

Nathan shrugged and took another long, satisfying drag, exhaling and once more disappearing momentarily in the white cloud. *And there's that sci-fi movie feeling again. I bet he went to a parallel universe, or something.* Saul waited until he reappeared again.

'You're up next,' he said.

'Don't remind me,' Nathan shuddered. 'Is there anything I need to know? Anything you want me to include? Or anything I need to keep to myself?'

'No television show comparisons, please.'

'Nope. Definitely not going to do that.'

'Your testimony will make or break this,' Saul told him.

'No pressure then,' Nathan sighed.

'You will be fine.' Saul gave him a reassuring slap on the back. 'Put that away. It's time to go back in.'

Nathan was nervous and felt like he was on trial. What he was about to tell the panel was the crucial part of the whole process. And possibly the most damming. Having the Prime Minister sitting there, listening to his every word and maybe make a decision based on what he was about to say, made him all the more nervous. He admired the man and had voted for him, but to have to speak in front of him on this particular subject was more than a little daunting. For all his bulk and tough-guy appearance, Nathan felt like a terrified puppy that had just peed on the living-room carpet.

The analogy was almost apt because he hadn't bothered with a bathroom break, opting for a vape outside instead. Now he regretted his decision.

Saul kicked his shin underneath the table and he sat up straight and glanced around the room. At the faces staring at him, including the face of the Prime Minister. Waiting for him. He swallowed and prayed that he wouldn't lose his capacity for speech.

None of the people in front of him knew him, so Nathan took a deep breath and began by briefly telling them who he was. He gave them his credentials and a quick summary of what his work entailed. He kept it brief and to the point as Saul had instructed him to do. Then he paused and waited for any questions they might feel inclined to ask him. No one spoke. They either didn't want, or need, to know or they knew more about him than Saul thought they did.

It was time to tell them about Jennifer, backtracking a little as he explained the process he used – the door scenario – and how it worked very well in an extremely high percentage of his cases.

'Why not a hundred percent?' one of the women asked.

'Some, a few people, just cannot be hypnotised,' Nathan explained. 'Usually they tend to be –'

She stopped him with a wave of her hand. 'It's okay. It is enough to say that this woman, Jennifer, can be hypnotised.'

'Sorry. Yes.' He took another breath. 'Jennifer was relaxed and compliant as I instructed her to count back from ten, visualise the door and walk through it into the dream. The door seems to be the key. Once I instructed her to walk through it, she was able to slip into REM sleep very quickly and I –'

'In effect you are suggesting what she should dream? Yes?'

'No. Definitely not. All I did was suggest she step through the door. It's the same as telling someone to fall asleep on the count of one to ten. This just takes it a step beyond that. The door is me telling Jennifer to go ahead and dream. But what she dreams about is entirely up to her and her subconscious. Prior to her hypnosis we did discuss what she should be looking for, but it wasn't a suggestion in that sense. The only suggestion I planted in her mind was that she used the door to come back and that she would remember all the details of what she experienced in her dream state.'

The woman in front of him frowned. 'I see. But from

what I can remember from my dreams, they don't make a whole lot of sense and tend to be a jumble of many things. How is this different?'

'Before we started this process, we had no idea if it would work or not. Jennifer could have just woken up with a crazy mixed-up dream about… well, about anything. But from what we had learned of her experience when she was in the induced coma, it appears she is able to lucid dream. That's where a person can direct the contents of his or her dream, where he or she can set a chosen path within the dream and stay on it. In Jennifer's case the peripheral surroundings differed and she had little or no control over them, but the events and everything she could see, took place, to a certain degree, as she experienced them – within her dreams.'

'How is that possible?'

'I don't know,' Nathan admitted.

'You must have some idea.'

'Well, and this is just my opinion – my professional opinion, it is possible that the head injury she received activated something in her brain that awakened a part of her consciousness allowing her to lucid dream almost naturally. Studies have shown that people can have their first lucid dream within three to twenty-one days. Now, that's on average. They have to be committed and practice every day. However, this is only a guide. It can often take months to learn how to lucid dream. But some people naturally possess the skills. In Jennifer's case, she claims that she never was able to lucid dream. She had heard of the concept but put it down to something that only 'hippy-dippy flower children' would believe in. Um, those were her words. Yet, she seems to have wakened from her coma with the ability to lucid dream. Maybe we all have it, this ability, but maybe it lies dormant in most of us.'

'Do you believe that, Doctor Cohen?'

'If you'd asked me a week ago, I probably would have said it was highly unlikely, but now…'

'Now?'

'Now? Now, I can't say for certain that we *all* have this dormant ability, but I can say with absolute certainty that Jennifer Ben-Levi has it.'

The PM shifted around in his seat, dug into the inside pocket of his jacket and produced a pen and a small note pad. He frowned as he opened the pad and scribbled down some notes. When he had finished, he closed his notepad and listened intently to the hushed conversation that was going on around him. But he did not make any contribution.

Nathan hoped they were about to tell him they were finished with him. But no, they wanted more.

'How do you know for certain, Doctor Cohen that Mrs. Ben-Levi had a genuine conversation with her husband while in a dreaming state?'

'I, uh…'

'I can answer that, Leah,' Saul spoke up.

'I'm all ears,' the woman called Leah smiled.

'Ilan and I discussed this about a month before he went to Syria. Both of us knew there was a likelihood it was a one-way trip for him. He accepted it but I didn't. I couldn't. Not only is he one of our best officers, I consider him a good friend and I personally hated the thought of losing him. But the loss to the organisation, and to Israel, of his skill, his years of experience, his courage... well, that would be too great a loss. And if there was any way, any chance, we could avoid losing him, I vowed to do my upmost best to find it. Then I remembered what he had reported to me when he came back from his trip to England with his wife. I mentioned it to him and he hit the roof. He –'

'Typical Ilan,' Gavi said with a wry smile.

'Typical Ilan, yes. I didn't expect anything else of him. So, I let him rant and rave for a while. Swear at me and shout at me. Threaten to quit. Threaten to write his memoirs. Threaten to shoot me.'

This was met with nods and some muted laughter that quickly turned to silent sadness. They all knew the man in question and their loss was as great as Saul had said.

'Eventually he calmed down,' Saul continued. 'And eventually I managed to talk him into considering what I wanted to do. I assured him that Jennifer would not be harmed in any way and that her part in this would be known to only a few people. It took a while but he gradually came around to my way of thinking, but he wasn't happy about it. I don't blame him, but he knew his chances of surviving, should things go wrong, could increase if messages could be channelled back to us through Jennifer.'

'And this proves it how?'

'Jennifer and Ilan have their own security phrase that they have used over the years. I don't know what it is. She told me that, in her dream, she had whispered it to Ilan and he had believed it was her. But I knew this wasn't conclusive proof. She could have just dreamed that she whispered the phrase to him. But between us, Ilan and I devised our own phrase, about the two of us retiring and going fishing, that he would say to Jennifer and I would recognise it when she relayed it back to me. She did so without fault and that was all the proof I needed that she had met with Ilan in a lucid dream.'

'Whoa. Hold on a moment. Is Ilan a lucid dreamer too?'

Saul shook his head. 'No. It would appear that Jennifer is able, within her dreams, to enter someone's consciousness, provided they are also asleep, visualise what they are dreaming about, and interact with them in that dream. Even if they don't remember having a dream when they waken up. Ilan suspected this, but he wasn't sure it would work. It seems that it did.'

Still unconvinced, Leah frowned and made a few notes before moving on. 'The transcripts show that Jennifer met Ilan in an hotel. In a bar. As he is, or rather was, in Syria how are you able to account for that?'

'The surroundings are not important, other than they are probably places where Jennifer would feel normal meeting with Ilan. A bar or a restaurant is a typical place to meet,'

Nathan interjected.

'Okay, I can imagine that. But how do *you* account for Jennifer being able to, in her last dream, walk through the compound and see Ilan being shot?'

'Um, this came as a bit of a surprise to us,' Nathan said and looked to Saul for guidance. Saul gave a slight nod of his head and Nathan continued. 'It would appear that Jennifer is also capable of remote viewing.'

Saul observed the wide-eyed stares of the people gathered around him as even the air in the room stilled and his words seemed too loud in the silence. Gavi frowned. Leah looked mystified and the remainder, including the Prime Minister, looked as if they wanted to get up and storm out. Angry at the waste of a perfectly good afternoon.

Well, that's set the cat among the pigeons, to use an English expression.

'It's getting late,' Gavi looked at his watch. 'I think we'll take a break for the day. I want everyone back here at nine o'clock in the morning.'

'Did we blow it?' Nathan asked as he walked alongside Saul to the carpark, puffing frantically on his e-cigarette.

'Not yet. But we do need to locate the compound as quickly as possible,' Saul replied.

'I know it's not within my paygrade, but are we, you, close?'

'Getting there.'

'And then what?'

Saul shrugged as he unlocked his car, glad to be going home for the evening. 'We'll see.'

Chapter 27.

Saul needed coffee. He glanced at his watch. He had time to spare so he made a beeline for the cafeteria and spotted Gavi in the line for breakfast. He tried to turn and back out, but Gavi waved for him to join him. Reluctantly, he made his way forward and ordered a coffee, black no sugar. He was too nervous to eat anything. *I'll end up with an ulcer at this rate.*

'That was some tale you told us yesterday, old friend.'

'Not a tale, Gavi,' Saul replied, wincing inwardly.

'You believe it, yes?'

'I believe it.'

'Join me for breakfast. I want to pick your brains some more.'

Saul followed him to a corner table overlooking the swimming pool. Neither man knew it, but it was the same table that Jennifer had sat at when she had talked to Nathan about hypnotherapy.

'I know your word is law in the Mossad but this will be a military operation and as such the eyes of the world will be on us. We have a couple of doubters and we cannot go ahead unless everyone is on board. Do you think you can convince them today?' Gavi asked between mouthfuls.

'Yes.'

'And we will need the PM to agree. Nothing will happen without his say so.'

'I know,' Saul replied and took a sip of coffee.

'He will want to speak with you individually, and possibly, with Mrs. Ben-Levi again.'

'I'll speak to him later. But I doubt she will come back here. She was naturally distraught at the death of her husband and all she wanted to do was go home and get on with her life. Such as it is now.'

'Do you think Ilan is dead?' Gavi asked.

'Sadly, yes. But that is irrelevant. Even if he isn't dead, there is nothing we can do for him. He knew the risks. He knew the completion of the mission – stopping whatever it is the terrorists have planned – was more important than his life. Even if his wife is incorrect and he is still alive, which I doubt, he would approve of a military strike to stop them.'

'I believe Jennifer positively identified Qahtani.'

'She did.'

'So, as we suspected, he is behind it.'

'Yes.'

'Remote viewing, eh?' Gavi chuckled.

'I know what you're thinking, but she does have the ability. I have seen her. I know her and she is capable of it. She is adept at it.'

'But remote viewing. I thought that shit had died with dead letter drops and honeytraps. It's very – old school.'

Saul shrugged and set down his coffee cup. 'Sometimes old school still works.'

Gavi's eyebrows shot up in surprise. 'I know you were involved with it back in the day. But it never came to anything that was of use to us. You want to reopen the program again? With her?'

'Maybe,' he said with caution in his voice.

'Would she be on board?'

'That I don't know. Probably not.'

'A shame. It would be – interesting.'

'Let's wait and see,' Saul dismissed the suggestion.

'How close are your people to locating the compound?' Gavi picked up on the older man's dismissal and changed the subject.

'Very close. A couple of days at the most. Sooner, hopefully. Jennifer's description has narrowed it down considerably for us. The courtyard she described was a godsend. It's only a matter of time until we identify it.'

Gavi finished his breakfast, drained his coffee cup and stood up. 'When you speak to the panel tell them what you said to me. Maybe play down the remote viewing part and concentrate on the satellite imagery search. Tell them she has identified Qahtani who was already our number one suspect.

Tell them about the laboratory she saw in her dream. We suspected he was planning a bioweapon attack. You guys did too. The how and the where of the attack is not important at this stage. But the when is. We are half way through December and our intel leads us to believe they are planning their attack to coincide with the Christmas holiday time across Europe and the United States. Maximum terror. Maximum effect. It is vital that we locate them and stop them. By any means necessary.'

'I will,' Saul promised. *And if Jennifer is wrong and Ilan is alive, it means sacrificing him. But that's what he signed up for.*

The thought lay heavily on his heart.

Less than two hours later Saul was back at his desk in his office on the top floor. He had done what Gavi suggested and told the panel what they needed to know. It was up to them now and all he could do was wait for a decision. The Prime Minister had not returned due to other pressing commitments, but he would be brought up to speed as soon as possible and he would make the final decision.

Saul checked a few reports and filed some older items, all the while watching the clock and waiting for the phone in front of him to ring, relaying to him the decision whichever way it would go. He was expecting two calls. One to tell him they had located the compound and one to tell him the decision to carry out an armed strike on the compound had been given the go-ahead.

Of course, the strike couldn't take place until the location had been confirmed, but Saul was confident that they would accomplish this. Jennifer's description was good enough for the search to begin, they already had several likely possibilities, but they needed an exact match. They would narrow it down, eliminating the ones they were certain did not hold Qahtani and his men, and eventually they would find his lair. A drone flyover would then take place for final confirmation and they would be good to go. Provided the military agreed to it. This was the tricky part. Would they take the word of a woman who had dreamed the whole thing?

It sounded insane. It probably was insane. But if it saved lives, it was equally insane *not* to do it.

His thoughts were interrupted by a knock on the door. Without waiting for permission Gavi opened it and stuck his head through.

'It's more or less a go,' Gavi said. 'As soon as your people come through with the location. The PM will make his final decision then. But I think he will decide in our favour.'

Chapter 28.

Jennifer pushed herself upright on the sofa and looked around her. The only light came from the blue screen on the television, still tuned to a radio channel where soft music was playing. She fumbled for the remote and switched it off and the room was immediately plunged into darkness. She quickly turned the television on again to give light, got to her feet, took a step forward and almost tripped over the throw which had fallen to the floor in front of her. She muttered a curse and picked it up.

Her head was spinning and her vision was blurred. She could barely make out the empty bottle of wine on the coffee table.

She stumbled over to the light switch and turned on the recessed ceiling lights, using the dimmer to reduce them to a less painful glow.

I must have fallen asleep. Jennifer eyed the empty bottle and the glass beside it, drained of all but a mouthful of its contents. The second bottle, also empty, was on the floor beside the table. *Or passed out, more likely.*

It was late. Later than she thought it would be. There wasn't much else to do but crawl into bed and worry about her hangover in the morning. And the rest of her life. She had that to worry about too and for that she needed a clearer head. She switched the television off again, left some dry cat food in a bowl on the kitchen floor for the cats who were both asleep, gulped down a large glass of water and, using the wall to steady herself, made her way along the hall to her bedroom.

The bedroom door was shut. *That's odd. I always leave it open for Holly if she wants to sleep in there. Must have forgotten.*

The door wasn't locked. It had been closed tightly and now it was sticking. Maybe because, with no heating on for a couple of days, the rain and the dampness had swollen the wood. Jennifer cautiously turned the handle and, with a gentle shove, opened the door. The bedside light was switched on and Ilan was sitting on the edge of the bed, bathed in the warm glow of the small lamp.

He stood up and smiled at her as she stepped into the room. 'What have you done with your hair?'

'What?' His question stopped Jennifer in her tracks.

'You've got a few copper highlights. They suit you. I love them.'

'My hair? Fuck, I don't know. Who cares about my hair? I thought you were dead.'

Ilan smiled and opened his arms to her. 'As you can see, I'm not dead Jennifer.'

'I don't believe it. You're a ghost just like Lucy. Or I'm hallucinating, or something.'

Ilan caught her wrist gently and pulled her towards him, his eyes never leaving her face. Afraid, Jennifer tried to pull away but he held her tightly. She flinched as his hand gently touched her face and his fingertips traced a line from her ear along her jawline to her mouth.

'Am I dreaming?' Jennifer whispered. Her lips moved against his fingertip.

'Yes.'

'Then you are dead. This is just a dream.' A sob escaped her.

'It is a dream, neshama, but I am still alive. You know that. You know it in your heart even though your mind has told you otherwise.'

Jennifer closed her eyes and leaned her head against his chest, feeling her husband's arms tighten around her. She bathed in the warmth of his body against hers as she listened to the steady, reassuring beat of his heart against her cheek. If this were only a dream then she wanted to stay asleep forever.

But it's impossible to stay asleep forever, unless you're dead or in a coma. Even in a coma there's always the possibility you'll waken up again. The reality is that dreams never last.

Jennifer sighed and pulled away slightly from Ilan. She looked into his eyes, taking another moment before she burst her bubble forever, then she pushed herself out of his arms. Ilan frowned and reached again for her hand but she angrily snatched it away.

'Don't lie to me. I saw you get shot,' Jennifer told him as she stood up and stepped away from him. She shivered and grabbed a throw from the nearby chair and pulled it around her shoulders. The warmth of it hugged her as she folded herself into it. 'You had been beaten badly and they dragged you in front of a crowd of men. They had guns and you couldn't stand up so two of them had to hold you up. You were a mess, covered in blood and barely conscious. Two other men were standing there watching you and they were talking. About you, I presume. And then suddenly one of them…'

Jennifer stopped and stared at her husband. Her eyes filled with tears. 'One of them pulled out a gun and shot you. You were dead. You are dead.'

She began to cry. Hot, angry tears as she screamed at him over and over again. 'You're dead. You're dead. You're dead.'

'Jennifer that was not me,' Ilan said. He got to his feet, held out his arms and reached for her but she let the throw fall to the floor to the ground and she slapped him hard on the face, her palm striking his cheek. Shocked, he stepped back. He rubbed his face and shook his head in denial.

'I don't believe you. I saw it.' Jennifer cried, almost hysterical now. 'I saw that man, *that monster*, shoot you.'

Almost as agitated as Jennifer now, Ilan turned away from her and paced the room, unable to look her in the face. Stepping away from her seemed to do the trick for, although she was still crying, a combination of shock and grief and anger had quietened Jennifer. He walked over to the bed and sat down on the edge, patted the space beside him, and invited her to sit down with him.

'Jennifer, please,' he said. 'Come and sit down and I

will explain.'

Jennifer stood still, rooted to the spot, her arms folded defensively in front of her. Her eyes were red from crying and her face was a mask of anger.

Ilan patted the bed again, once more inviting her to join him. 'Let me explain, please.'

'What is there to explain?' she said. 'I saw you getting shot. I saw you die.'

'It wasn't me,' Ilan told her, almost reluctantly.

She snorted derisively. 'Who was it then?'

'His name was Eitan,' Ilan sighed. 'He lived in Tel Aviv, just a few blocks from our house. He had a wife and three children and he was a good friend and colleague. Motorcycles and camping and horses were his greatest passions. Shoshana – that's his wife – hated camping but she put up with it for his sake, and because the kids loved it.'

'I remember how she would complain about it,' he smiled at the memory. 'But she told me that if it made him happy and helped him relax, she was quite prepared to spend her weekends camping for the rest of her life. He was the worst chess player I have ever met, and in his spare time he was a football coach at a nearby school. He was the prisoner you thought was me. I was the man you saw shoot him.'

'I don't understand,' Jennifer said. She remained where she was but her posture had relaxed slightly. She wiped her eyes with her hand and sniffled. Ilan looked around for a tissue but couldn't find one and Jennifer wiped her nose on her sleeve.

'He was my contact on this operation. I couldn't use a cell phone in case it was discovered so he was nearby and we had a dead drop where I could pass information to Saul. But something must have happened before we moved to the new location and Eitan must have been compromised in some way and he was captured. It could have as easily been me but it wasn't. I got lucky. Sayeed was spooked enough to move location earlier than we anticipated and I had no choice but to go with him as we needed the intel on his new location as well as what he was planning. I didn't know that they had captured Eitan and brought him along.'

'How could you just shoot him like that?'

'Jennifer, I had no choice.'

'Why not?'

'He was barely alive. He had been tortured and his wounds were beyond critical. They were not survivable. Sayeed told me he hadn't broken – hadn't told them anything. I know Eitan and he would have held out as long as he could. Sayeed was going to allow the guards to continue beating and torturing him for their... sport. That is how evil Sayeed is. When I looked at Eitan, he was begging me to let him go. Begging me to release him from his suffering.'

'And you shot him? Like he was an injured animal at the side of the road?'

'Yes… He was my friend… and I shot him like an injured animal. I had to. To put him out of the pain he was suffering from and because there was a risk he would eventually talk. I had no choice.'

Jennifer swore softly as she remembered what she had seen in her dream and tried to imagine Ilan's state of mind when he could simply pull out a gun and shoot dead someone that he called a friend. She looked at him – this stranger disguised as her husband.

How can he be a stranger? I know who he is. I know what he is. He's a spy. A spook. A Mossad officer. Of course, he has killed people. It's a part of his job. But he killed his friend and colleague. Shot him in cold blood. But he was dying anyway, wasn't he? I'm married to a killer. No. You're married to a good man who had to do a terrible deed. Think of how he felt when he pulled that trigger. Yeah, I'm trying to.

Jennifer's thoughts were in turmoil. They zig-zagged back and forward from acceptance that her husband could carry out this act, to denial of his words and back to acceptance again. She sat down on the bed beside Ilan. Close, but not touching. She kept her head down, unable to look at him but she reached for his hand and he gave it willingly. She laced her fingers through his.

'I thought you were dead,' Jennifer told him. 'Everyone thinks you are dead. I told Saul what I had seen in my dream and now they all think you are dead. Even Nurit. She is heartbroken.'

Ilan breathed in sharply and Jennifer looked at him.

'It's okay,' he said.

'It is not okay. I have to tell them you are still alive. That's what all of this was about. Finding you. Wasn't it?'

'Not exactly,' Ilan said as he let go of her hand and shuffled up to the head of the bed. He swung his legs up and lay down. He looked at her as he stretched out and waited for her reaction. Would she lie down beside him?

'What do you mean – not exactly?' Jennifer frowned at him and remained where she was.

Ilan took a long while to answer. His response when he did finally speak, chilled her to the bone.

'They wanted you to complete the mission,' he said.

'I don't believe you,' Jennifer said. Denial was her best defence. Her only defence at the moment.

'Think about it, neshama,' Ilan reasoned. 'What did Saul ask you to do?'

'To help him find you, of course.'

'And each time you awakened from your dreams, did he ask you about me or did he ask you where you thought I was located?'

'He asked me about both,' Jennifer told him, a note of triumph in her voice.

'What else did he ask you?'

Jennifer puffed out her cheeks as she thought about it. The last few days had blurred already. The endless questions. The boredom when she was awake. The dreams when she was asleep. It was hard to tell which parts were real and which were elements of this dream, this nightmare, she was caught up in.

'He asked me lots of questions. I can't remember

everything but I do remember that he asked a lot about the village and the little courtyard. I had to look at satellite images to see if I could recognise it. I found a few that were similar but none that I could say was an exact match. And the man I saw when I thought you had been shot. Saul made me look at dozens and dozens of photographs until I picked him out. Oh, and he was very interested in the room I saw that looked like a laboratory.'

'You saw all of that in your dreams?' Ilan's eyes widened in amazement.

'Yeah,' Jennifer shrugged and picked at a thread on the bed cover. 'But all of that was so they could find out where you are and then they could go and rescue you.'

'Did Saul tell you that?'

She thought about it. 'Not in so many words. No. But surely that's what he meant.'

Ilan sighed. He rubbed his eyes wearily and sat upright on the bed. 'Saul is a good man and a good friend. Has been a good friend to me for many years. But for all the goodness in him he is, first and foremost, an officer. And he is an excellent manipulator. He is an expert at getting people to do what he wants and, at the same time, lead them to believe it was something they wanted. He used your love for me, manipulating it, and you, and you believed it was all about me. I am so sorry, Jennifer. Had I known he would do this I never would have told him.'

'Told him what?'

'About you. I told him about your experiences when you were in the coma after the accident. I never mentioned it again until about two years ago when you told me you thought you had been able to control what you were dreaming about a couple of times. I was having a beer with him one evening and he asked about you and if you were okay now. And I told him. I never thought any more of it. Never thought he would either.'

'For fuck's sake!' Jennifer's eyes narrowed as she glared at him. 'I didn't really *control* my dreams. I happened to be thinking about something before I went to bed and I ended up dreaming about it.'

'I know. I remember you telling me. And I am truly sorry for mentioning it to Saul because he seemed to believe that you could. Then when this operation came up, we knew that there was a possibility that I could be captured and killed, and he asked me if you could be brought on board to help if required. I told him it was out of the question. That I would never use you in this way but, like I said, Saul is an excellent manipulator and he convinced me you could, and would, do it. Maybe not for the greater good, but you would do it for me.'

'Oh, you bastard!' Jennifer hissed at him as she covered her face with her hands. 'I can't believe you let him do this to me. To us. How could you, Ilan?'

Without waiting for an answer, Jennifer jumped up, quickly turned towards the door and reached for the handle. As she began to open it, Ilan yelled at her to stop. He was up in a flash, off the bed and beside her in a second. He slammed the door shut, grabbed her by the arm and pulled her around to face him.

'No!'

'Let go of me,' Jennifer shouted as she struggled to break free and get through the door.

'Don't open the door,' he said as he held her tightly in his grip. 'Don't go through it. You will waken up. Stay here, Jennifer. Stay with me for a few minutes more.'

I have to get up and feed the cats. I really should get up. But it's too warm and cosy. I think I'll roll over and sleep for a while longer.

But the door beckoned to her.

'Let go of me, please, Ilan,' she said.

'Jennifer, listen to me. Saul had to use you. And I knew you would do this for me. There was a high probability that this mission was going to be a one-way trip for me. I knew that and I was prepared to die if necessary. But I don't want to die and, if I can avoid it, I will. You are my failsafe. You are the only one who can help me.'

Ilan continued in this manner. Whispering to her and cajoling her. He told her he loved her and wanted to be with her, repeating the words over and over again. He gathered her into his arms and held her tightly to him, ignoring her struggle as she tried to pull away from him.

Gradually, Jennifer seemed to give up her attempts to break free and her body relaxed against Ilan's. He refused to release her from his arms. Not yet. She could still turn and run through the door.

'You should have told me.' She admonished him, her voice muffled against the fabric of his shirt.

'I couldn't Jennifer.'

'Why not?'

'Because I could not be sure this would work. I could not give you hope if there was no hope.'

'It hasn't worked though, has it? You're still there and I'm alone in our bed dreaming all of this.'

'I need you to do one more thing for me, neshama. I need you to pass a message to Saul from me.'

'What kind of message?'

'Co-ordinates for the compound. I need you to memorise them and pass them to Saul. Tell him they are the exact location of the laboratory.'

'And what then? What will he do with them?'

'There will be a military strike,' Ilan said and a note of confession crept into his voice.

'No,' Jennifer said, shaking her head vehemently.

'No what?'

'I won't do it. Not if it's going to get you killed.'

'I need you to do this. For me.'

Jennifer took a deep breath. 'I want my life back and I want you back. For over eight months now I've been waiting for you to come home and every day I'm here in an empty house and this is not how I want my life to be. I want you back in my life. But if I pass these details, these co-ordinates, on to Saul then you *will* die. I won't do it. I will *not* be responsible for your death.'

'Many lives will be lost if they go ahead with their plans.'

'I'm sorry, and I know how awful this sounds, but I don't care.'

'Jennifer please. I will do my upmost to get away before the strike but I cannot guarantee it. If you refuse to do this then I will have to try something myself and that considerably lessens my chances.'

Jennifer considered what he had said. 'Do you promise me faithfully that you will try to escape?'

'Of course.'

'How will you know when the military will attack?'

'When you give Saul the co-ordinates, explain to him that he must time it to take place at three o'clock on Tuesday morning. Everyone, except the guards, will be asleep as they are leaving at nine that morning.'

'They can plan an attack that quickly and time it that precisely?'

'More or less.'

Jennifer placed her palms on Ilan's chest and pushed herself away, out of his embrace. She caught the wary hesitation in his eyes.

'It's okay. I'm not going to make a run for the door,' she told him.

She walked around the room and stopped to stare out of the window for a moment. Clouds hid the stars. Clouds that were heavy with impending rain. Already, Jennifer could see drops land on the windowpane and they trickled down the glass like tears. She folded her arms around her as she stared out into the darkness.

'How do I get the co-ordinates to Saul?' she asked.

'I will dictate them to you and you will memorise them,' Ilan told her.

'What if I forget them when I wake up? Can't you write them down or something?'

Ilan laughed. And it was a genuine laugh, full of

humour. She missed that laugh, even if, this time, it was directed at her.

'Do you think you will waken up clutching a piece of paper, my love? I'm sorry but it doesn't work that way.'

'That is some ask. Expecting me to remember co-ordinates!'

'You may be useless at maths but I have never met anyone who can remember numbers the way you do. Most people struggle to remember their pin numbers but –'

'I even know yours,' Jennifer told him.

'I will keep that in mind next time I check my bank statements,' Ilan jokingly warned her. 'But you can rattle off the whole account number so I don't think you will have difficulty with these numbers.'

'Yeah. But under these circumstances?' Jennifer held out her hands, not at all confident she could do what he was asking of her.

'You have nothing to lose,' Ilan told her.

Not true. I have everything to lose.

'Okay. I'll try. What are the numbers?'

Ilan recited the co-ordinates he needed her to remember and Jennifer repeated them several times at Ilan's insistence until he was sure she had correctly memorised them and would be able to forward them to Saul when she awakened in the morning.

'Just promise me you'll get away before they attack,' she pleaded.

'I will do my best,' he told her. His arms went around her and he pulled her close to him. Jennifer leaned her head on his shoulder.

'Where will you go?'

'I'll make my way to a spot approximately one kilometre to the east. Tell Saul that, and if I'm not picked up there then I'll find my own way back.'

'In the dark? At night? In a hostile country? You won't stand a chance, Ilan.'

'I know the terrain well. I can make it to the border and

from there home. Or if it's absolutely necessary, I can cross over into Jordan.' He did not tell her that it was unlikely he would get that far and that capture was not an option. 'Don't worry.'

'That is something I won't ever be able to do,' Jennifer sighed.

'Repeat the numbers again,' Ilan said and she did so. Rhyming them off perfectly, proud of herself for being able to do so. But remembering them when she spoke to Saul would be the real test.

'Once more.'

'I've got them, Ilan.'

'Just once more, please.'

Jennifer repeated them twice more until he was satisfied. Ilan glanced at his watch, put his arm around her and once again gathered her into his embrace. He held her tightly, reluctant to let her go, and Jennifer could sense the tension in him. She wanted to ask him what was wrong – apart from the fact that he was stuck in Syria, in a terrorist compound, and had killed a friend and colleague – but she was afraid of the answer he would give her.

His arms released her and he stood up. He caught her hand and pulled her to her feet. He tilted her chin up and kissed her gently on the lips.

This is a goodbye kiss. You're not going to make it. You're going to die.

Her tears began to fall again and they splashed onto his hand. Ilan put his forehead to hers.

'I love you,' he whispered.

'I love you, too.'

'You have to go now, neshama. You have to walk through that door and waken up.'

'I don't want to.'

'I know. I don't want you to go but you have to.' He pushed her gently away.

Jennifer nodded slowly as she reached for the door handle. One last look back then she opened the door and walked out of their bedroom.

Jennifer pushed herself upright on the sofa and looked around her. The only light came from the blue screen on the television, still tuned to a radio channel which played soft music. She fumbled for the remote and switched it off. With the curtains still closed, the room was plunged into darkness. Turning it on again quickly, she got to her feet, took a step forward and almost tripped over the throw which had fallen to the floor in front of her. She muttered a curse and picked it up.

Her head was spinning and her vision was blurred. She could barely make out the empty bottle of wine on the coffee table.

She found her way to the light switch and turned on the recessed ceiling lights, using the dimmer to reduce them to a less painful glow.

How did I end up here? I could have sworn that I got up and went into the bedroom. I must have just nodded off right here on the sofa. Jennifer eyed the empty bottle and the glass beside it, drained of all but a mouthful of its contents. The second bottle, also empty, was on the floor beside the table. *Or passed out, more likely.*

She checked her watch. It was early in the morning and not daylight yet. Her head was aching and her mouth was as dry as sandpaper. She stumbled, barefoot, to the kitchen as the cats weaved in and out of her legs and threatened to trip her up. Jennifer shooed them out of her way and quickly fed them, holding her breath against the smell of the wet cat food. *Please don't let me throw up. All that wine I drank last night is going to taste horrible coming back up again.*

The cats fed, Jennifer poured a large glass of cold water and drank all of it down. It helped. A little. She switched on the coffee machine and popped two slices of bread into the toaster.

As she waited for the toaster, memories of her dream

came back to her. But they were foggy. The hangover she was suffering from saw to that. Something about getting highlights in her hair, which she had been considering for a while now, and something about Ilan and how he wanted to tell her something important. She couldn't remember anything more.

Then she remembered that he was dead and a sob escaped her. Ilan was dead. *Maybe I'll dream of him every night now?*

The toast popped up, interrupting her thoughts. With a sigh, Jennifer placed the two slices onto a plate, smeared butter on them, got a packet of paracetamol out of the cupboard and poured a mug of strong coffee. But she had no appetite for even the coffee. The toast went into the bin underneath the sink, the coffee down the sink and the paracetamol back in the cupboard.

Chapter 29.

In his undercover persona as the terrorist named Jamal, Ilan Ben-Levi knew that the end was approaching and he was consumed with doubts that his hare-brained plan had any chance of succeeding. Even if it did, the likelihood of him surviving ranged from slim to zero. But he was alive now and he would do his utmost to remain that way and, at the same time, complete his mission. Although the two were not mutually exclusive.

As long as Jennifer relayed the message to Saul, that slim chance existed. He was confident Saul would believe her. When they were discussing the mission and Ilan had inadvertently suggested that Jennifer could dream his escape, he had meant it, not so much as a joke, but rather as an attempt to lighten the sombre mood after Saul told him it would most likely be a one-way mission. But Saul had leapt on the idea immediately and had even begun talking about what they would need to do and who he would need to get in order to make it happen.

Ilan refused to even contemplate involving Jennifer, and told Saul in no uncertain terms that his wife would *not* be a part of this. He even threatened to quit the service. But once the idea had been planted in Saul's mind there was nothing Ilan could do to stop him. He knew he had put his foot in it and he knew that Jennifer would kill him if she ever found out, but Saul – like a dog with a bone – refused to relinquish the idea. In the end, faced with Saul's expert manipulation skills, Ilan had no choice and he reluctantly agreed to allow Saul to bring her on board should she be required. He just prayed that, if he *did* survive this, Jennifer never found out that it was his fault she was involved.

Saul had been much more enthusiastic about the project than Ilan was. Of course, Saul didn't have as much invested as he did, his wife's mental health and well-being for one thing, and his own life, and he suspected the older man saw this as a chance to reboot his career. If it was successful, and there was still no certainty that it would be, he suspected Saul imagined himself as the new head of the newly-formed, top secret Remote Viewing Department, or whatever they would eventually decide to name it. Saul would see it as a golden opportunity to stave off retirement for a few more years.

It had been Saul who had persuaded him to return to operational missions after nearly three years behind a desk. Always good at reading people, Saul had known he was bored and itching to get back into the field again, despite his promise to Jennifer that he would stick to coming home every evening and not working weekends. Saul had known it was killing him inside. When Saul had dropped by his office and placed the file on his desk in front of him, Ilan made the decision to step away from his desk before he had even read it.

Do I regret it? Yes and no. I regret what I did to Jennifer. But the mission, provided it is successful, is more important. I can make it up to her when I come home. Maybe a holiday. Somewhere exotic perhaps? Or a cruise? Anywhere as long as she can relax and we can catch up again.

Ilan conjured up an image of his wife as he lay on his cot. Shortly, he would arise and join the others in morning prayers, his pretence of being a good, devout Muslim still a necessity. Even more so at this late stage in the game. But right now, it was early and he could afford a few moments escape by thinking about her.

He imagined her up and about. She was an early riser. Anything after seven o'clock was a lie in, and reserved for a rainy day or a bad hangover. Normally, by now, she would still be in her dressing gown, feeding the cats and waiting for the coffee to brew. But this morning she would have wakened from her dream, relieved and happy in the belief that he would be coming home to her very soon. She would shortly be in Headquarters, relaying the good news to Saul and she would give him the co-ordinates he had made her memorise.

How does she do that? She is terrible at maths – her talents lie more in design and art – but her memory for numbers is phenomenal. Oh, I miss you darling. So much more than you will ever know. I hope this works but I have no way of knowing because I hardly ever remember my dreams. Did you come to me in my sleep and did I tell you where they could find me when they have ended this?

Doubt began to set in. What if? *No. Don't think that way!*

No matter how hard he tried, Ilan couldn't shake off the feeling that this fanciful idea that he and Saul had concocted would come to nothing. Jennifer's dreams had been the result of a brain injury. What were the chances they could recreate a similar scenario to the state she was in just after the accident? Not a medically induced coma of course, as Saul had promised to investigate other avenues. Hypnotherapy being his preferred choice, and he had told Ilan that he already had someone in mind to work with them.

Yet, it all came down to Jennifer being able to control her mind and her dreams. Ilan suspected she would. She was a strong woman. Determined in so many ways. And a perfectionist. *And she loves me. She would make sure she could do it. For me.*

But Ilan still had no way of knowing if the scheme had worked. For all he knew, Jennifer could have refused to participate. Or she had embraced it wholeheartedly, only to have it fail. Or it had worked perfectly, and right now she was relaying the details and the all-important co-ordinates to Saul. He did not know.

He needed a back-up plan. Some way of destroying the compound if there was no air strike. *But what? What could one man armed with only a handgun do against so many? Nothing. Nothing of consequence. I could take out a few before they gun me down or capture me, but what would that achieve?*

Gunned down or alive but captured, Ilan knew they would finish him off and go ahead with their plans. Nothing would change other than the fact that he would be dead, and the lives of many thousands of innocent civilians would be lost. In the most horrible and painful way imaginable.

Ilan wracked his brain for some sort of idea. Some plan of action. If only he had explosives. But, despite his frequent covert searches, he had found none. Was there any other option? The guards? Could he win a few of them over? Doubtful. They were all as fanatical and devoted to the cause as Sayeed. He considered the ones he knew. The few he had more than a passing acquaintance with. None of them could be considered amenable to a change of ideology. Not even his cigarette-smoking buddy, Ali. He had seen the gleam in Ali's eyes when they had spoken a few words over a smoke. No, Ali was as fanatical as the rest of them.

The best idea Ilan could think of was to break into the lab and smash as much as he could before they caught him. Again, this option meant certain death, from exposure to the virus if not from a gunshot. But even this was not enough. It was the best he could do and he would attempt it tonight if the airstrike did not happen.

The call for morning prayers came and he rose to his feet, resigned to the idea that he would put this plan into action if nothing else came to mind. He forced all thoughts of Jennifer and home out of his mind as he prepared for another day in the skin of Jamal the terrorist.

Chapter 30.

Saul Mueller paced the confines of his office while he waited. He rubbed his face with his hands in a vain attempt to ward off the exhaustion and the sense of despair that washed over him. His palms brushed the stubble and realised he hadn't had a shave in, how long? Since all this began by the feel of it. That was fine for a day or two spent at home, his wife ordering him to do some gardening, but it was not how he liked to appear at work.

The euphoria from yesterday was all but gone. So far Qahtani's compound had not been located and there were more than a few people who were beginning to doubt, not only Jennifer's description, but if it even existed. They didn't say this aloud, not to his face, but he could see it in their eyes. Sympathy mixed with a 'it was a fucking crazy idea' roll of the eyes that he deliberately ignored as he kept up the appearance of quiet confidence that only he knew was beginning to fail him. Could he have been wrong? Could Jennifer have simply dreamed something that was not connected, or at least connected only by a slender thread, to Ilan's whereabouts? He didn't think so. Jennifer had repeated the phrase they had concocted – that casual comment about the two of them packing in the job and going fishing. How could she have known that if Ilan hadn't whispered it to her?

Maybe we should have done that, Ilan. Maybe you and I should be sipping beer beside a riverbank somewhere and wondering if we were ever going to catch anything? And not caring if we didn't because it's the beer and the comradeship and sitting by the water that makes fishing such a great pastime.

And there it was again. That thing that made him close his eyes in grief. It was always there underneath all the stress and worry, and the doubt. It was that hot seam of molten lava that bubbled and spurted up to the surface in a torturous reminder that a good man was dead. And there had been no contact from Eitan Katz whatsoever, so it was more than likely he was also dead. Ilan had been an old, dear friend and Eitan had his whole life in front of him. Both good agents. Both were a loss that would be hard, if not impossible, to replace.

There would be memorial services for both men in the next few weeks. Quiet and dignified with only service personnel and immediate family members present. The public would never know what had been lost. And after that life would go on. But if Qahtani was not stopped, then both Ilan's and Eitan's deaths would be meaningless. And many deaths would follow.

Saul stopped pacing and sat down in front of his desk. He picked up the phone and dialled an extension.

'Anything yet?' he demanded as soon as it was answered.

The person on the other end of the phone told him there was nothing and Saul's shoulders slumped in despair. They were close, but not close enough.

Tempting though it was to crawl back into bed and spend her hangover beneath the comforting warmth and darkness of the duvet, Jennifer hesitated. There was something she was supposed to remember that kept niggling at her as she stumbled and suffered through her morning.

This was possibly the worst hangover she had woken up to in a long, long while. The two bottles of wine she downed last evening were on the kitchen counter where, like two stern teetotal old ladies, they sat there and judged her. They frowned and tut-tutted and told her, in no uncertain terms, that she should have more sense at her age. Jennifer refused to listen to them any longer and she grabbed them up and took them out to the garage where they could cluck and complain all they wanted from the inside of the recycling bin.

Maybe if I eat something, I'll feel a bit better.

She placed the pan on top of the cooker and lifted a carton of eggs out of the fridge, with the intention of making an omelette, but the thought of actually eating it sent her flying to the bathroom where she threw up in the toilet.

She flushed the remains of her liquid supper from the night before away and leaned against the wash-hand basin to steady herself while she splashed cold water on her face. Jennifer glanced at her reflection in the bathroom mirror. Her face was pale and dark circles smudged the skin around her eyes. Her ash-blonde hair looked washed out against the paleness of her skin and she remembered a fragment of a dream in which Ilan had commented on the copper highlights in her hair. *What a weird thing to dream? Wish I could remember the rest of it.*

Her nausea had abated for now and her empty stomach rumbled with hunger. She walked slowly back into the kitchen where she whisked the eggs, poured them into the pan, put a slice of bread in the toaster and held her breath as she cooked them. So far, so good. But eating the omelette would be the real test.

Still in his office on the top floor, Saul checked his watch. It would be lunchtime soon and his stomach rumbled at the thought. But he was too nervous, too uptight, to eat anything. The worst part was not the waiting but not being in control. All he could do was sit at his desk and wait. Or pace and wait. Or stand there and wait. His hand reached for the phone again. Maybe if he asked again, the answer this time would be the answer he wanted to hear. His hand hovered over the phone. Near the phone. His fingers twitching to pick it up and dial the extension again. Then it dropped to the desk, his fingers splayed across the hard surface. He checked his watch again and continued to wait.

Jennifer swallowed the last piece of egg and toast and waited. Would it stay down? Or would she have to make another dash for the bathroom? A minute passed. Then another. And another. So far, so good.

Gingerly, she stood up. No nausea. That was good. That was brilliant. *Maybe I'll survive.*

She poured a glass of water and took a blister strip of paracetamol tablets from the cupboard above the counter near the fridge.

Jennifer quickly swallowed two of the tablets along with half a glass of water and hoped they would kick in soon. *Please let them kick in soon. And please don't let me throw up again.*

Back in her comfortable spot on the sofa, Jennifer pulled the throw around her and stared at the television screen, not caring that it was switched off. Her husband was dead. There was no reason to care anymore. She tucked her legs under her, and stared at the blank screen. She tried to remember what it was she knew she was supposed to remember.

Hunger finally lured Saul out of the office. Down the five floors to the canteen where he waited in line for the coffee and the sandwich, he knew was all he would be able to eat. He acknowledged anyone who spoke to him with only a gruff nod as he put a lid on the coffee container and, instead of finding a quiet table and taking his time over his meagre lunch choice, he hurried back upstairs. He could hear his office phone ringing as he approached the door. Hope flared in his heart as he dashed into the office and set the sandwich and coffee down onto his desk, almost knocking the Styrofoam cup over. He steadied the cup and grabbed the receiver.

'Ken?'

Saul closed his eyes and rubbed the space between them as he listened to the forensic accountant giving his verbal synopsis. It was unconnected to Ilan's operation, but it was important and it demanded his full attention. It was something that, at least for a while, would take his mind off the search. The search that was going nowhere. He politely thanked the caller and asked for the report to be emailed to him immediately and hung up.

While he waited, he opened another folder on his laptop. It was an operation that was still in the planning stage but one that was already showing great potential. The only difficulty was that it would take place on American soil. The Americans weren't keen on others playing in their toybox. They could, of course, bring in the US authorities but it would be preferable not to. Fine, if it was successful – no one would ever know. A political and diplomatic disaster if it failed.

Saul added a few notes to the report, then opened another one but his concentration kept lapsing and his thoughts returned to the search in Syria.

Jennifer leaned forward on the sofa and held her head in her hands. *What's wrong with me? Why am I sitting here nursing my hangover and not crying over him? His presence is all around me. His clothes are hanging in the wardrobe. I can see his favourite books and DVD's mixed with mine on the bookshelf. His car is in the driveway. Oh, wait, it isn't. It's parked in the carpark at Headquarters. I suppose I'll have to go and get it back somehow. But all his other stuff is here. Everything of his is all around me. Everything that's him is here. Well, almost everything. The part of him that took him away from me isn't here. It was never here because it was never a part of him and me.*

When do I start clearing out the wardrobe? Packing up his clothes for the charity shops? His books and DVD's too. They're not ones I'd read or watch. They can go. For fuck's sake! What's wrong with me? Why am I not sitting here bawling my eyes out? Why do I feel nothing? No grief. No sense of losing him. Shouldn't I be broken with grief? He's only been dead a day and a... wait a minute. Was he dead?

Jennifer sat up straight on the sofa and frowned. *Where did that thought come from?*

She shook herself and stood up. Folded the throw and placed it over the back of the sofa. Plumped up the flattened cushions, fed the cats and left some out for the feral cats waiting in the garden and then she paced.

She paced the floor from one end of the living room through to the kitchen and back. Then down the hall to the bedrooms and bathroom and back again. She walked the length of the house – north to south and east to west. It was not a massive house. Too big for two people but probably cramped for a family of four. They had found it together by chance one day when they were out for a drive and had fallen in love with it. Maybe not as much as they loved the house in Cyprus, but it was close. That house had been the one they bought back when their relationship had been all new and shiny. Jennifer smiled as she remembered the good times they shared in that house. The sex had been awesome. It had been frequent and fun.

It didn't end when they moved to Israel and bought this house. But it did change. Maybe they were older and more sensible now, and less inclined to risk getting arrested by making love under the patio lights where the neighbours could watch and learn. Or watch and phone the police. Maybe it was the circumstances. Having to flee the home you had made together and move to another country and look for another house because you needed one definitely made a difference.

Their relationship was softer. More loving. Less sex for the fun of it. Though they still did that. In the shower. On the sofa. On the rug in the darkness with only soft music and candles for company.

Jennifer laughed aloud, remembering one occasion when Possum climbed up on top of Ilan's naked back and settled down for a snooze while he was on top of her.

Obviously, I haven't had sex since before he went away. Over eight months. Why am I thinking about some of our best moments now? Is that a stage of the grief process? Remembering the good times? Surely that should come later?

So why am I not going through all the other stages? I feel like I've shut down. Like I'm hibernating for the winter, maybe. Oh, I sound like a wildlife documentary. Yeah, grieving is a bit like hibernating. I'll shut down. Lose my capability to feel anything. Unless I meet someone else. If that ever happens. Or is this just me quietly acknowledging the fact that he's dead and I'll never feel his arms around me again? Or see his smile and hear his laughter? Or feel him inside me again?

Or is he dead?

What is it with this voice in my head? Questioning me? Asking me if he really is dead? Making me think back to all the good times? Is this normal? Is this what one is supposed to do when their spouse dies? Or is it something else?

Jennifer's frantic pacing around the house lead her once more to the bedroom that she had shared for so long with Ilan. She pushed open the door and walked in. As she stood there in front of the bed, she frowned and narrowed her eyes. It was almost as if she could see him sitting there, waiting for her.

All these thoughts of sex and already I'm imagining him sitting on the bed waiting for me to climb in beside him so he can screw my brains out.

And then it hit her. The dream she had last night came back to her in a fragmented rush of emotions and images.

But she couldn't remember all of it. There was still something important that she couldn't remember. I don't know what it is. I don't know. I don't know. Then you need to figure it out. But how? These are your thoughts. Why are you asking me? Because you are my thoughts, you idiot. Oh, right. Sorry. Now, can we get on with this? Sorry, I don't know the answer.

Jennifer stopped pacing. Her headache was almost gone

and she no longer felt she was going to throw up. She filled a large tumbler with water, lifted the stack of mail from the counter, went out to the terrace where she sat down and watched the afternoon unfold. The rain had cleared and, although it was cool enough for a sweater, the sun was shining and the sky was almost an unbroken blue. Except for a few white clouds on the horizon that, for a moment, reminded her of her dream of the day at the café with Lucy and how they had talked about the dreams they were exchanging. What she had been doing with the Mossad was basically the same thing, but it had moved on considerably from what she had experienced with Lucy while in the coma.

She sighed. It had been such a great idea, Saul was correct about that, but it had come to nothing.

From behind her sunglasses, Jennifer gazed out over her garden and, beyond the wall that enclosed the property, at the streets in this quiet suburb of Tel Aviv. It was indeed shaping into a lovely afternoon, which was ironic because this was the worst day of Jennifer's life. Yet she felt okay apart from the remnants of her hangover and a stiffness in her neck – from the position she was in when she fell asleep on the sofa. She felt almost, but not quite, happy. *It probably just hasn't hit me yet.*

Jennifer ran her fingers through her short hair, remembering again Ilan's remark in her dream about copper highlights. It had been something she was considering but he never knew that. She'd only thought about it a couple of months or so after he left. And it was only a passing thought.

Strange. Downright weird even.

Jennifer placed her feet up on the table, tilted the chair back and began to sort through the pile of mail. The junk mail and advertising flyers went to one side to be dumped in the recycling bin later and she opened the first of the remaining three envelopes. It was a new credit card she had applied for.

Great. Another number to memorise.

'Fuck!' Jennifer's feet dropped to the ground and the

chair slammed forward onto all four legs again as it all came rushing back to her, so quickly it was almost overwhelming.

Chapter 31.

Saul picked up the phone and dialled the operations room number.

'Anything?' he asked when it was answered.

'Nothing yet sir,' came the reply.

He hung up the phone and went back to his paperwork.

Jennifer sat rooted to the spot at the small patio table as she remembered her dream of finding Ilan in their bedroom and how he had explained that what she had seen in her dream of the compound she has misinterpreted. She had cried and refused to believe he was still alive and then her shock when he had told her he had been the man holding the gun and shooting the prisoner whose name was… what? She couldn't remember his name but he had been a friend of Ilan's and Ilan had killed him. Put him out of his misery. She shuddered at the memory.

And then when he finally managed to convince her he was still alive, Ilan told her what he wanted her to do.

The numbers! The bloody numbers he made me memorise!

She leapt to her feet and ignored the unopened envelopes that had spilled to the ground. She hurried into back into the house and grabbed a pen and a notepad.

'Now what?' She spoke aloud as she looked at the numbers she had written down. To the best of her knowledge, they were the correct numbers – the ones Ilan had made her repeat over and over, again and again. Normally, she didn't doubt her ability to recall card numbers and phone numbers, even car registration numbers, but with so much at stake were these ones correct?

They have to be. They're exactly what Ilan told me. I think. Oh, please let them be correct. I need to tell Saul. I need to tell him where Ilan will be. What if they've already located it? What if they are already attacking it? And they're blowing it up right now? Ilan won't stand a chance.

She picked up her phone to dial the number. But this was one she didn't know and, obviously, it wasn't in her list of contacts. She could call Nurit. No, she couldn't contact Nurit and get her hopes up. She dialled Reuben's number.

But Reuben wasn't answering his phone. She dialled again, then again, but to no avail. Jennifer set the phone down and pressed her hands against the table, willing herself to calm down. There must be some way she could get in touch with Saul. She just had to calm down and think. She closed her eyes.

I can't drive there, I'm probably still well over the limit. I could take the chance, though. What are the odds? But then if I'm stopped and breathalysed and I explained where I was going. Yeah, that'll work. They'll just think I'm nuts as well as half-drunk. What about Talia? No. Talia might still have her old car and a driving licence that might or might not still be valid but she hardly ever drives now. I can't even remember seeing her on anything other than her bicycle. Who else? Think, Jennifer. Think.

Then the obvious solution dawned on her and she grabbed her bag, stuffed her phone and the piece of notepaper into it and wasted a few precious moments looking for her house keys.

A fragile seed of hope took root in Saul's heart when his phone rang. He held his breath as he answered and his heart thumped in his chest.

'There is someone in the lobby to see you, sir,' the voice told him.

Saul groaned inwardly, closed his eyes and massaged his brow as his hopes were dashed once more. 'I already told you I am not seeing anyone today. For any reason,' he barked.

'I'm sorry sir, but this woman is very insistent. She spilled out of a taxi outside the front gates and she claims she has important information in relation to an operation you are running. She mentioned you by name and she said that she is going nowhere until she speaks to you and only you. To be honest sir, I think she's slightly drunk. I can smell alcohol on her breath and she's a complete mess. Crying and yelling at me to let her in. Insisting she needs to talk to you urgently. Of course, she could be just some crazy in off the street. You'd be surprised how many of those we –'

'What is her name?' Saul demanded.

'She says it's Jennifer Ben-Levi, and she claims that you and she worked together recently.' The security guard snorted derisively at the notion of the drunken, dishevelled woman standing beside him working with Saul Mueller.

Saul remained silent as he mulled over his options. The most sensible thing to do would be to have her escorted from the building with a stern warning that she would be arrested and charged if she showed up again. Although the Jennifer he had come to know these past few days probably wouldn't take no for an answer. She was more likely to chain herself to the railings than leave peacefully.

'Have her escorted up to my office,' he said.

Saul opened the door and stood back, shocked by the sight of the woman who came crashing into his office. He barely recognised her with the wild look in her eyes and the expression on her face – glee mixed with panic. She looked as though she had slept in her clothes and her whole body jittered and jumped with nervous energy.

'I know where it is.' Jennifer told him. 'I know where the compound is. Where Ilan is.'

The words spilled out of her in a breathless rush. He could smell the stale wine mixed with minty toothpaste and possibly a hint of vomit.

He reached out to take her arm, to guide her to the chair until he could call security back, but she slapped it away.

'I have the co-ordinates for the… for the compound,' she said as she brandished a page torn from a small notepad in front of him. 'I have them written down on this. Because I remembered. You see, I had another dream. And Ilan is alive and he's here. I mean there. And he wants you to... he needs you... he made me memorise them and he said... he said he liked the… the highlights in my hair. But he's never seen them because I don't have highlights in my hair. I was only thinking about getting my hair done,' Jennifer frowned in confusion as she momentarily lost her train of thought.

She stared at the floor as she concentrated then took a deep breath and looked at Saul, her eyes wide and pleading. 'And he said I was really good at remembering numbers so he made me remember them... he made me repeat them over and over again until I remembered them. But I forgot until now. I forgot he'd told me. I'm sorry. I woke up and I felt so bad that he was dead that I just forgot. Then when I got my new credit card and saw the numbers on it, I remembered. I just remembered now. Well, a while back. At the house. So, I came here. To tell you. And he told me… told me to tell you that this is where he is. And now you have to stop it. You can do it with these numbers. And you have to go and get him. You have to save him. Please.'

'Jennifer, I am so sorry.' Saul knew this was all his fault. The woman in front of him wasn't merely drunk. She was suffering from a mental breakdown brought on by what he had forced her to endure. That, and her grief at losing her husband. He had to help her.

'Why are you sorry?' Jennifer frowned. 'You should be happy.'

'Please sit down. Here, let me help you.' Saul took Jennifer's arm and attempted to guide her towards the chair but she shrugged his hand away and stared at him.

'I don't have time to sit down. I have to give you these numbers. You don't have time. You have to save him.'

'Calm down Jennifer. And sit down. Now.' His voice was stern and cut through her near-hysteria. 'I have to tell you something.'

Jennifer stepped back in surprise and looked at him. Confusion was written on her features, but she groped behind her for the chair and only just managed to sit down on it.

'I ... I don't understand,' she stammered. 'What?'

'Jennifer,' Saul kept his voice calm. 'You have been a great help to us. And I appreciate your hard work very much. We all do and we are heartbroken that the result wasn't the one we had hoped for. You did your best and we came very close. And I am so very sorry for your loss. Ilan was a great man and he commanded the respect of so many and his death grieves me deeply – he was a good friend to me over the years and I know how much he loved you. He once told me that meeting you and –'

'What the fuck are you talking about?' Jennifer said.

'I beg your pardon,' Saul blinked in surprise at her words.

'All this crap about how you're sorry for my loss and what a great man Ilan was. What are you talking about? You're making it sound as though he's dead.' Jennifer's eyes filled with angry tears.

My God. She's in complete denial. She's still convinced that Ilan is alive and we can rescue him. We can't even stop the terrorists, let alone find and retrieve him. But what if she really was wrong about his death and she was able to contact him in another dream? A natural dream wherein he gave her the co-ordinates to his location? Or is she so grief-stricken that her mind conjured this up as a defence mechanism? But if these are the co-ordinates likes she says, the very least I can do is check them against satellite imagery. If it gives us a credible, potential location then this changes everything.

Jennifer reached into her handbag and Saul's stomach clenched in fear.

She has a gun!

He only relaxed when she tucked the note she had been holding inside her bag, and produced a tissue. She dabbed at her eyes and blew her nose then put the tissue back in her bag.

'Give me the numbers and I can have them checked,' he said.

'No. I can't. Not yet.'

'Jennifer, please try and understand. We cannot locate the compound. We have been searching the satellite images and we cannot find any abandoned village with the courtyard you described. We… you have to understand, unless you give me the co-ordinates, I cannot locate the village.'

'Then you're not looking in the right places. I saw it, Saul. I walked through it in my dream.'

'I'm not doubting that, Jennifer. But maybe your memory played tricks on you. After all, you witnessed Ilan being shot and witnessing something like that could have distorted your memory. Maybe the courtyard, and now this latest dream, was a defence mechanism that your brain... your mind conjured up so it wouldn't have to deal with the death of your husband.'

'No. I saw it. And I saw the shooting. But it wasn't Ilan. It was the other guy.'

'What do you mean – the other guy?' Saul frowned.

'It was your other guy. The one who was helping Ilan. His contact. Or his back-up. I don't know. His name was... his name was... dammit, I can't remember. Ilan told me his name. But I can't remember. Why the hell did I drink so much?' Jennifer frowned as she rubbed her forehead and tried to concentrate. Tried to remember.

'Think Jennifer. Who was the other guy?' A seed of hope found its way into Saul's heart and threatened to take root and grow like a weed in the hard, rocky soil of disbelief. *Could it be possible?*

'Ilan told me he was a friend and they were working together. I'm sorry I can't remember his name.' Jennifer said. 'But it was Ilan who shot him.'

'What?'

'Ilan shot him. Ilan was the one with the long, grey hair and the gun. I couldn't see his face because his back was to me. But the prisoner. I read it all wrong. It's understandable, isn't it? He was beaten and covered in blood, and I couldn't make out his face so I just assumed it was Ilan. I'm sorry.

Ilan is still alive and that's why I dreamed about him last night.'

If she interpreted this incorrectly what else did she get wrong? The courtyard? Have we been searching all this time in completely the wrong place? The blood drained from Saul's face and his hands grew clammy at the implications. He reached for the desk and placed his hand on it to steady himself. His chest felt tight and beads of sweat formed on his brow.

'You're imagining things!' His voice was both fearful and accusatory. It was his turn to be in denial.

'Saul, I promise you I did dream this last night,' Jennifer said as she spread her arms wide, palms up, in a pleading gesture. 'Ilan told me what happened. And he told me to tell you where and when to attack. Why don't you believe me? You believed me when I was lying on that bed in the 'sleep room' hooked up to all those monitors and stuff. Why don't you believe me now?'

'I don't know,' he admitted.

'What can I say to make you believe me?'

'Tell me the name of the other Israeli. The one you claim Ilan killed.'

Jennifer screwed her eyes shut and rubbed the bridge of her nose. Her headache was coming back with a vengeance. She searched her memory for the name. It was on the tip of her tongue but she just couldn't recall it.

'Can I have a glass of water, please,' Jennifer said. 'Or maybe a coffee?'

Saul took a bottle of water from the small fridge in the corner of his office and handed it to Jennifer.

'Thank you.' Jennifer opened the bottle and took several mouthfuls and then set it down on the desk.

'His name, Jennifer?' Saul asked again.

'I'm trying.'

'What was his name?'

'I don't know. He was younger than Ilan and he was married with kids. Three, I think. Ilan said he liked motorcycles and… and… what was it? Oh yes, camping! He liked camping and his wife didn't, but she put up with it for him. His name was Evan. No, that's not it. Ethan! Yeah, I think that's what Ilan said. He was called Ethan, or something very close to that.'

'Eitan. His name was Eitan Katz. And yes, he had three children and loved camping.' Saul quietly corrected her. *And I know this because I take the time to become acquainted with my operatives before I send them to their potential deaths. And I do this because I need the guilt and the pain of loss to be real.*

'Do you believe me now?' Jennifer asked.

'Yes. I believe you, Jennifer.' Saul looked at her. *Yes, I do believe you but I'm not sure what good it is going to do.*

'Then you'll send a rescue mission to go and find Ilan?' Jennifer said. She smiled as she looked up at Saul. Her shoulders slumped in relief and the nervous tension that had built up since she awakened that morning flowed out of her body.

Saul could see the hope in her eyes and he hated to dash that hope but he had no other choice. He walked to the front of the desk and stood before her.

'It's not as simple as that Jennifer,' he told her. His voice was a gentle murmur laced with genuine sympathy.

'Why not?'

Saul closed his eyes and rubbed his forehead as he formulated an answer for the woman seated in front of him.

'As much as we prefer to bring our people home, and we always try our upmost to do so when we can, staging a rescue mission for Ilan is… impractical in the current situation. The threat that this group poses has to be our highest consideration and something we *must* deal with. You must understand that they have to be stopped. And I need those co-ordinates in order to do so.'

'Okay. I had a feeling you were going to say that,' Jennifer said as she opened her bag and took out the note once more. 'But you are going to do it my way, or not at all.'

She handed it to him.

The expression on Saul's face turned to rage as he found himself staring at a blank piece of paper.

Chapter 32.

Since early morning the compound had been a flurry of activity. People rushed from one end of the old village to the other as they packed up boxes and crates and left them ready to load into the trucks that would carry them and all their belongings away. By tomorrow they would be completely gone, and any trace, any evidence, they had ever been in this place would be gone along with them.

Like everyone around him, Ilan was on edge and charged with nervous energy. It coursed through his body, and made the hairs on his arms and the back of his neck stand up as he shivered with more than the cold. His breathing was shallow and he forced himself to take long, slow deep breaths to calm his racing pulse. He mimicked the wide eyes and nervous glances of those around him as he pretended to be one of them, and he kept his head down as much as possible. All the while he attempted to formulate some sort of back-up plan.

He had one gun. It might as well be a child's toy water pistol for all the use it was to him.

What he needed was explosives. He searched among the boxes and equipment as he packed but he found nothing he could use. Nothing he could secure away in his clothing.

He slipped away and searched through the abandoned houses and it was in a room, in a house that no one was using, that he found an old box containing ten hand grenades. They were old by the look of them. Maybe too old. But they were a gift from heaven. He lifted the box and searched for a more secure place to hide them. The building he was in had once been a home and, like most of the village, it had now fallen into disrepair, destroyed by time and the elements. The remnants of furniture – wardrobes, cabinets, and desks – lay scattered around but there was nowhere suitable for a hiding place. Ilan checked out the other rooms. The remains of a kitchen held a broken sink and an old oven and he placed the box inside the oven in the hope that no one would have reason to look inside. He would retrieve them later.

Once he had hidden the box of grenades, Ilan made his way outside to the trucks that still had to be packed up. Still on the lookout for anything that could be useful, he was rummaging through another crate when Sayeed called his name.

Frustration and fear made him angry and he almost snapped back a reply. He took a deep breath, set down the box he was holding and turned to face the leader of the terrorist group.

'What do you want, my brother?' The words almost stuck in his throat but Ilan was once more wearing his Jamal persona around him, like a well-fitting winter coat, and he could detect no suspicion or doubt in Sayeed's eyes. *But that doesn't mean it isn't there. Tread carefully. He would kill me in a heartbeat if he thought it necessary.*

'Walk with me, brother,' Sayeed indicated in the direction of the main building.

Jamal inclined his head and strode beside the other man as they walked past the troops – the workers and the heroes. Not one of them made eye contact with Sayeed and his right-hand man. Their fanaticism may have come from belief in their misguided cause but it was strengthened and nourished by a liberal dose of fear in the man who led them.

'You look worried,' Sayeed remarked as the two men walked back towards the village.

Jamal glanced quickly at Sayeed. He gave a slight shake of his head and his mouth twisted in a grimace. 'Worried, no. Concerned, yes.'

'Why?' Sayeed asked.

'There is so much that could go wrong. I know we have prepared as well as we could and everything is on track for tomorrow. But now... now it is out of our hands.'

'It is now in the hands of Allah. He will safeguard them as they complete His mission.'

'I know,' Jamal replied.

'Do you not have faith, my brother?' Sayeed's eyes

narrowed in suspicion.

I have faith in the ten hand grenades I found earlier. That may be enough to stop you if my other plan, the one that involves my wife, fails. And fuck you for doing this and making me drag her into it.

The grenades were all he had and if there was no airstrike, if Jennifer had failed him, he would use them.

She hasn't failed. I have to believe that. I have to have faith in her.

'Yes, I have faith,' Jamal told him. 'But not all our people will make it through.'

'That is true. It is unfortunate but throughout history there have always been casualties of war. This is no different. But as long as enough of them make the journey to Europe and North America we will win. Allah will win.'

Jamal nodded, unable to meet the other man's eyes. Afraid Sayeed would see the anger and the hatred in them.

'I do not enjoy this, my brother,' Sayeed said.

Oh, but you do.

Sayeed opened the door and led the way inside. Jamal followed him; his lips set as though in stone as he forced the anger down into his soul. *If I killed him now, would that be the end of it?*

Tempting though it was, Ilan knew killing the man in front of him would not stop the action. Like cutting off the head of the hydra, someone else would step up to complete the mission. Not him. Although he had inadvertently become the de facto second in command, there were others in Sayeed's tightly-knit inner circle who would fight each other like cats and dogs to the death in order to take his place and carry out the so-called Allah's Will attack. Killing Sayeed right now would, at best, delay it for a day.

Let it play out a while longer. If all else fails I have the grenades.

With his head held high, and still in the guise of Jamal, Ilan followed Sayeed into the room Sayeed used as his private office.

Two men – Sayeed's personal guards, dressed from head to toe in black – stood like statues in the room. They were armed with machine guns and their faces were covered. Only their eyes, unblinking and cold, were visible.

The furniture in the room had been rearranged and the far wall was now clear. Empty of everything save for a black sheet that had been pinned up from corner to corner. Although the sheet now hid the old, crumbling plaster from sight, this had not been done from a decorative point of view. Sayeed hadn't looked around and decided the place needed sprucing up. His motive didn't have that homely feel to it.

Arabic writing in white covered the top quarter of the sheet. It read 'Allah's Will Shall Prevail'.

Shit. He knows who I am. He's figured out I'm the second Israeli spy. Did Eitan talk? No. Probably not. Another source? Maybe, but not likely. How long has he known? The blood in Ilan's veins turned to ice as suspicion dawned on him as to what Sayeed was planning next. He had seen this kind of situation before. In videos, posted on the internet. In operational briefings. And on one occasion, one that still gave him flashbacks and occasional nightmares, he had seen it in person.

Witnessing a beheading, even via a video feed, was not for the faint-hearted. But to be there and see it in front of you was the worst horror imaginable. To see the terror in the eyes of the victim. To smell his fear and hear his pleas as he begged and whimpered for mercy. No one, not even the strongest, failed to beg and plead for his life at such a time. Some did it silently, only their lips moving as they whispered a frantic prayer. Others shouted and screamed. Everyone's last moments on this earth were as unique and individual as they themselves were. But their actions at the moment they faced their death, were not a judgement of their character or their bravery, or lack of bravery. Their actions were merely a manifestation of regret and sorrow and, very often, an uncompromising and futile denial that they were about to look death in the eye.

Ilan remembered all too well the beheadings he had witnessed and he now pictured himself kneeling in front of the camera. Would he beg? Scream? Fight helplessly for his life? *Or would I merely accept my fate and the regret that comes with it knowing my life is over? I am so sorry, Jennifer. I hope you can forgive me.*

'It will take a few minutes to get set up.'

Sayeed's voice cut into his thoughts and Ilan raised his eyebrows in confusion.

'I am going to record my video message to the world,' Sayeed answered the unspoken question.

Ilan glanced quickly around. The nearby table held a laptop, a bottle of water and a sheet of paper. The handwriting on it he recognised as Sayeed's. The words written on the paper he recognised as part of the notes he had seen earlier. The scribbles and corrections were gone now and, in their place, a neatly handwritten speech. Ilan wondered how many times Sayeed had rewritten it before he was satisfied.

The laptop was powered up and connected by cable to a small digital video camera mounted on a tripod. It was positioned in the middle of the room and facing the wall with the black sheet. On the screen there was a reproduction of the part of the room from the perspective of the camera. The cursor, as though waiting patiently, hovered over the 'record' icon.

Sayeed lifted the sheet of paper and quietly read it, memorising the salient points and nodding to himself as he did so. When he seemed confident that he would remember it all, he set the paper down on the table, picked up the water bottle, opened it and took a long drink. He declined to share. He wasn't that sort of man.

'I need you to click this icon once I am ready to begin,' Sayeed said.

Ilan fought the urge to moisten his dry lips with his tongue and nodded.

'I will indicate when I am ready,' Sayeed told him.

Ilan kept his face – the face of Jamal – impassive as he took up position on the other side of the small table, his hand poised over the laptop.

Sayeed took another drink of water, wiped the excess moisture from his lips and stepped in front of the camera. He scrunched his shoulders up and down a few times, as if to loosen them, and twisted his neck to ease his perceived tension. Ilan suspected from the slight smirk on the man's face that he was, in fact, relaxed and relishing the thought of what he was about to do. Not only the speech, but the action that would begin tomorrow morning.

Sayeed bowed his head and closed his eyes momentarily. When he opened them again, he held up his hand in a 'wait for it' gesture to Jamal. Then he pointed to the laptop, cleared his throat and indicated with a snap of his fingers that he was ready. Ilan clicked on the record icon and Sayeed, his eyes fixed on the camera in front of him, began to recite his speech. In English.

Initially he spoke about the history of the plague as a weapon of war from the fourteenth century until the second world war. It was not unlike a lecture in a college. A war college – the stuffy kind – with long, monotonous lectures verbalised to students by a boring old professor on a hot afternoon. They would hear it but not hear it, though some of it might sink into their brains to be regurgitated at exam time.

But there was nothing stuffy, nor monotonous, about Sayeed's delivery. It was his favourite subject and he told it with a fervour and a passion that was chillingly gleeful. Ilan felt sick to his stomach as he listened. His face was still. Without expression, giving nothing away.

Sayeed paused for a moment as he got to the gist of his story. 'My holy warriors have gone out into the world and they carry with them the will of Allah,' he said to the camera. 'They will mingle with the infidels. In the airports. The train and the bus stations. The cafes and the bars. Cinemas and sporting arenas. They will walk among you as silent, unseen ghosts. They will bump into you as you walk down the street.

Shake your hand. Exchange money with you. Then you in turn will go home to your families. You will go to your places of work and your churches. Your bars and cinemas. These silent ghosts will follow you. And you will not know them. As you fall ill and those around you fall ill, you will not know the cause. But you will know that there is no cure and you will suffer and die. And this world will be purged of you. In the name of Allah. Because it is His will and I do this in His name!'

It wasn't a speech full of fervour that would rally the troops. Raise them up to fight and die. Kill or be killed. Because this speech was not for them. This speech was for the victims. It was a warning and a threat. More than that, it was a promise. It was chilling and doom-laden and told them that an act of evil had already been perpetuated against them. Not that Sayeed saw it as an act of evil.

As Jamal, he listened to the words with a sense of awe and a sense of pride that he was a vital part of it – having been so immersed in his undercover role he could identify with their ideology to the point where he almost believed in it himself. As Ilan, he was filled with revulsion at the horror of it, and terror at the thought of not being able to prevent it. But at the same time, a small, secret part of him as trying not to laugh aloud at the image Sayeed portrayed to him. *If he holds his pinkie finger up to his lip like Doctor Evil in the movie, I'm going to lose it completely.*

And those thoughts were wrong. So wrong. There was nothing funny. Nothing to laugh at. Because the words and the man, and the act itself, were evil. *And I have to find a way to stop him.*

Chapter 33.

'Yes, I'll give you the co-ordinates, but on one condition,' Jennifer said without looking up. Exhausted and emotionally drained, she leaned forward on the chair with her head lowered. Her elbows rested on her knees and her hands cupped her face.

From his own chair on the opposite side of his desk, Saul could only see the top of Jennifer's head. His eyes narrowed.

'You are not in any position to set conditions,' he said.

Jennifer's head shot up and she glared at him. They had been arguing back and forth for the best part of ten minutes now. When Saul had asked her for the co-ordinates she had written down, only to discover the piece of paper was blank, he was so angry she thought he was going to hit her.

'They're in my head, Saul. Do you think I'd be stupid enough to write them down and just hand them over?'

Saul picked up a small notebook and slid it across the desk. A pen followed it.

'I don't have time for this,' he said. 'Write them down.'

'No,' Jennifer said and her voice was firm. 'I don't think you understand me. I'm not writing anything down until I get what I want.'

'I could have you arrested.'

'Yeah. You could,' Jennifer nodded and shrugged her shoulders in an I-don't-care gesture.

'You would spend the rest of your life in prison.'

'For what? Refusing to reveal the contents of a dream? I don't think your courts would go along with that, Saul – not even the military courts.'

Saul spread his palms on the desk and took a deep breath. Threatening the woman sitting opposite was getting him nowhere. He needed to try something else. Maybe appeal to her sense of right and wrong. Her duty. Her humanity.

'Jennifer, if this attack goes ahead, if it is successful, do you realise how many people will die? How many thousands? Hundreds of thousands?'

'Yes, I know. And, believe me, if I could then of course –'

'That's just it, Jennifer,' Saul interrupted her. 'You *can*. But you won't, because the only thing important to you is one man.'

'And that one man is my husband, Saul. And I get it. History is littered with people who sacrificed themselves or a loved one for the greater good. I'm not that heroic. I'm not one of them. And I don't want Ilan to be one of them either. So yeah, I get it. Boy, do I get it and, until you do it my way, I am not giving you the co-ordinates.'

'We need them now, Jennifer. If you continue to stall then I will have no other choice,' Saul said as he picked up his desk phone and punched in an extension number.

'I need a security detail to my office,' he said and put the phone down again.

He's bluffing. He can't arrest me because he needs me and... oh fuck! What if they've found the place already? No, they haven't found it. He would have thrown me out by now if they had.

'Are you going to have me tortured, Saul?' Jennifer asked.

'I don't condone torture. Never have, never will. But, since you are refusing to give me information you have that could prevent an act of terrorism, I will have no problem seeing that you are locked up for a long, long time.'

Jennifer knew that she was playing a risky and, ultimately, a dangerous game. She had no intention of keeping the co-ordinates to herself. She wanted to give them to Saul – they were spinning around and around in her head and she wanted rid of them. But the timing had to be right. She needed to know the lead time for a night raid because that way she could stall for as long as possible, then reveal her information and they could launch their attack after enough time had elapsed for Ilan to get away.

If she gave the numbers up now, Saul would go in all guns blazing and Ilan would not stand a chance. That wasn't her plan. Getting her husband back, safe and sound, was the reason she had signed up for this insane experiment in the first place and she wasn't going to throw it all away now. Not when she was so close.

But something told Jennifer that she was running out of time. And the look on Saul's face told her she could wind up in very serious trouble if she wasn't careful. His threat to have her arrested frightened her. *Would they put me in prison for that? Yeah, they would. Withholding information doesn't sound serious, but if it's about a terrorist threat then it's really fucking serious. How many years would I get? Probably a lot. Saul means what he says and, even though it was a dream, knowing him, he'd figure out some trumped-up charge to get me into prison.*

'This is crazy,' Jennifer shook her head. 'I *will* give you the co-ordinates. I never said I wouldn't. I just want you to do what Ilan asked – wait until the middle of the night to give him a chance to escape. What's so wrong with that?'

She jumped in surprise at the light knock on the door.

'Last chance, Jennifer,' Saul said. He stood up and within a few steps he was at the door, his hand on the handle, ready to open it. He gripped it and looked at her, his eyebrows raised in a question.

Jennifer sprang to her feet. She placed her arms out in front of her in a pleading gesture. 'Whoa. Wait a minute. Let's talk about this, please.'

She remembered what Ilan had once told her about Saul. How he was a good man to work for. Loyal and dedicated. But he could be an egotistical bastard at times. *And that's what I need to play on. His ego.*

'I don't have any more time to talk.' Saul's hand was still on the door handle.

'I'll make a deal with you.'

'Too late,' Saul said and began to open the door.

'No, wait. Listen to me. Please.' Jennifer caught him by the arm and pulled his hand away from the door.

'I'm not sure you have anything left to deal with other than the co-ordinates that will end this and save many lives,' he said. His voice was cold.

'I'll work for you,' Jennifer blurted the words out, worried that she might have jumped in too early. But it was all or nothing. She had to do all she could to save Ilan and so she dived in with both feet. 'This experiment you roped me into. It worked. I was able to go into my dreams and find what you wanted me to find. Well, almost. I gave you enough to find it. Think of the possibilities, Saul. Think what we, what you, could accomplish. You could use me to find anyone or anything you want and there'd be no risk to anyone. No need to send operatives undercover into dangerous situations. I'll do it. I'll be happy to do it, if you promise to do this one thing for me.'

'Go on,' Saul said and motioned for her to take a step back. He invited her to sit down and continue with her argument.

'I'll give you the details just before you launch the missiles or whatever it is that you are intending to do in enough time for you to hit the compound at three in the morning. Ilan said he will make his escape just before that and he'll be at a drop point a kilometre away so he can be picked up safely. If you do this – if you give Ilan enough time to get clear – then I promise, I swear, I will work for you on the Sleep Program for as long as you need me. Time off and salary to be negotiated. Okay, I'm kidding about that part,' Jennifer said in response to Saul's angry glare.

'Go on,' he said.

'All I want is a promise, preferably in writing and with witnesses – Nurit and Nathan Cohen would be ideal – that you won't launch until the right time and you will send a recovery team, or whatever you call it, to pick up Ilan. Exfil, I think, is the term you use. And for that, I will work for you. I'll do anything you want me to do.'

Saul stared as Jennifer's proposal rang in his ears. He was convinced the program would be useful, not only in the fight against terrorism but in all kinds of criminal investigations. It wouldn't require a lot of funding – both Miriam and Nathan had already said they would be willing to devote a few days a week, more if required, if it was initiated – and it could be as covert or overt as necessary. It would keep him from retirement for a few more years. That was the plus side. The negative side? Would those above him believe in it?

'It is called the Dream Information Capture Initiative. DICI,' Saul informed her with a note of pride in his voice.

'Sounds dicey,' Jennifer told him and made a face like she had tasted something not to her liking. But she knew she had him hooked.

'I beg your pardon.'

'DICI. Dicey. When you say it as a word, which most people will, it sounds iffy. You know, dicey – dodgy or dubious. It doesn't really inspire a whole lot of confidence.'

'What would you suggest?'

'Well, I haven't really thought about it in great detail but I'd be inclined to stick with Sleep Program. Or maybe something involving the words – Lucid Dreaming or remote Viewing since that's what it is. Or maybe…' Jennifer paused and thought about it, but nothing suitable came to mind. 'We can work on the name.'

She looked at Saul and could see that he was mulling her offer over in his mind. *You know you want it. Go for it.* She crossed her fingers. Then another rap of knuckles on the door made her jump and her breath caught in her mouth when Saul pulled the door open.

'Is everything okay, sir?' the uniformed security guard asked. His eyes were narrowed in suspicion and his hand was on the grip of the gun in his side holster. Being called to the director's office was not a trivial matter.

'Yes. Sorry. It was a false alarm. You can go now,' Saul told him.

Jennifer let out a long sigh of relief. She knew she was close to winning Saul over now. All she had to do was push him a little bit more.

'It makes sense, Saul,' she said. 'I'll do it willingly for as long as you need me. Provided you bring my husband home. Bring Ilan home safe and sound and I swear I'll spend all my nights lucid dreaming, or whatever you want to call it, for the Mossad. And for you.'

Still he hesitated, and Jennifer racked her brains for something that would convince him. She knew she was winging it. If she said the wrong thing, Saul would shut down the conversation and call the guards back to haul her away. She needed something.

'Think of the intelligence you could gather. With no risk to anyone. No one would have to go into the field, risking his or her life. Not even me. I'd be safely tucked up in bed but at the same time, I'd be anywhere you want me to be – listening, watching and learning. Of course, it wouldn't hold up in court or anything like that, but it could be a pointer. It could lead you to what or who you want.'

'And you would do this willingly? Yes?'

'Yes,' Jennifer said. She knew she could be promising her life away but she didn't have a choice. *Maybe it won't be that bad. I'll be on call only when it's necessary. Probably not all that much. Better than losing Ilan and going to prison.*

Saul watched her carefully and Jennifer knew he was swaying towards agreeing with her suggestion.

He paced the small room and rubbed the back of his neck while he considered Jennifer's surprising offer. He stopped and turned then paced some more as he weighed up the options. Retrieving Ilan wasn't the priority. Stopping Qahtani was. But saving the life of one of his best operatives was a bonus and getting Jennifer on board with his program was a lifetime of bonuses all rolled into one.

'I'll have to take this to the Prime Minister. He is the one who makes the final decisions,' he told her. It wasn't exactly true but it wouldn't hurt to have her squirm for a few moments.

'How long will that take?' Jennifer asked.

'I have no idea. Hopefully not long. Wait in the cafeteria. Have a coffee and something to eat while you are there because, once the decision is made by the PM, I suspect it is going to be a long night for all of us. I will meet you there once the decision is made.'

'One question,' Jennifer raised her index finger. 'How long does it take from when I give you the co-ordinates until you launch?'

'We can launch in around ninety seconds. Why?'

'Okay, two questions. How long does it take after the launch for the missiles to strike their target?'

'We use the Delilah missile. It's an air-to-surface missile designed to target moving and re-locatable targets with a CEP, that is a circular error probable, of one metre. It differs from typical cruise missiles, which lock onto a pre-programmed target prior to launch, because the unique feature of the Delilah is that it is able to loiter and survey an area before the operator in the aircraft identifies the specific target. Launched from an aircraft and once launched, it is effectively a drone. It can observe, relay images in real-time, function autonomously and receive real-time instructions from the weapons operator.'

He began to lecture her about the missile's specifications and capabilities but Jennifer quickly stopped him with a dismissive wave of her hand.

'That sounds truly fascinating, Saul,' she said and rolled her eyes. 'But please, I neither need nor want a lecture in weapons technology. I just need the time frame.'

'The aircraft are already on standby and the missiles are loaded. We can launch in ninety seconds and be over the target in approximately fifteen minutes.' Saul narrowed his eyes as he told her and wondered what she was planning. He studied Jennifer as she glanced at the digital clock on the wall and, with a concentrated frown, did the mental arithmetic. He knew she would wait until the optimum moment, to ensure Ilan made it away from the camp, before giving them the details they so desperately required. Although angry at her, he could not fail to be impressed by her audacity and her bravery in the face of his threat to have her imprisoned.

'And then what happens?' Jennifer asked.

'If you are sure of the co-ordinates, then the Delilah won't have to search and destroy – merely destroy.'

'I am sure,' Jennifer said. *At least I think I am. No. I'm definitely sure.* 'So, what happens when I give them to you? Is it instantaneous?'

'Almost,' Saul told her. 'It is read out over a secure link and then read back to confirm. About a minute and a half to double-check.'

'When that is done, how long until they strike?'

'If the drone needs to seek and destroy based on only visual clues, it will take several minutes. But if the co-ordinates you give us are already keyed in, then around one or two minutes.'

Saul told her and she suffered through the mental arithmetic again.

'Okay then. I'll give the numbers to you in enough time to strike the compound at three o'clock.' When he remained silent, Jennifer continued. 'Ilan will have left by then and be at the pick-up point. Just like he said. Oh, and I want to be here when it happens. And I want Nurit with me.'

'That's quite a list of demands,' he said with a wry smile. 'Anything else?'

Jennifer shrugged. 'Nope. That's it.'

Chapter 34.

As soon as he was as certain as he could be that everyone but the guards were asleep, Ilan slipped outside. Even though he was under the cover of darkness, he avoided the open spaces as best as possible, as well as areas where he knew guards were posted. No one saw him and he made his way to the old building where he had hidden the grenades. With only ten he had to use them to their best effect. Sayeed intended to have the plague virus administered after morning prayers and before they moved out and Ilan had discarded his initial plan to booby trap the laboratory with the with grenades, on the grounds that it carried too much risk. The lab was too well guarded and he would have no chance of breaking into it to carry out his act of sabotage.

The vehicles were his second choice and, when he thought about it, probably the better option. Probably the only option.

He set to work and carefully planted a grenade under the wheels of the first truck. The lack of light was not a problem. Ilan scooped a handful of dirt away from behind the front wheel on the driver's side. He used his hands to guide him and placed the grenade underneath the wheel then packed the dirt around it to ensure there was no movement. Once he was sure it was steady, he checked with his fingertips that the handle of the grenade, or spoon as it was known, was tight against the tyre and would remain in place, becoming the safety mechanism, until the vehicle moved forward. Then the spoon would release and the device would be activated.

When he was satisfied that it was tight against the wheel, Ilan removed the firing pin. This was the moment when it could go horribly wrong.

Ilan swallowed hard, concerned that the grenade would shift in the dirt. But nothing happened and he let out the breath he had been holding then made his way around to the passenger side of the vehicle, where he repeated the exercise.

Two down, eight to go. There were four trucks so he could either use all the grenades or keep two over as spares. He elected to use them all.

It took him thirty precious minutes but he refused to rush. Haste, in this instance, equated to clumsiness and that could be fatal. So, he worked steadily and quietly, all the while expecting to be either discovered or blown to pieces. Both results would be bad. Finally, he positioned his one remaining grenade under the rear wheel of the fourth, and last, truck. He had already placed two at the front but another one would have extra impact and possibly more fatalities. He checked the spoon would not move and carefully pulled the pin out of the last grenade.

They would not be seen and they would explode when the vehicles moved forward, disabling them and, hopefully, killing or seriously incapacitating some, if not most, of the occupants. It was the best he could do and it should be enough to prevent them moving out in the morning. With no driveable trucks, any survivors had no means of escape and would be trapped in this remote area. Then the men Sayeed had infected, those that weren't killed by the grenades, would manifest symptoms, become ill and then die.

Ilan had not given up on the belief that Jennifer had been able to convince Saul Mueller who, in turn, had convinced the military and the Prime Minister that she knew the location of the camp. He had to believe that the plan, involving his unknowing wife, concocted more than eight months ago would work. That his people would strike in an hour or so and these men would all die a lot more quickly and a lot less painfully than what Sayeed had planned for them. And the world would never know exactly what they had planned.

I have to believe that. I have to believe that Jennifer came to me in a dream last night and I told her where I am. I thought about her before I fell asleep. But did it work? Had any of it worked?

It was a bitterly cold night. The air was crisp with frost

and the black sky was full of stars. A thin sliver of the new moon afforded no light but, in the darkness, Ilan counted all ten firing pins as he slipped them into his pocket. It wouldn't do to have them lying around the vehicles come daylight. Once he was certain he had all ten, he made his way through the old village that had been his reluctant home. He trod lightly and carefully for fear he would stumble and someone would hear him. He carried his gun but prayed he would not have to use it on a startled guard for he had no silencer and a gunshot would awaken the whole camp. It had not occurred to him to steal a knife from the kitchen of one of the abandoned houses. He regretted that oversight now.

He wrapped his coat around him to ward off the cold. There was no wind tonight. But an occasional fluttering breeze stirred around him and seemed to chase away the last remaining traces of the terrorist named Jamal. As he walked, he became Ilan more and more with each step. And it felt as though he was finally going home.

He was almost clear of the village when a dark figure armed with a rifle stepped out in front of him.

'Hello brother.'

It was Ali, his cigarette smoking buddy.

Ilan's heart almost stopped beating in his chest, but he recovered quickly. 'I cannot sleep, brother. And I need a cigarette. Do you have one to spare?'

Perhaps reluctant to part with even one more from his dwindling supply, Ali hesitated and glanced uncomfortably at the ground.

'I will buy you a carton of them when we get to Damascus,' Ilan promised.

The enticing prospect of a whole carton of smokes did the trick. Ali set his rifle down against the wall and reached into his pocket. He produced a crumpled pack, then dug out a lighter from his other pocket.

He offered the pack and Ilan took one from it. Ali flicked the lighter and held up the tiny flame. The cigarette dangled from his lips as Ilan leaned forward to light it. He drew hard on it, inhaled the smoke deep into his lungs and relished the heady rush of nicotine. *Will I ever be able to quit?* The thought fluttered through his mind. *She will make me quit when I am home. Don't go there! You are not home and safe yet.*

Lady Luck, or God, or even Allah himself, was on Ilan's side because a gentle gust of wind appeared out of nowhere and caused Ali to turn away and cup his hands around his own cigarette to light it. With the man's back to him, Ilan saw his opportunity and took it. He threw his cigarette to the ground, took a step forward, and grasped the guard with both hands on either side of Ali's head. Ali had no time to react and Ilan twisted his head around and snapped his neck. It was silent, quick and effective. Ali was dead before he hit the ground.

'Rot in hell, Ali,' Ilan whispered as he picked up the discarded rifle, grabbed the dead guard by the collar and hauled his body a few metres across the hard ground, where he stashed it behind a rocky outcrop. It would remain there undiscovered until it was too late. He knew the rotas – Ali was here on post until first light. No one would come to relieve him. He broke the rifle in two and left it beside the body. He had no need for it.

It occurred to him that he was a thief and he smiled grimly in the darkness as he quickly rummaged through Ali's pockets until he found the pack of cigarettes. He reckoned he would need a smoke or two before the ground forces arrived to take him home. He slipped the pack into his pocket along with Ali's lighter. He still had the lighter Ali had given him when he last bummed a cigarette off him, but he took this one as well. *I stole this from a dead Jihadi.*

Ilan walked away from the village into the night. He did not look back.

Chapter 35.

The kid who introduced himself as Rafi was a big bulky kid. But bulky in an athletic way – from hard training and sports. He exuded ferociousness and strength and looked like he should be doing a hundred press ups before breakfast or sweating his way through a fifty-kilometre hike in full combat gear.

He definitely didn't look like someone who should be sitting at a desk only three weeks into his army basic training. And he wouldn't have been sitting at a desk if his right leg hadn't been encased in a plaster cast.

'Training accident?' Jennifer asked as she took a seat beside him.

'No. I was playing with my kid brother on weekend leave and I fell off his swing,' Rafi told her with a self-depreciating shrug.

'Ouch,' Jennifer winced. Her sympathy was more for the reason for his injury than the injury itself.

He blushed and tucked his encased leg under the desk as Nurit snorted with laughter, but he still risked a smile in her direction.

As a married woman with two small babies and senior in rank to him, she gave him a stern look and chose to ignore his smile and the puppy dog eyes that gazed at her in adoration. But Jennifer knew she secretly loved it and, although it was neither the time nor the place for laughter, it was good to hear Nurit laugh again.

Rafi pulled his chair closer to the desk, positioned his hands above the keyboard. With a nod, he indicated to Jennifer that he was ready and, one number at a time, Jennifer recited the co-ordinates and watched as he typed them into the search computer. Saul and Nurit stood on either side of her as though she was a prisoner and they were her guards. In a way they were.

'There it is.'

Jennifer had no idea who spoke. It could have been Rafi or it could have been any one of the six personnel tasked with staring at the screens. They all knew what to look for from the description Jennifer had given them. It didn't matter who had called it first.

A ripple of subdued excitement spread around the large room. Jennifer glanced up at Nurit who raised her eyebrows. Is this it? Jennifer nodded and shrugged her shoulders. Yes. Maybe.

But Saul needed a verbal confirmation from Jennifer herself and he adjusted the screen beside her. He swivelled it around so she could see it clearly.

'What do you think? Is this the courtyard you saw in your dream?'

Jennifer studied the screen carefully. So much depended on this moment and she had to be sure. Rushing it was not a good idea. The image on the screen was in black and white and it had been taken from above, but the features did look familiar. The stone bench-type seats and the large terracotta pots with the dead plants were the same as the ones she had observed when she walked past them in her dream. The old buildings, decrepit and decaying, that surrounded the little courtyard were familiar to her. She saw the door she had walked through into the large room – the school or meeting house, or whatever it was. She remembered the people gathered there and the prisoner in front of them, awaiting his fate.

Jennifer swallowed. It was not a memory she wished to remember.

'Is this it?' Saul asked her and his voice was gentle, as though he knew what was in her mind.

Jennifer nodded.

'Are you sure? One hundred percent?'

'Yes, Saul. I'm sure. This is the courtyard from my dream. That door there,' she pointed to the screen. 'It leads to the room where I thought Ilan was killed. And that door is into the room that looked like a laboratory.'

Saul picked up a phone and dialled the Prime Minister's office. 'We have visual confirmation, sir.'

He listened for a moment then nodded and set the phone down again. He turned to Jennifer and Nurit. 'We have a go.'

'What happens now?' Jennifer asked.

'The co-ordinates are being entered into the Delilah's system,' Saul told her.

'And then?'

'We wait.'

In Syria, crouched behind a large boulder and sheltered from the worst of the cold wind, Ilan cupped his hands around the lighter as he lit another cigarette. He took a deep, satisfying drag, tightened his coat around him and sat down on the hard ground to wait. He wore no watch but he knew the time was near.

To Jennifer's surprise, Saul had permitted her to remain in the Ops Room as long as she remained in the background and out of the way. Her investment in the outcome was so much more personal, yet she could only be an observer. She was thankful that he hadn't banished her to an office or a waiting room because that would have killed her. It was nerve-racking enough but, at least here she could see what happened when it happened.

She was seated at a small desk – out of the way but close enough. She smiled in thanks as Nurit handed her a coffee, and she appeared calm but under the desk one of her legs bounced up and down with jangling nervous energy. *Do I really need more caffeine?* But she took a sip anyway.

Nurit paced back and forth a few times before stopping beside Jennifer. Her training finally took over and she stood as still as a rock beside her stepmother. She appeared in control of her emotions but she chewed at her lip and her eyes were wide and fearful. Jennifer reached for her hand and

Nurit took it willingly. Both women needed the physical contact as they waited and worried about the fate of the man that bound them together.

Saul remained nearby, also an observer, for his job was done and the success or failure of the operation was now in the hands of the military – both here and in the air. And on the ground. He seemed calm and collected, but Jennifer could see the strain on his face that was so much more than tiredness. She wanted to take his hand too, but it didn't seem proper in the circumstances.

'How long?' Jennifer asked and her voice was a hoarse croak. It seemed hours had passed when it had only been a few minutes.

'Not long,' Saul replied.

Almost in answer to her question, the telephone rang and all three of them – Jennifer, Saul and Nurit – jumped in startled surprise. Even Rafi looked up from his keyboard. Jennifer stared at it and wondered what news it would bring.

Saul picked it up, listened for a moment then nodded and replaced the phone on the desk. 'That's it. They've launched and they are on their way.'

'How… how long until… until?' Jennifer asked.

He told her and she glanced at her watch. The seconds seemed to tick by so slowly.

The cold had found its way into his bones and Ilan shivered despite the heavy coat he was wearing. Hunger gnawed at his stomach and he reluctantly pulled his hands out of his pockets to light another cigarette as he waited. He had one left in the pack.

His eyes remained fixed on the horizon in the direction of the village from where Sayeed Qahtani planned to mount his act of terrorism. It wouldn't be long now until Qahtani would be destroyed and the horror of what he had planned would be destroyed along with him.

When it came, it came quickly. The Delilah missiles found their targets and a series of loud, rapid explosions lit up the night sky. Immediately afterwards, Ilan heard several smaller explosions. It was the grenades he had planted. Their spoons released by the movements of the vehicles, or possibly the movement of soil underneath the wheels as a result of the missile strike. Either way, they exploded. Ineffective now, but they gave Ilan a small sense of satisfaction knowing that his improvisation would have had some effect should it have been needed.

Moments later came the second wave and another series of explosions which obliterated every part of the small village. Nothing was left intact and it was doubtful if anyone was left alive. Sayeed Qahtani's base of operations was destroyed forever.

Ilan stood up and watched the light show for a few moments, lit his last cigarette and smoked it as he watched. Once finished, he flicked the butt into the darkness. He watched the faint red ember as it died.

A footstep behind him made him jump and he turned sharply to see a figure approach him out of the darkness.

'You ordered an Uber?' A voice spoke to him in Hebrew.

'Loh. I ordered a stretch limo. But I guess an Uber will suffice,' Ilan replied also in Hebrew. His native tongue was easy on his lips once more.

'Sorry about that, sir. Maybe this will compensate you.' There was a note of humour in the voice as the figure stepped forward. Ilan could now see his face in the moonlight. He didn't know him, but he did recognise the uniform and the Captain's insignia on his arm.

The Captain reached into his jacket, underneath the body armour, and produced a small hip flask. He handed it to Ilan.

'With the compliments of Saul Mueller,' the Captain said. 'L'chaim.'

'L'chaim,' Ilan sighed as he unscrewed the cap and put

the flask to his lips. He took a mouthful, swallowed and took another. After eight months the whiskey tasked like heaven. He took a third gulp.

'Better pace yourself with that, sir.'

Chapter 36.

It had been a long couple of hours. Strong coffee had kept them going. But waiting for the plane, a C-130 military transport, to land and the passengers to disembark and walk through the doors felt like the longest wait of Jennifer's life. One passenger in particular seemed to take forever to appear and she was beginning to think they had lied when they said they had found him and were bringing him home.

So far, only one man had come through who was not wearing a uniform. He was a dirty and dishevelled man, with a long grey beard and haunted eyes, and he was dressed in navy blue sweatpants and a matching sweatshirt. He looked dangerous. He looked like someone who should be in ankle shackles, handcuffs and wearing an orange jumpsuit. And there should be armed guards surrounding him. Jennifer had no idea who this man was.

The man had stopped and he was watching her. *Why is he staring at me? Who is he?* He seemed surprised to see her. And there was something about him. Something familiar. Jennifer frowned as she scrutinised his features.

Then she recognised him. She let out a heart-wrenching sob and raced forward towards her husband.

In a heartbeat, she was in his arms and he was holding her. He was squeezing the life out of her and trying to kiss her and speak at the same time. He could manage neither, so he gave up and simply held her.

'You're safe! You're alive and you're safe. And you are home! Oh, thank god! You have no idea how…' Jennifer grimaced. She wrinkled her nose and tilted her head back to look at him. 'You stink to high heaven!'

'I'm sorry,' Ilan breathed, his voice hoarse with emotion. 'I need a long shower. I haven't had one in a while.'

Then Nurit was beside them with the widest grin on her face and tears of relief and happiness streaming down her cheeks as she waited for her turn to wrap herself in her father's arms. Ilan reached out his hand to her and pulled her into his embrace and the three of them stood there, Ilan with his arms around both women. He held them tightly with no intention of letting them go.

Jennifer felt as though her knees would buckle as she realised Ilan was leaning on both her and Nurit to keep from falling. *He's exhausted. Probably starving, too. I need to get him home.*

Nurit nodded to Jennifer in unspoken agreement as their eyes met. *He'll be fine once he is home.*

But before the trio could make a move, Saul stepped forward. He had been hovering nearby to give them a few moments together, but it was his turn now. He reached out his hand to Ilan.

'Well done. It was a complete success. Welcome home,' he said. 'I'll need a detailed report from you as soon as possible.'

Ilan met his eyes and gave an almost imperceptible shake of his head – not now, Saul.

Saul's hand fell to his side and he took a step back. 'We can talk during the debrief.'

Jennifer turned on him and her eyes blazed with a quiet fury. 'He is coming home with me. You can debrief him all you want later but, right now, he needs a hot shower, food and a good night's sleep.'

Startled by the venom in Jennifer's voice, Saul could only nod quietly at her. He cleared his throat and glanced at Ilan once more. 'Good work. Do what your wife says and go home and rest. We can go over your report tomorrow.'

This elicited another angry glare from Jennifer.

'Or maybe the next day,' Saul added hastily.

Someone, Saul most likely, had arranged a car for them. A driver in civilian clothes stepped out and opened the rear door. Ilan almost collapsed into the car. Nurit took the front seat and Jennifer climbed in beside her husband. She held his hand in hers as they sped through the city. Ilan stared out of the window at the passing buildings as if he had never seen them before.

In no time at all they pulled up outside the house in the sleepy suburb and Nurit was out of the car in a flash. She opened the rear door and asked the driver to wait for her as she took Ilan's arm and helped him out of the car.

The familiar houses and cars seemed strange, almost alien, to him. It would take a while for him to adjust.

Nurit gently touched his cheek. 'Hey. I'm gonna get a lift home with this guy, give my husband and babies a big kiss and then get some sleep. I'll call you later. Okay?'

Ilan wrapped his arms around her one more time. 'Kiss them for me, please.'

'You want me to kiss Reuben for you?'

Ilan laughed. A genuine, happy laugh. He planted a kiss on her cheek. 'Sure. Why not.'

He watched the car as it disappeared from sight then turned to his wife. Jennifer dangled the front door keys in front of him.

'Shall we?' she asked.

'Do you still love me?' Ilan asked.

Jennifer looked at the thin, scruffy man standing in front of her. Right now, she wanted to… she swallowed the anger. It would keep for later. He was alive and he was home. That was all that mattered now.

'Yes. I still love you.'

Amanda Sheridan
October 2020

If you enjoyed this book, I would love to see your review on Amazon.

Or you can find it on Goodreads and leave a review there –

https://www.goodreads.com/author/show/20338737.Amanda_Sheridan

Please check out my Facebook page –

https://www.facebook.com/Amanda-Sheridan-104074121231229

Instagram –

https://www.instagram.com/amandasheridanauthor

Twitter –

https://twitter.com/amandas26597105

Acknowledgements

Once again, I have to thank my husband, Hugh, for feeding me keeping me stocked up with tea/wine while I was writing this book.
David Kessler for his help and advice. For correcting all my mistakes. And for some really useful facts and figures regarding Israel's Delilah missiles.
Amy Hunter Designs for the wonderful cover from a photograph by Claudio Scott, the illustrations by Clker-Free-Vector-Images and Callum Ramsay.
Kari Holloway (KH Formatting) for preparing the manuscript for publication.
And last but, by no means least, I would like to thank everyone who bought a copy of Rapid Eye Movement, read it and told me how much they loved it. Thank you so much.
I hope you love this one, too.

Amanda Sheridan
October 2020.

Printed in Great Britain
by Amazon

79263700R10181